Author's Note

Once again, I would like to thank Marla and George Engel of Book Creations and all the staff of that firm, who have helped me with this, the fifteenth volume of the *Children of the Lion* Series. My gratitude is due in particular to Laurie Rosin, whose kind support and incomparable editorial skills have been indispensable in bringing this book to fruition.

Finally, I thank my loyal readers, whose expressions of interest in the Children of the Lion have sustained me for more than a decade.

A CHOSEN PEOPLE AND A SACRED CLAN SWEPT INTO A FIERY CONFLICT THAT WILL SET THEIR WORLD ABLAZE WITH FORBIDDEN DESIRE, DARKEST TREACHERY —AND A SHATTERING BETRAYAL

ABIMELECH—The illegitimate son of the great Israelite commander Gideon and a Canaanite slave, he would set into motion a bloody plan to make Canaan the greatest kingdom on earth, but only at a terrible cost to his oppressed people . . . and to the woman he secretly loved.

MIRIAM—After her brother Gideon's death she saw her beloved homeland torn apart by the ambition of her own nephew, a man whose anger and lust would threaten her world in one brutal night of violence.

NUHARA—High priestess of the maenads, she was the most powerful woman in Thrace. Traitor to husband and family, she stole the sacred treasure of the Children of the Lion and, with her secret allies, now plotted to wipe them off the face of the earth.

NAVAN—Cruel and barbaric, the powerful Phoenician overlord gathered his army against the hated Canaanites while using a beautiful Israelite dancing girl to destroy his most dangerous enemy: the self-proclaimed king of Israel.

HELA—Forced to flee Egypt, she sought refuge in the Sinai desert, where she would save the life of a young girl branded by the mark of Cain . . . a child possessed of an ancient power that could change the course of a nation's history.

Volume XV

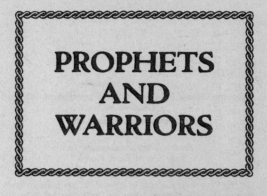

PROPHETS
AND
WARRIORS

PETER DANIELSON

 Producers of **The First Americans,
The Frontier Trilogy,** and **The Holts.**

Book Creations Inc., Canaan, NY • Lyle Kenyon Engel, Founder

BANTAM BOOKS
NEW YORK • TORONTO • LONDON • SYDNEY • AUCKLAND

PROPHETS AND WARRIORS

A Bantam Domain Book / published by arrangement with Book Creations Inc.

Bantam edition / January 1993

Produced by Book Creations Inc.
Lyle Kenyon Engel, Founder

ISBN 0-553-56132-4

Published simultaneously in the United States and Canada

Bantam Books are published by Bantam Books, a division of Bantam Doubleday Dell Publishing Group, Inc. Its trademark, consisting of the words "Bantam Books" and the portrayal of a rooster, is Registered in U.S. Patent and Trademark Office and in other countries. Marca Registrada. Bantam Books, 666 Fifth Avenue, New York, New York 10103.

PRINTED IN THE UNITED STATES OF AMERICA

RAD   0 9 8 7 6 5 4 3 2 1

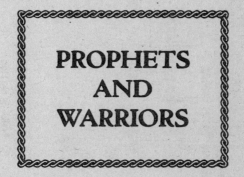

PROPHETS
AND
WARRIORS

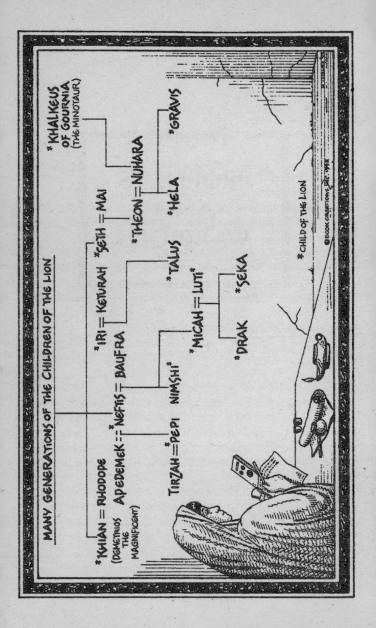

MANY GENERATIONS OF THE CHILDREN OF THE LION

*KHIAN = RHODOPE
(DEMETRIOS THE MAGNIFICENT)

APEDEMEK == *NEFTIS = BAUFRA

*IRI = KETURAH

*KHALKEUS OF GOURNIA (THE MINOTAUR)

*SETH = MAI

*THEON = NUHARA

*HELA   *GRAVIS

*TALUS

TIRZAH = PEPI   NIMSHI*

MICAH = LUTI

*DRAK   *SEKA

*CHILD OF THE LION

© BOOK CREATIONS, INC. 1988

Prologue

By dusk the caravan had reached the base of the cliffs. The descent, started at dawn, had been long and perilous. Several travelers had stumbled and hurt themselves. One hapless fellow had lost his life after falling to the rocks below.

The wanderers had expected to find water and grass and softly rolling hills on the other side of the mountain pass. What they saw instead was a vast, boundless, parched desert that gleamed red in the sunset. Nothing seemed to be alive. There was no breeze. There were no creatures.

In despair the travelers sank to their knees. They wept and screamed and beat their breasts. The children, frightened by their parents' wretchedness, wailed piteously.

Suddenly they heard the familiar chant of the Teller of Tales. His mere presence was a comfort; here was a man who had endured worse trials than the one they now faced.

"In the name of God, the merciful, the beneficent . . ."

The old man strode out onto the desert ground, then turned and faced the travelers. His long, white hair curled like vines about his neck and shoulders. His dark eyes were fierce. His gaunt body was held straight, erect, proud. His robes also took on the red of the sun. The Teller of Tales raised his magnificent carved staff with both hands and cried out, "Cowards! O ye cowards! Where is the iron in your bones? Where is the love in your heart? Where is the faith on your lips?"

The adults' wailing stopped abruptly. The gathered wanderers looked upon the old man, and sheepishness crept over their faces.

He shook the staff at them. "Why are you afraid of this desert? Does it have claws like the beasts? Does it have sharp, curved swords like the Bedouin? Does it have teeth like the great serpent that lurks in the shallow waters?"

The children's cries lessened into whimpers and then stopped altogether as the parents regained control of their own emotions.

"True, a man lost his life today, and we grieve for him. But could it not be that his lessons on this earth had been learned, and it was his time to leave us?"

Silence had been won. The Teller of Tales lowered his staff. His eyes swept across all the members of the caravan.

"Let me tell you of true courage! Hear my tale of noble Theon and his companion Talus. Together they challenged the mighty god Dionysus. Together they raised their banner against the Thracian hordes to recover what was theirs—the treasure of the Children of the Lion."

The old man paused. He lifted his staff, then stabbed it into the sand to punctuate his words. "Listen to the struggle of gentle Miriam, sister of the great Gideon. Hear how she, above all the Israelites, possessed the love and inner strength to transcend her own suffering and thus freed her people from the king who would lead them all into the pit of death and blasphemy.

"And hear of the strange black-skinned child Tuk, found in a desolate camp, thrown into the whirlwind of war and treachery. Listen to the story of her courage as she discovered within herself powers so startling and limitless that they changed the course of history for the Children of the Lion.

"Listen to my tales, learn from them, and you shall triumph. Hear how the prophetess Luti and her husband, Micah, journeyed into the very womb of deceit—the palaces of the great Phoenician empire—and pried from the usurpers the secrets that would have blessed Babylon."

The old man took a threatening step toward his audience

as if his anger for their weakness could no longer be contained. Those seated closest to him recoiled and clutched their children in a protective embrace. But it was only a feint . . . a humorous feint on his part to test their courage. He stopped and smiled knowingly as the people tried to regain their dignity, pretending that they had merely shifted their position for greater comfort.

"Listen to my tale of the beautiful Hela," his voice boomed out. "Hear how Theon's daughter was worshiped as a goddess and then betrayed into the jaws of death, only to rise again.

"O my children," the old man intoned, "hear my words. They speak of men and women who did not flinch from the evil that confronted them . . . of children who brought truth and clarity to a world gone mad . . . of heroes and heroines who struggled mightily against the ambitions that worked to subvert the one living God."

Suddenly, a tiny child escaped his mother's grasp and ran out toward the old man. The Teller of Tales picked the child up and, slowly straightening his back, held the babe. Tears of love and triumph shone in the old man's eyes as the little one, unafraid and cooing, buried fat, dimpled fingers in the long, white beard. The old man chuckled as the toddler's young mother came forward to extricate her darling from the storyteller's beard and embrace. She bobbed her head in respect, then scurried back to her place beside her man.

There was no sound now except for the breathing of those waiting for the old man to begin.

PART
ONE

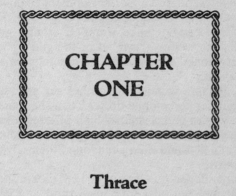

CHAPTER ONE

Thrace

The first rays of morning light were slanting over the massive low bed. Nuhara was wide awake. The naked man next to her was asleep; but his was a troubled rest, and his body jerked and thrashed. She grimaced every time he moaned. If he awakened, he would want more sex, and she had no desire for another so-called erotic bout with that fool. He really believed that she desired him; she had played her part too well.

The only reason she was sleeping with Heraclitus, the high priest of the Dionysian cult, was because he was the guardian of her fortune. In return for his guardianship he received a generous monthly stipend to finance his proselytizing activities throughout Greece . . . and she gave him her body whenever he wanted it. In the meantime, she was

7

secretly planning to liberate her fortune from the cave where it had been safely hidden by the priest. Then she would resurrect the shipping empire of the Children of the Lion, the clan whose financial network had been destroyed in an attack on their island headquarters called Home.

Her eyes wandered about her opulent chambers. Heraclitus's walking staff leaned against a far wall. She could make out the carved snake wrapped around grapevines etched into the wood—a symbol of the god's power. The priest's ceremonial robe was folded carefully on the divan beside the staff.

Why, Nuhara wondered, had her servant Hipparchia also laid out her ceremonial dress? Then she remembered: Today she was to be invested as high priestess of the maenads—the young women who flagellated themselves in the service of the god and then abandoned themselves to wild erotic behavior.

Nuhara slipped quietly out of bed, careful not to disturb Heraclitus, put on a long linen robe, and padded on bare feet into the hallway. Hipparchia was sleeping quietly on a woven mat against the wall. Nuhara delivered a vicious kick to the maid's ribs. "Get up," she hissed, "and be quiet!"

Hipparchia jumped up, her face registering pain and carefully controlled hatred.

Nuhara walked quickly down the hall to her father's room, and the maid hurried silently at her heels. Old Khalkeus was already up, sitting disconsolately upon a divan. The once feared pirate, leader of all brigands working the Great Sea, was now a shadow, a sick, trembling old man. But the moment he saw his beloved daughter, his face brightened.

"Ah, Nuhara, today is a great day! I will be so proud of you when you become queen."

"High priestess, Father, not queen," Nuhara corrected gently. Her father, she realized, was a weak fool who actually believed all that resurrection nonsense about Dionysus. According to legend, the god had been chopped up and then miraculously reassembled, like an ivory puzzle. But Nuhara's love for Khalkeus allowed her to forgive him this folly; he was, in fact, the only man Nuhara had ever loved.

She kissed him softly on the soft, wrinkled skin of his forehead. "Are you cold, Father?"

Before he could answer, she barked at her maid, "Get my father a blanket and wrap it around his shoulders."

Hipparchia quickly followed her orders.

"Now get out!" Nuhara shouted at her. "Prepare my bath and wait for me in my room."

Hipparchia left.

"You are very harsh on her, darling," Khalkeus said.

Nuhara did not respond. In his old age he had become solicitous of the slaves' feelings. She tucked the blanket more securely around her father's neck.

"How can I ever thank you, my dear," he said, "for bringing me to Thrace? If it were not for you, I would never have been able to worship the great Dionysus. I would never have been able to conquer my fear of illness and death. I am the luckiest father in the world."

Nuhara picked up his high-veined, clawlike hand and pressed it against her cheek. She and Khalkeus had come so far together; they had suffered so much. But now they were close to triumph.

"Listen to me, Daughter," Khalkeus whispered, suddenly weak. "I had a dream. And in that dream I saw my grandchildren. I saw the twins, Hela and Gravis. They were safe and well, thank the god. And they were coming toward us, to Thrace."

"I pray, Father, that your dream comes true. But so far no one has been able to find them. My spies have returned empty-handed again and again. All trace of the children has been lost."

"If only Theon were in Thrace! He would know how to find them."

Nuhara said nothing. Her father did not know that her husband, Theon, was already in Thrace . . . hiding in the

mountains, gathering men to fight against her. No, her father knew very little about anything. And that was the way
it must remain.

"I need to prepare for the ceremony, Father," she
said, then kissed his palm and released his hand. "I'll see
you at the temple." She made sure he was bundled up, and
then returned to her chambers. Luckily, Heraclitus was
gone. She bathed, with several women attending her. Her
toenails were cut and lacquered. Her skin was kneaded
with rose-hip jelly, then anointed with fragrant oil. Her
mouth and eyelids and nipples were daubed with dried
pollen—a golden color. By the time the special robe was
slipped over her head, a contingent of priests was waiting
to escort her to the temple of Dionysus.

The ceremony was scheduled to begin at noon. The
hundreds of Thracians who had been invited lined the path
between the palace and the temple. They stood in respectful silence as the powerful woman and her entourage
passed by. Then Heraclitus raised his hand. The slow beat
of drums commenced at his signal, soon to be joined by the
eerie beauty of the dual flutes.

Suddenly the temple was overrun by goats, who had
been released with their throats just slit. Their hooves
clicking on the marble floor, the beasts ran wildly around
the altar until they died. The audience cheered. Each goat
symbolized the dying god. Like Dionysus, each of the goats
would rise again.

The beat of the drums increased as the line of naked,
oiled maenads snaked into the temple's rotunda. Each
young woman, her long hair unbound, was more beautiful
than the last.

Nuhara looked around until she found her father. The
old man's eyes were lit with pride and excitement. The
maenads, chanting, moved sinuously, thrusting their hips
forward, and formed a circle in the rotunda.

Three priests of Dionysus broke through the circle of
maenads. Each man carried a long vine, which was used as
a whip to beat the ecstatic women. The lashes raised hor-

rendous welts on the maenads' perfect young flesh. Their
white limbs were streaked with blood.

The women ran faster, their blood spotting the pol-
ished marble floor. Pain mixed with ecstasy as their faces
contorted with agony and pleasure.

The cheers of the assembled audience grew louder,
urging the women on. They moved to encircle their new
high priestess. Nuhara's whole body began to tremble. Her
loins felt moist, warm, aching with need. Although she felt
no allegiance to Dionysus, even she, with all her cynicism,
could not withstand the incessant, driving beat, inspiring
the flesh to seek sexual release.

Then the music stopped abruptly. The maenads collapsed to the floor around her. The high priest, Heraclitus,
walked regally around and over their bodies and approached his lover. In his hand he held a short gold staff.
The head of the staff was carved in the shape of a male
sexual organ. He held the object out to her.

"Take this, Nuhara," he intoned, his voice loud and
officious. "Take this in the spirit of Dionysus, whose power
is beyond all reckoning." He bowed to her, and when she
accepted the staff, the temple walls reverberated with the
cheers of the people.

Once the ceremony was over, physicians came in to
attend to the maenads. In the meantime the invited guests
left the temple and hurried into the courtyard, where tables laden with food and drink had been set up. There
were whole roasted lambs and enormous vats of stewed
peppers. There were bowls of grapes, dates, pears, raisins,
and persimmons. There were platters of bread. And the
deep, dark wine was everywhere—ladled by slaves into
porcelain bowls.

Nuhara was just about to join the festivities when she
saw Heraclitus beckoning to her, then moving out of sight
into an alcove. The high priest was visibly upset. Smiling,
she excused herself from the well-wishers who surrounded
her, then went to find him.

Heraclitus pulled her into the small alcove. "I have

very bad news," he said in an urgent whisper. "Theon is with his men, only twenty miles from here, in the Valley of the Skull."

"Is that what is worrying you? Poor Heraclitus." Nuhara laughed contemptuously. "What would it matter if he was only a mile away? What can he do? For more than a year he has been trying to raid the temple, and each time he was beaten back."

"Maybe he has more men now, and better fighters," Heraclitus said.

"I doubt it. He has no money. He recruits those poor, dumb peasants. He promises that great treasure is hidden here. No one believes him anymore. Don't you under-stand? Theon is pathetic, a fool. He's living a fantasy. Let him play in the mountains for as long as he wishes. There is no danger from him."

"You are too arrogant, Nuhara," the high priest warned.

She rubbed against him, smiling, silently promising him another night of erotic bliss. But still agitated, he moved her gently but firmly away. His reaction disturbed her. For the first time she realized it might be necessary to destroy that idiot Theon and his young companion Talus— and to do so immediately. For her own security she had to keep Heraclitus at his ease . . . and under her thumb.

She remained silent for a long time. Finally she said, "Very well. I will remove them. Can you send me one of your elite guards this evening?"

"Why?"

"Don't ask questions. Can you send me such a man?"

"Of course. I'll send you the best I've got. His name is Crates."

"Fine. Make sure he is at the door of my chambers by sunset." She turned and walked away, to join the banquet.

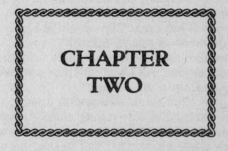

CHAPTER TWO

Kingdom of Babylon

A small oxcart moved slowly along the dusty road that ran parallel to the northern Tigris River. A coarse cloth, wet with dew, covered the rear of the cart, and a simple wooden plank functioned as a driver's seat. On that plank sat Luti and Micah. Behind them their son, twelve-year-old Drak, and their eight-month-old daughter, Seka, lay asleep under the cloth.

Micah grasped the reins tightly and clucked to the weary, skinny beast pulling the cart. The travelers were approaching one of the snaking, poorly graded bends in the road that made it treacherous. Micah glanced at his wife. Her eyes were closed, but he could tell by the way her arms were folded across her breasts that she was not sleeping. She was daydreaming, perhaps, or seeing the future.

13

He shrugged and turned his attention back to the road. The moment the route straightened, Micah saw a village.

"Is that the one we want?" he asked Luti. "The village called Rum?"

She did not answer. Micah cursed, pulled the beast up so that the cart stopped, and snarled at his wife. "Answer me, woman! Answer me when I talk to you!"

She opened her eyes. "You won't be happy until you wake the children—is that it, Micah?"

He lowered his voice into an angry whisper. "I don't want to wake anyone. All I want to know is whether or not that village in front of us is Rum."

"Yes, it's called Rum," she said in disgust.

Micah started the cart rolling again. It was obvious that Luti was in one of her bad moods, and it was best for him to back off—to ignore her and to keep his own counsel. These dark emotions had come upon her more frequently lately, he realized. And he knew full well what they were all about: She just could not accept her new life with its poverty and hardship. Worse, she blamed him for her lack of fortune. She still believed that if he had been willing to use violence, to fight and kill the slave who had betrayed her and usurped her property, she never would have lost her lands, her house, or her wealth. Yes, she still believed that in her heart. Her anger spilled out of her mouth like lava from a volcano—hot and unending. And her fury grew even stronger after Seka was born. *That was all my fault, too,* he thought.

The cart reached the outskirts of Rum, then rolled on. Micah was appalled at the poverty of the settlement. The mud buildings were crumbling. The brick wall around the tower in the center of the village had large holes in it. Apparently no one was awake. The place seemed deserted.

"Dismal," Micah muttered. Even the weather was damp and gray.

"Go to the square," Luti ordered. "The western edge of the square."

Micah guided the ox to the area that Luti had designated. A couple of stray dogs ranged silently over to the ox, sniffed its hooves, and then ambled off.

A head popped out from behind the cloth and thrust its way between Micah and Luti.

"I'm hungry," said Drak, his dark hair tangled and standing on end.

"I told you that you'll wake the children," Luti said to Micah.

"It was time he got up anyway," Micah retorted.

Luti searched around in her large bag, which was beside her on the seat. She pulled out a piece of dried fruit and handed it to her son. He grabbed it and, remaining between his parents as he chewed, ate it quickly.

"Where are all the people?" he asked.

"Still sleeping," his mother replied.

"Or dead," Micah interjected. "Maybe all the people who once lived here have long since floated down the river."

Drak asked his father what "floating down the river" meant. Luti explained to her son that it was the custom of the villagers in the northern part of the kingdom to dispose of their dead in the river—to tie the corpse to a raft and just float it away.

"Now go in the back and make sure your sister is still asleep."

Drak obeyed his mother, vanishing back under the cloth-covered part of the cart.

Micah parked the cart on the edge of the square. He leaped down lightly and slid underneath the cart, where a large linen banner was rolled in canvas and tied. He brought the bundle out, unfurled it, then carefully fastened it with ropes to the side of the cart, as he had done a thousand times before.

He stepped back to look at his handiwork. The banner was straight and clearly visible. On it was written: LUTI THE BIRD DIVINER! KNOW YOUR FUTURE! REASONABLE RATES! On either end of the banner was drawn a large blue heron.

Then Micah glanced up and caught his son staring at him. The boy's expression registered contempt. Ashamed, Micah felt sick to his stomach. Drak was bitterly disappointed in his father. For the first years of his life, Drak had been told how his father was a great hero of the Israelites—a worthy soldier and the daring man who had assassinated the hated overseer Eglon of Moab. And Drak had been told how his father was, for many years, the feared bandit known as Blood of the Judean Wilderness. But now all he saw was a pathetic man who was supported by his wife, a man who would not raise his hand in anger or violence, an old soldier going soft.

Micah could not bear to see that look on Drak's face, for everything he had read in the boy's eyes was true. He wheeled around and put his back to the cart. He saw one of the mongrel dogs digging into the ground for a scrap of food.

Is that what I have become? he asked himself silently, bitterly. *If I ever have the chance to get away from her before she destroys my manhood completely, I won't have to think twice.*

CHAPTER THREE

Tyre/Lebanon

As Cotto hurried through the narrow streets, her luminous beauty caused more than one man to stop what he was doing to admire and desire her. The long afternoon shadows followed her steps. Her thoughts were on the new dance routine she had developed. Tonight would be the first time she performed it before an audience, and she wanted very much for her employer, the powerful Phoenician Navan, to approve. He had invited a very special group of people to his palatial estate. Usually she danced for wealthy but uncouth businessmen from Tyre. By the time she started her performance they were already drunk and could not care less what she did as long as her dance showed enough flesh.

Tonight, however, the audience would be primarily the

ruling clique of Phoenicians. These men were much more restrained and sober, and they fancied themselves as patrons of the arts. Yes, they would pay close attention to her because of her exalted reputation as a dancer. The fact that she was known to be an Israelite would make her all the more attractive to them. No doubt they all had heard the story of how she had betrayed her lover Talus to Navan. That scandal would make her even more interesting, she was certain. Phoenicians were masters of machinations.

The streets widened as Cotto approached the port area, and in a few more minutes she saw the freshly painted delicate pink walls of Navan's mansion and the carefully pruned fruit trees of his garden. One of them had gorgeous pink blossoms. As the sweet fragrance floated to her on the late-afternoon air, she wondered for a moment if the Phoenician had selected that particular tree because its flowers matched the color of the walls. It was the kind of thing that Navan would do. At the very least he would have hired a gardener who knew and shared his sensibilities. The only thing that obsessed Navan as much as money and power was beauty.

What a strange and interesting people these Phoenicians are, Cotto thought as she approached the gate. One moment they were indescribably cruel, and the next moment they could express great sensitivity and tenderness. One moment they were miserly, and the next moment they spent gold freely for insignificant items. She herself had seen Navan pay out twenty talents of silver for a single bolt of embossed linen.

When she came to the estate's gate, the Sea Peoples guard straightened, pulled back his shoulders, and stuck out his massive chest. It was the same routine every night. "Got time for me tonight after the show, Cotto?" he asked, his blue eyes twinkling and hopeful.

"Not on your salary," Cotto answered flippantly.

The guard shook his head with exaggerated disappointment, and his heavy golden hair swung from side to side. Then he saluted professionally and opened the gate. Cotto glided through. She could feel the guard's eyes on her as she entered the courtyard.

Servants were already setting out tables laden with fruit and breads and jugs of wine. Others cleaned and re-arranged the divans scattered about.

Cotto walked into a wing of the mansion, went down a hallway, then entered her cubicle quickly and shut the door. She hung her shawl on the hook behind the door and headed toward the dressing table.

A young woman, a stranger, was seated there.

"Who are you?" Cotto demanded.

"Amalie," the woman said, smiling.

Younger than Cotto, Amalie had long, luxurious brown hair made into many braids and a lean strong body encased in a diaphanous costume. There was no doubt about it—she was a dancer.

"Well, I am Cotto, and this is my dressing room. You must have made a mistake." Cotto kept her anger on a tight leash. She did not want to get upset before performing her new dance. She just wanted the intruder out of there quickly so she could calm down and regain her concentration.

"But I was told to dress in here," Amalie explained. "I'm dancing later on."

"I don't care what you're doing later on," Cotto exploded with rage. "Get out of my room!" She flung the door open.

Amalie did not budge. Infuriated, Cotto looked around for an object to fling at her.

A long shadow crossed the threshold.

Cotto turned. Navan was standing in the doorway and glowering at her from behind his heavy beard. A dangerous light glittered in his dark eyes. Behind him Cotto could see his two Philistine bodyguards—squat, powerful men with bronze breastplates and ugly double-edged swords in their side scabbards.

"I'm sorry for my screaming, Navan, but I'm trying to get this fool out of here."

"She belongs here," Navan said quietly.

"This is my room!"

"You don't need a room, Cotto. You are no longer dancing for me."

His words made her legs go weak. She held on to the door frame. "What?"

"Time has caught up to you, my dear Cotto," Navan continued in a matter-of-fact manner. "You are no longer a woman who inspires admiration."

"What are you talking about? Everyone loves me. And I have a new dance that I will perform tonight. It will be the most beautiful and daring of all." She reached out after she spoke and grasped the sleeve of his long garment.

With one strong swipe of his hand he knocked her hand away, as if it were diseased. "I have made my decision. I have another kind of dancing in mind for you."

"If I can't dance here, then I wish to return to my people," she demanded.

"You will go where I say you will go. I own you, Cotto."

"Please! I beg of you."

"Begging will accomplish nothing. Do you think I was stupid enough to believe you had nothing to do with the theft of my gold? Your young Talus never could have managed that alone! The time has come for you to pay up, my pretty one." Navan nodded to his guards, then stepped out of the doorway. One of the Philistines grabbed Cotto's arm in a powerful grip and pulled her from the room.

"No, Navan! No! Please! I'll do anything—"

They dragged her down the hallway, through the courtyard, and through the gate. Once they were on the street, they released their grip and allowed her to walk.

"Where are you taking me?" she asked.

They were silent. The winding streets were dark now except for occasional flickering oil lamps hoisted over the doorways of the houses.

Cotto knew the guards were walking north and east, toward the old section of the city, farther and farther from the magnificent homes of the ruling Phoenician class. She had never been in this neighborhood before. She tried to maintain her dignity and act as if these men were her escorts; but they walked too quickly, and she nearly had to run to keep their pace. She grew tired. The night was cold. She trembled. It was like a bad dream.

They entered a narrow alley—so narrow that they had to walk in a single file. High walls bordered the way. The guard in front of Cotto stopped so abruptly beside a massive wooden door, she almost bumped into him. She squinted at the door. There was some writing with yellow chalk on it and a design, but the night was too dark for her to make out the writing. She could but dimly perceive the meaning of the design.

Then, like a chilling wind, the awful realization hit her. When her brain fully understood what her eyes could not see, she felt as if she had been struck in the stomach by a blunt instrument. They had taken her to The Nail. It was the most horrible brothel in all of Tyre—a filthy den of perverted whores who serviced the scum of society, men dredged up from the sewers and dungeons and holds of the ships.

"No! No!" she screamed.

When the wooden door swung open, Cotto tried to run away. But the narrow alley provided no opportunity for escape. One of the guards picked her up, flung her over his shoulder, and carried her into the brothel. The stench of sex was strong.

Fighting for breath in this close, stale place, she kicked and scratched and bit the guard, but the powerful arm that held her did not flinch. He carried her up a flight of stairs and down a long hallway. The shrill sound of a woman's laugh came from behind a door.

Cotto was flung into a small room, and the door was locked behind her. Only then did she hear one of the guards call out, "Enjoy your new dressing room! Enjoy your new dance assignment."

All was silence. She sat up. A small candle of poor-quality wax was smoking in the corner of the room. A thick mat was visible and, next to it, a low table with a chipped washbasin.

She stared dumbly at the walls. She began to make out more sounds from adjoining rooms—groans and curses and harsh laughter.

The horror of her situation began to envelop her. She was now a common whore in the most hideous place in Tyre. In one brief hour her life had been shattered, her aspirations destroyed. She banged on the door and screamed for help. She shook the handle, but to no avail. A deep voice boomed at her to shut up—or else. Cotto could not risk the man's wrath. She collapsed in the corner of the room and wept.

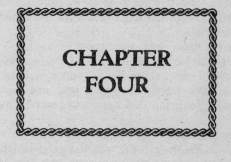

CHAPTER FOUR

Egyptian Desert

The once powerful army of the revolutionary movement, derisively called the Milk Drinkers by their foes, had been broken by the Egyptian chariot forces. The rebels were called milk drinkers because their banners bore the ancient symbols of the most hallowed gods of the delta: the shepherd's crook of Osiris and the cow of Isis.

The rebels' attempt to overthrow the reigning pharaoh, Ramses III, was now only a memory. For safety they retreated to the vast and alien desert.

But even the desert would not succor them. A terrible plague had broken out in their midst, and now the moans of the dying drifted over the wasteland. Their tents were filled with the sorrow and the keening of the bereft. The dead were being consumed by the bonfires that burned day and night, sending the sickening sweetish odor of charred corpses over the encampment.

The twins Gravis and Hela, children of Nuhara and Theon, stood at the entrance of their magnificent cream-colored tent and stared at the smaller shelters of their followers, those who had rescued them from slavery. These poor souls believed that the twins were the reincarnations of Osiris and Isis.

Their mistake was understandable, for Hela and Gravis were blessed with a physical perfection that was otherworldly. Their golden hair, green eyes, and tall, supple bodies were nearly identical, and one had to look closely before realizing that the youths were a male and a female.

The twins' beauty was enhanced by their delicate linen garments. On Gravis's tunic was the gold insignia of the shepherd's crook. And on his sister's, the cow of Isis, the symbol of fecundity, had been embroidered.

"We must help them, Gravis," Hela said in a trembling voice. "We cannot stand by and watch them suffer like this."

"There is nothing we can do," he replied.

"But they believe in us. They see us as their protectors. They saved our lives! We owe them everything." Her eyes clouded. "Perhaps we owe them the truth."

"Stop talking nonsense, Hela. We had no choice. If we had denied that we were reincarnated gods, we would have died either at their hands or Ma-Set's. Or they would have abandoned us in the desert."

Tears began to run down Hela's cheeks. She turned away so that her beloved brother would not be able to see her grief.

But she could not hide from him. He knew her every thought, just as she knew his. "Don't cry, Hela, please. Believe me, if there was something we could do for them, I'd be the first to try it."

Hela nodded and sniffed.

"Look!" Gravis said. "It's Ma-Set!"

Hela turned back and saw the soldier walking toward them. The former chariot commander in Ramses III's crack legion had become father and mother to the twins. It was impossible to know whether or not Ma-Set still believed in the twins' divinity; they certainly had failed in their efforts to assure him of success in overthrowing the pharaoh. But he still addressed them as Holy One and viewed himself as their protector. No one could speak to the youths unless the audience was cleared first with Ma-Set.

He was carrying a staff in one hand. His other hand rested on the hilt of the sword in its scabbard. He bowed with difficulty and spoke to Hela. The urgency in his voice was unmistakable. "Holy One, you must come with me now."

"What is it, Ma-Set?" she asked.

"You must come now," he repeated without giving specifics.

"Wait for me here, Gravis. I'll be right back," Hela said.

But as the girl moved to follow the soldier, Ma-Set shook his head quickly at Gravis. *This may take awhile,* his expression said.

Together they walked through the camp. Hela was immediately recognized, and the people bowed low until she had passed. Ma-Set took her on a circuitous route. Thick, black smoke from the funerary pyres burned her eyes, and the wails of a dying person's relatives were sometimes so loud that she had to flatten her hands over her ears.

Darkness was almost upon them by the time they reached a small, poorly erected tent. "In here, Holy One," Ma-Set said, holding the flap open. "Keep your face covered."

Inside, Hela found herself staring at a woman who was lying on the floor. Moaning and writhing, she had obviously been struck down by the plague.

Ma-Set cautiously moved closer to the woman. Hela

followed. "She is dying, Holy One," Ma-Set explained un-necessarily, "but she has a request of you."

Hela knelt near the stricken woman.

"What is her name, Ma-Set?"

"I know not, Holy One. I'm not even sure when or how she came to be among us."

The woman rasped out a few words, but Hela could not make them out. The woman strained with the effort to make herself heard. "Watch . . ."

That was the first word. Hela nodded, echoed the word, then moved closer until her ear was against the woman's veiled mouth. "Watch . . . over . . . her."

Yes, Hela was certain she had heard correctly. She turned to the soldier. "I don't understand, Ma-Set. Watch over whom?"

Ma-Set pointed into the dark corner of the tent. There, sitting cross-legged on the ground and sucking the first two fingers of her left hand, was a tiny girl.

"Her name is Tuk," Ma-Set said quietly.

The child, about five years old, sat absolutely still. Her skin was black; her hair was cropped short. She was naked. She appeared to be neither agitated nor frightened by the woman's terrible suffering. Hela was confused. The dying woman was fair complected, and bore no resemblance to the girl. Hela went to the child.

"Is that your real name? Tuk?" she asked.

The child did not answer. Her large, dark brown eyes unblinking, she stared at Hela. The steady gaze was discon-certing.

The girl, Hela decided, was adorable to look upon but very strange. Why wouldn't she talk? Why wouldn't she answer the question? Why was she so unemotional while her protector was dying? Hela felt she should reach out, gather the child into an embrace, and comfort her, but she could not bring herself to do so.

Ma-Set picked up a crude oil lamp that burned low near Tuk's guardian. "Please, Holy One, I wish to show you something." He joined them in the corner and told Tuk to stand. Without hesitation she did so. He motioned that the child should turn around, then gestured for Hela to come close. He pointed at Tuk's tiny round rump.

Hela stared at the child's body, where the dim lamplight flickered. She gasped, unable to believe her eyes! Tuk bore the mark of the Children of the Lion: the lion's paw print, on her lower back. But the birthmark was unlike any Hela had ever seen; it seemed to be sketched with yellow chalk on the child's brilliant black skin.

After Hela had recovered from the initial shock, she told Ma-Set to get a damp rag to run over the mark.

The man vanished, then returned in moments with a rag. He rubbed the mark briskly, then stepped back. The mark was still there. Hela narrowed her eyes, wondering if the mark might be a trick. But after close scrutiny, she knew it was a genuine birthmark.

How could this be? she wondered. "We must show the child to Gravis," Hela said to Ma-Set. She looked around the tent for the little one's clothing, but there was none to be found.

Ma-Set took off his short cape and handed it to Hela, who used it to cover Tuk's nakedness. It totally enveloped the strange child. In so doing, Hela inadvertently touched Tuk and recoiled—the child's skin felt peculiar, simultaneously hot and cold. She pulled her hand away as if the skin might infect her with some kind of deadly magic.

"What about the woman, Holy One?" Ma-Set asked.

Hela knelt by the plague victim. "Woman, is this your child?"

The miserable eyes, the plague-parched lips, answered no.

"I will make sure she's cared for," Hela promised. When she saw the woman was trying to communicate, Hela bent low again, positioning her ear to the cracked lips.

"Not . . . all . . . murdered. Three   graves . . . two children . . ." And, that said, she died.

Hela had no idea what the woman was talking about.

She repeated the words to Ma-Set, but he, too, was sty-mied.

They left that place of death and walked hurriedly through the desert night. The soldier carried Tuk. A wind was blowing, sending smoke and embers from the pyres into their tearing eyes.

When they entered the twins' large and lavish tent, Hela called out to her brother. "Gravis! Come quick."

There was no response. Then Ma-Set and Hela heard a low moaning. Hela rushed toward the sound. She found her brother lying on a mat. The dread lesions of the plague covered his face and neck and belly. He was bathed in sweat. His limbs trembled. The moans seemed to be forced out of his constricted throat by a demon within.

"No! No!" Hela screamed, and collapsed on the ground beside her beloved brother. Tuk, sucking on her two fingers, looked on silently, impassively.

CHAPTER FIVE

Canaan

As the men lowered Gideon's body into the open grave, the slender young woman staggered and almost fell. If only she had been able to speak to her brother before he died! If only she had been able to embrace dear Gideon just once more. Quickly Miriam shifted the baby in her arms and fought to regain her composure. She pulled the shawl away from her face so that she could breathe more easily.

Miriam closed her eyes. She knew that Gideon had sunk into terrible debauchery during the last year of his life. She knew that he had come undone by the strain of organizing an army and leading it into battle. Then, after his success, he had become crazed with his glory and power and had repudiated Yahweh—Who had given him that glory and power. But the only things in Miriam's heart now were love for her brother, and remorse.

She closed her eyes. She knew she should not have come to the funeral. But how could she have stayed away? Around her the people began to recite the sacred prayer for the dead. In their voices she heard love and respect. They were glad that the great Gideon was being buried near the Spring of Harod, where he had waged his first great victorious battle against the well-armed, experienced Bedouin armies.

She opened her eyes. A space beside the open grave had been created by the mourners, and an old man, assisted by a young boy, walked forward. Miriam froze. It was her father, Joash, and Gideon's son Jotham. The sight of her father was like a knife to her heart. How deeply she had missed him! How acutely she had suffered from his anger and rejection! He had publicly mourned her as dead because she had conceived and given birth to a child whose father was a Bedouin. She forced her eyes away from her father's hunched form.

Where was Shulamith, Miriam wondered. Gideon's wife surely was there! But Miriam could not find her in the crowd.

Around her father the seventy "sons" of Gideon stood in a semicircle. They were resplendent in their armor and helmets. But she could not bear to look at them; she hated them. They had taken upon themselves the name of son, but in truth they were evil men who held no love for Gideon. Once, they had been his greatest warriors; now they had brought ruin and rapine and Baal worship back to the land of the Israelites. The inhabitants cried out for mercy and relief from their violent rule.

Again she stared at her father, at his bent back, at the face so ravaged by time and grief. She could not restrain herself. She pushed forward through the crowd, and like a woman possessed she finally burst into the clearing and stood across the grave from her father.

The boy Jotham spotted her and cried out joyfully,

"Miriam!" He started to move toward her, but the old man's hand caught him in a tight grip and held him back.

"Father," she called out, the tears falling down her cheeks, "it is I, Miriam, your daughter!"

A hush fell over the crowd. All prayers ceased. For a moment the old man's face seemed to collapse, and his eyes filled with tears. Then he covered his face for a moment, and when he pulled his hand away and spoke, his words were brittle and cruel. "Liar! I have no daughter. Once, I had a daughter named Miriam, but she became a whore. So I mourned her for dead, and dead she will remain."

His words were like a sword ripping into her body. Miriam stared down at her brother's corpse, wrapped in a white linen shroud and resting on a simple pine plank at the bottom of the grave.

She lifted her child in her arms. "Have mercy, Father," she cried out, "for Gideon's sake."

Old Joash reached for a pike and held the weapon high. "Kill that bastard of a Bedouin in your arms, and you shall be my daughter again. Kill him if you are truly my daughter, my Miriam."

Fearful, she pulled the child back into her protective embrace.

"Never! My child is beloved of Yahweh," she called out, her voice trembling with fury and pride and anguish.

"Bastard child of a whore!" Joash screamed in response.

"No! My child will bring glory to the people of Yahweh," Miriam cried, now holding the swaddled infant up for the many mourners to see. "It was all foretold by a messenger from God! It was. . . ."

Her words were choked off by a scream of rage from her father's lips. And then the old man flung the pike at his daughter, across the grave of Gideon. It missed her by inches, embedding its sharp point in the grass. The shaft trembled.

Her heart filled with sorrow and fear, Miriam turned and fled.

After the priests had recited the final prayers over Gideon's open grave, Joash took his grandson's hand and approached the burial pit. They were followed by the deceased commander's seventy closest adherents.

A great hush fell over the gathering. One of the priests handed the old man a spade. Joash scooped up some dirt and held the blade over the grave. He closed his eyes, and tears fell down his cheeks. He seemed to waver, as if he would fall, but young Jotham took tight hold of his grandfather's arm. Steadied, Joash tilted the spade, and the first dirt rained onto Gideon's grave.

One by one the seventy sons of Gideon followed suit, picking up the spade, lifting some dirt, and dropping it into the burial pit.

Suddenly the solemn ceremony was interrupted by the sickening thud of iron-tipped arrows slamming into the earth. The first landed only inches from the gravesite, and then there was another and another. The mourners began to scream. Only the people standing near the attackers knew from where the arrows were being shot and, thus, where to run for safety. The soldiers among the grievers drew their swords, but there was no defense against a hidden archer.

Then a large man stepped into the clearing. He grasped a powerful bow and a quiver of arrows in one hand. His hair was long, and his black beard was full and impressive. He was dressed simply, in the garb of a shepherd—unbleached sheepskins laced together by leather thongs. He wore no shoes.

The archer strode arrogantly to the edge of the grave. The powerful muscles of his big-boned body rippled as he walked. When he reached the pit, he called out in a loud, brutal voice that everyone could hear. "I come to claim my rightful place at the grave of my father. Gideon had many daughters but only two sons: one, the child Jotham; the other, myself, Abimelech, true son of the great Gideon. True successor! True warrior!"

Joash blinked. No one had seen Abimelech in years, but rumor had it that he was living as a half-mad recluse in the hill country.

"Go away, you crazy fool!" Joash shouted at the intruder.

"*You* are the fool, old man. Gideon's blood runs in my veins as truly as your blood ran in his."

Joash was losing patience. First the terrible scene with his daughter, and now this. He reached for the spade and flung it at the intruder. But the old man had little strength to put behind the throw. Abimelech sidestepped nimbly and contemptuously.

"Your mother was a slave woman from Shechem," Joash called out scornfully. "You are not of our people. You are the bastard child of a single night's play, when my poor son was so drunk he would have coupled with a she-goat."

"Acknowledge me as Gideon's son!" Abimelech shouted back, brandishing the bow.

Joash signaled to the seventy sons of Gideon. The warriors moved quickly to surround the stranger. Their sharp-edged short swords pointed toward his throat.

But Abimelech contemptuously spat at them. He addressed the crowd, turning to face them all. His eyes were wild, and the veins in his thick neck stood out like taut ropes. "Hear me, Israelites! Before the harvest festival begins, all of you will beg to kiss my feet. All of you will bow in my presence."

But the Israelites began to laugh—titters at first and then guffaws until the laughter rang out like thunder in the sky. The seventy sons, bent double from the hilarity, lost their grip on the weapons and abandoned their offensive position encircling the intruder.

Abimelech leaped across the grave and, before any of Gideon's warriors could stop him, clutched Joash by the shoulders and kissed him soundly on the lips.

The old man wheeled away and fell to the earth. He

spat, then wiped his mouth with the back of his hand. His face contorted with shock and revulsion.

"I give you the kiss of death, old man. Now you can save time and trouble and throw yourself into the grave with Gideon. The worms are already eating your body and mind."

Then Abimelech raised his massive bow contemptuously over his head and walked slowly away through the stunned crowd until he had vanished into the woods beyond. Young Jotham helped his grandfather up, and they watched in grim silence as the proceedings continued and the grave was filled with dirt.

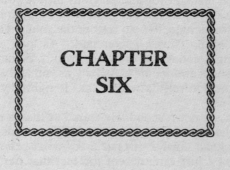

CHAPTER SIX

Thrace

Theon pulled the tattered lynx-skin robe tighter around his lean frame, but there was no defense against the bitter night chill of the mountains. The fire in front of him was flickering and would go out soon. Beside him on the ground was a Greek sword in its scabbard, the bronze hilt discolored. On the other side sat his young companion Talus, hunched over and muttering against the cold.

"I remember," Talus said angrily, "when we could look around and see twenty campfires other than our own. Now there are only two."

"We can't expect our followers to live on promises alone," Theon soothed. He had felt a similar anger when his men deserted, but he had come to realize that it was inevitable.

Talus turned toward the older man. Although Talus was young, his face was drawn, his eyes were dull. "Oh, Theon, I've lost faith in this whole venture. Even if we could ever get close enough to Nuhara to destroy her, we wouldn't survive the battle. There are too few of us."

Theon leaned over and playfully hit the younger man on the back of his head. The blow was meant to be consoling and affectionate, to help restore the young man's confidence. "Listen, Talus," Theon said. "As long as we two have strength enough to draw our swords, Nuhara and all she represents are doomed. As long as you and I keep our eyes on the future, the wealth that is rightfully ours will return to us."

Talus did not respond. He stared at the six shepherds who huddled around their campfires a few yards away. He shook his head slowly. "It's not that I don't believe in you, Theon, but I just can't accept the fact that our army has shrunk to a force of eight."

The wind kicked up and howled through the campsite. Above, clouds and the twisted trees obscured the moon. Talus and Theon leaned closer to the fire and thrust their hands so close to the flames that their nails were singed.

"It's just that sometimes I am afraid I will die here," Talus said pathetically, "in these horrendous mountains. And there will be no one to mourn for me."

"We have a long way to go together, Talus. Our journey won't end here. Believe me!" Theon spoke in a soft but intense voice. He watched the younger man to see if his words had restored Talus's confidence. But there was no way to know; Talus had closed his eyes and was gently rocking in front of the fire.

Theon glanced away. A stab of sadness suddenly came over him. Once, there had been many journeys and challenges and companions in his life. He had come from a powerful, illustrious background. His education had been the finest available. He had been loved and indulged. Now he was fighting for his survival and for that of all the Children of the Lion. The Fates had been treacherous to him.

They had offered him love and then stolen it away. They had lavished him with wealth and luxury, and then sucked his memory dry so that for years he had wandered the Great Sea like a homeless dog. And then they had restored him to health, only to see the island called Home destroyed, its people—including his twins, Hela and Gravis— killed or enslaved, and its treasure looted by his wife, Nuhara.

Theon closed his eyes and drifted into a half sleep, in which he was always on the cusp of remembering what had happened to him during the years of memory loss. He tried to bring back the faces of the children he had fathered and the woman he had married during those ten years. Their images were always close but never realized. They remained mere shadows to him. Nuhara, however, was always real . . . evil . . . dangerous—the woman he had once loved. But then betrayed by his amnesia, she transformed into the woman who had paid him back a thousandfold in misery. It was hard for him to reconcile the fact that his beautiful twins could have been born to a succubus such as she.

He woke abruptly from his half sleep, his senses fully alert. He had heard a sound from the underbrush. He looked quickly at Talus. The young man was dozing and had heard nothing. Theon waited silently, tensely. When the sound came again, he reached slowly for the sword beside him. The disturbance might have been caused by an animal, he knew. The mountains of Thrace were home to lynx, wolves, wild hogs, and goats. But as the noise came again, it was clearer, like a moan, as if a wounded beast might be inching its way through the brush.

Theon shuddered. These mountains were primeval. The people and the beasts who lived in these forests led short, brutish lives. The rule was kill or be killed. The strong ate the weak.

He leaned forward, ready to fight. His heart pounded. Could it be one of Nuhara's raiding parties? That did not seem plausible. He and his men had covered their tracks well, although they did not forgo the luxury of campfires. The smoke might have drawn Nuhara's men. But, he reminded himself, the soldiers attached to the temple of Dionysus did not like to fight at night.

Again the sound came, much louder—a deep, throbbing, pathetic wail.

Theon leaned over and shook Talus awake, first covering the young man's mouth so he would not cry out.

Talus's eyes opened and stared at him. Theon made a sign with his finger cautioning silence, then pointed to a torch that lay near the fire. Talus nodded, picked up the torch, and lit it in the embers. Then he drew his own sword.

Moments later the two companions were moving silently toward the underbrush.

Theon led the way, and even though he was a large man and had spent most of his life in cities, he broke the path without a sound. Talus followed in his steps. The torch he held cast bizarre shadows.

The sounds grew closer. Theon paused and listened.

"There, Talus," he whispered, "by that lightning-scarred tree. Bring the torch down."

As Talus did so, Theon positioned his sword to the ready. They moved quickly now and reached the tree in a few steps. The torch light illuminated a sight so horrible that both men recoiled.

The sounds were coming from a human being, an elderly man who lay on his side. He had been beaten. One eye was swollen shut. Blood bubbled out of his nose. His lip was split.

The man's eyes widened in horror when he saw the torch. "Please," he groaned, "leave me alone. Don't hurt me any more. I beg you."

Theon quickly knelt beside him. "Have no fear, stranger. We will help you."

While Talus hurried back to camp for the water-filled bladder, Theon dug into the earth until he reached moisture and quickly placed the moist dirt on the man's most grievous wounds.

The pain evidently eased a bit. "Thank you," the man rasped. "Thank you!" The stranger tried to sit up, but the pain was too great.

"Don't try to move," Theon ordered. "We will carry you to our camp. You can rest there until you are well."

The next morning the brutalized victim seemed improved.

"Tell us your name, stranger, and who did this to you," Theon asked.

He was more willing than able to talk. During his beating, his teeth had gone through his tongue, so now he spoke slowly, very slowly, and sometimes his words were slurred. He managed to croak out a few sentences.

"My name is Circus. I am a poor old thief. That witch Nuhara did this to me. I stole some food from her banquet table. The servants caught me at it. Nuhara laughed while the soldiers taught me a lesson."

"Well then, you are not only safe here, stranger, but you are welcome," Talus chimed in enthusiastically. "We ourselves are the sworn enemies of Nuhara."

Circus's eyes widened in astonishment. He looked at Theon for confirmation.

"Yes," Theon verified, "we are determined to destroy her. You are not the first to suffer from her cruelty."

"You have saved my life," the stranger said. "And I will repay you."

"Rest now," Theon told him.

But the stranger would not rest. "No, listen: I can help you destroy her. We can have our vengeance together." The pain from the exertion caused him to groan and twist. But he continued. "I can lead you to the secret vault of the temple priests. I know the tunnel entrance that joins a vast underground cave. There you will find an enormous treasure, which people say was stolen by Nuhara from a distant land."

Talus stared at Theon. And then he hooted with joy. He performed a little dance beside the campfire. "Theon," he called out, waving his sword, "our luck has finally changed. Everything we have been fighting for has just fallen into our lap."

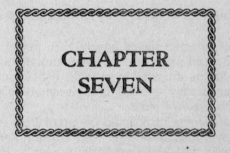

CHAPTER SEVEN

Kingdom of Babylon

It was a bad day for telling fortunes. By midafternoon only six people had paid for Luti's services. Obviously the villagers of Rum were too poor for such extravagances.

Luti squatted in front of a large blanket laid out by the side of the oxcart. On the other side of the blanket hunkered down a distraught old woman, barefoot and toothless.

Between them on the blanket were three feathers, a skull, and assorted bones—all from a blue heron.

"What questions do you have for me, old woman?" Luti asked.

"My daughter is childless. Will I die without seeing a grandchild?"

"Any other questions?"

"Yes. Seven nights ago the face of my husband appeared to me in a dream. The face was nearly unrecognizable because of his pain. I realized then that he was suffering in the netherworld because of some crime he committed while he was on this earth. Tell me what the crime was."

"Pay me, old woman, and your questions shall be answered."

The old woman sighed hugely, then pulled out from her robe a small piece of dirty linen, knotted on the corners. Her fingers struggled to untie the tight knot. Finally a single silver coin lay revealed. Luti plucked it up and put it quickly into her own purse.

The cries of a baby could be heard from inside the oxcart. It was little Seka. The wails became louder. *Why doesn't Micah feed her?* Luti thought angrily. *How can I support the family with all these interruptions?*

Then the cries ceased, and Luti regained her concentration. She leaned forward and picked up the skull and bones of the blue heron. Her eyes closed, she cradled them for a moment in both hands, then flung them upward.

They landed on the blanket. Two of the small bones, those from the pelvis of the heron, formed their own group, inches from the other objects.

"Your daughter will conceive and give birth within two years' time, old woman. But the child will die."

The old woman rocked back and forth and moaned, "Oh, I knew this would happen because I was old—too old —when I had my daughter. I gave the weakness in my bones to her. It is all my fault."

Luti waited patiently until the woman had recovered her composure. There was another question to answer. She picked up the three magnificent blue heron feathers, leaned over the blanket, and touched each feather to the brow of the old woman. But Seka began to cry again, this time much louder and much more persistently. Luti tried to concentrate, but she found it impossible.

"Wait here for me, old woman. I will be right back," Luti said.

She ran to the back of the cart and pulled open the curtain. Drak was nowhere in sight. Seka was lying on her lambskin. She was waving her fat little arms and howling. She was red in the face from her crying. And Micah was fast asleep, oblivious.

Luti shook Micah violently. "Wake up! Wake up! Is it too much to expect you to feed the child while I'm working?"

Micah cleared the sleep from his head. He glared at her with both shame and anger. "I was tired," he said defensively. "I spent the whole morning trying to drum up business for you. Drak was supposed to feed Seka."

"Well, Drak isn't here."

Micah picked up a small cloth that hung inside the wagon. He dipped one end of it into a jug of goat's milk. Then he took the cloth and held it against the baby's mouth until Seka sucked the goat's milk from the fabric.

Still angry, Luti stomped back to her customer, picked up the three feathers, and once again touched the old woman's brow with them. Then she released the feathers and allowed them to float down onto the blanket. The first and second landed with the quills facing south. The third landed on the first two, the quill pointing east.

Luti sat cross-legged and stared at the woman. The feathers never lied. And this time the way they fell signified a profound sin on the part of her customer's dead husband.

"Are you sure you want to hear the truth, old woman?" Luti asked.

"That is why I paid you," the customer answered.

"Then I will tell you. Your husband betrayed you. He lay many times with your younger sister."

The old woman blanched. She sat back as if Luti had struck her a blow in the face, and her eyes grew wide. "Liar! Liar! Charlatan!" she hissed, then jumped up and ran from the blanket as if Luti had the plague.

Disgusted and tired, Luti folded the blanket and climbed up to the driver's seat.

"Are you calling it a day?" Micah called from inside.

"Yes. I want to bathe and get some sleep."

"Let's go to that grove on the other side of the village," Micah suggested.

Luti nodded and guided the ox out of the village. Drak came running up and joined her on the seat.

The wagon creaked along the dusty road until it entered the cool glade.

"There's a small stream not far away," Drak enthusiastically told his mother. "I found it this morning."

Luti gently hit the ox on his right side, and the beast veered in the direction of the stream.

"Mother!" Luti heard her son's scream a second before a cry escaped from her own throat.

In front of them three figures on horses had suddenly appeared. The men's faces were concealed by bronze helmets.

In a moment the cart was surrounded by well-armed troops on powerful horses. The men's armor and bearing bespoke danger, brutality, and threat. Drak reached out to grasp his mother's hand.

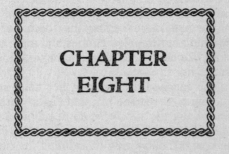

CHAPTER EIGHT

Tyre/Lebanon

The foul-smelling Hittite drover rolled off her. Cotto was nauseated, and her body ached. She closed her eyes tightly for a few seconds and prayed that this was a horrendous nightmare from which she would awaken.

"Bitch!" the man fumed. He stood and spat onto the floor. "I'd be better off humping a goat." Then he pulled on his coarsely woven clothes and stomped out of her tiny room, slamming the door behind him.

Cotto heard a crash from the next room, but she was too depressed to investigate. As Navan's employee, she would have been perfectly willing to make love to him or to his powerful friends. But never had Navan asked for her favors. She had been free to choose her partners as she desired. Now, to be at the mercy of filthy, common men she would not have noticed if they passed her in the street was painful and humiliating.

She rolled onto her stomach and stared through the tiny window at the first rays of dawn. That meant she would have to endure no more customers for a few hours; the brothel was open only from noon to dawn.

She sat up and winced. The pain in her body was great, but she had to get across the room, to the straw hamper that held her jumbled clothes and a jug of watered wine. Feeling like a whipped dog, she moved slowly across the cold stone floor.

When she reached the hamper, her hand snaked under the clothes, removed the jug, and eagerly brought it to her lips. She drank the sour wine so deeply and so quickly that liquid spilled out the sides of her mouth. She did not care. Wine was the only thing that dulled the horror, that brought her some peace, that enabled her to forget the perversions demanded of her.

She had opened herself to worse brutes than the Hittite drover, but these last hours of the night were always the ones she remembered with the most loathing.

Cotto drank more wine, and then more, greedily sucking at the jug. Her pain eased. She bent to examine her thighs. They were red, raw. A tear slid down her cheek as she fixed her eyes on the small window. This time the rising sun offered no consolation.

How many days had she been here? she wondered. She no longer remembered. How could she escape? She knew of no way. The brothel owner had been instructed by Navan to plunge a knife into the heart of any girl who tried to leave. She knew that—all the whores knew that—and the gold-hilted blade always dangled at the owner's waist. It was hard to accept how meaningless she was to Navan. She had not been aware of how greatly her position as favored dancer had influenced how she felt about herself. He cared more for his gold than for her life, in spite of her years of service to him. She shook her head ruefully and marveled at her own arrogance and stupidity. At one time, and not all that long ago, she believed she could control the Phoenician.

The wine was at last making her stuporous. She drained the jug, then set it on the floor. The morning light flooded the tiny, filthy room and hurt her eyes. She turned toward the far wall, putting her back to the high window.

Suddenly she saw the face of a man on the wall. She blinked. An apparition? It was Talus, the young man she had loved and betrayed. She reached out toward the vision, but it vanished. She dissolved into bitter tears and collapsed across the bed.

Why had she betrayed the one man who had loved her? Why had she double-crossed him and told Navan that it was Talus who had stolen the gold when she herself had been the culprit? Why had she denounced her own people, the Israelites, and chosen to live among the Phoenicians?

Tears stained her once lovely face. She had betrayed everything and everyone in a stupid quest for riches and power. She had deluded herself into thinking that her dancing skills and exceptional beauty would enable her to climb the ladder of wealth. Then she, too, would be counted as one of the lords of the earth.

She began to shiver and tremble. The ancient beliefs of her people in a God of vengeance infused her with terror. Yahweh, it was known, paid back the guilty in blood.

How she longed to touch Talus again! How she longed to see her family once more, to feel safe and secure in their arms! How she longed to be away from this filthy room and this city of perversion, sorrow, and pain.

Cotto, wishing for a new start, praying for the opportunity to put her hard-earned lessons into action, lay curled beside the bed until the wine brought blessed sleep.

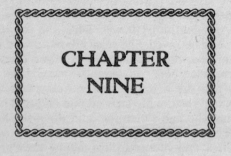

CHAPTER NINE

Egyptian Desert

"Momma! Momma!"

Gravis's moans woke Hela, who was dozing at his side. She reached for the damp cloth in the bowl of cool water and wiped her brother's sweat-drenched face.

For three nightmarish days and nights she had nursed Gravis and prayed fervently to the gods for his recovery, but he, like the many others in the encampment who were similarly affected, grew worse and worse. Hela and Gravis had always wielded strange powers, and Hela had tried all her tricks and concentration to return her twin brother to health. But since he had taken ill, her extraordinary abilities had faded. It was as if her supernatural skills could not function without Gravis's energy providing half the fuel.

In a helpless rage, Hela had literally driven her servants from the tent. She permitted only the soldier Ma-Set and the little black girl, Tuk, to remain.

Gravis could no longer eat or drink. His muscles convulsed, and his glittering eyes saw demons that did not exist. At times he was deathly pale, but always at night his cheeks burned with two hectic red circles of fever. He cried out, but Hela could not understand what he said. Tears welled up and hung from her eyelashes as she stroked his head. His golden hair was dull, lifeless, darkened now from constant sweating. Hela closed her eyes and, bereft, rocked back and forth. She remembered how happy they had been together on the island Home—in the safe and carefree days of childhood, when no thoughts of death had touched them.

"Holy One?"

Hela opened her eyes. Ma-Set, all concern, offered a blanket. She smiled wanly with gratitude, then covered her beloved twin, adding this blanket to the others that already swathed his shivering frame. It was, she knew, a futile gesture. Nothing could make Gravis more comfortable. Nothing, she feared, could save his life.

"He will not see the dawn," the soldier said sadly.

"Don't say that!" she cried out. "He mustn't hear you talk that way. You could kill him with your words. We have to hope for a miracle, Ma-Set. He cannot die here!"

"Forgive me, Holy One," Ma-Set said, bowing his head in shame. "Surely if anyone will be favored by the gods and made well again, it will be your brother."

Hela grasped her brother's hand and spoke to him directly, her voice rising in a hysterical curve. "You won't die, will you, Gravis? Please, you can't die. We've always been together. We've always looked out for each other. Live, Gravis, and I promise to take you back to Home." Hela, weeping, wrapped her arms around her brother and laid her head on his chest. "Please, Gravis, I don't know if I could live without you."

She felt another convulsion stiffen, then shake his body. He loosed a bone-chilling scream and fought with extraordinary strength against her embrace. She held him tightly, and Ma-Set helped to brace him. Then, with a final jolt, Gravis lay still.

"He's dead, Holy One," Ma-Set whispered.

"No, no, no," she moaned, the tears flooding her face. "You're wrong!"

The old soldier gently disentangled her from the corpse and eased her away from the bed.

"He's dead," Ma-Set repeated quietly. "You have done everything you could. You can do no more for him."

He helped Hela, limp and unresisting, to lie down. Then he covered her with a blanket, tucking it securely under her chin and around her shoulders. Next he pulled a blanket up to cover Gravis's face, then left the tent. Tuk sat cross-legged, watching silently from a darkened corner.

Hela lay beside her brother for hours. She could neither speak nor move. She felt numb. Her world had collapsed. Gravis had been her only companion, her only confidant, her only friend, her other half. He was more than flesh and blood to her; he was the seat of spiritual integrity and identity. His strength had brought them through all the horrors since the Phoenician invaders stole them away from Home. His words were the only ones she listened to—even though, because of the deep connection between them, the words were rarely spoken. She had read his thoughts as clearly and as accurately as he had read hers.

At dusk Ma-Set brought her rich goat's milk, but she could not drink. He brought her delicate chopped meats and vegetables, but she could not eat.

How will I survive now? she agonized. *Why should I survive? What is the point of anything? Why go on with all this lunacy? Why continue the charade that I am a reincarnation of Isis?*

She wanted to reach out and touch Gravis, to console him, but she did not have the strength to move. Suddenly she noticed that Tuk was looking at her from the far darkness of the tent. Her misery congealed into unreasoning fury. "Why don't you speak?" she screamed at the girl. "Why do you keep staring at me like that? Leave me alone! Don't you know that my brother is dead?"

The child did not respond.

Hela buried her face in the blanket and wept. Finally, she slept; it was the sleep of despair.

A hand was pulling at her. Hela sat up quickly, disoriented, not knowing where she was. She caught sight of the covered body next to her, and memories flooded over her with terrible clarity.

"Holy One?" said Ma-Set. His hand was still gently on her shoulder, to steady her. "A delegation from the people wishes to speak to you."

She looked past him and saw the group standing just inside the tent. They were edging toward her slowly, respectfully, bowing low with each tiny step. Then the group stopped, and one man came forward. He was one of the prayer leaders of the cult, an olive-skinned, dark-eyed man named Paht. Hela knew him to be both fearless and devout.

Ma-Set nodded at Paht, giving him permission to speak.

"Holy One," he entreated, "hear my pleas. Hundreds of our people have already perished from disease, and each dawn more are found dead. Only you can save us."

Hela's eyes flared with anger. Did he not realize that Gravis had died? Surely if she could not save her own flesh and blood, she would not be able to help anyone else. Why was he bothering her now, of all times?

"How do you think I can save you?" she asked bitterly.

"Holy One," Paht continued, bowing low, "if you perform the ceremony of the miracle, then the sick will get well, and those who have perished will live forever under the benevolent love of your father—Ra, the sun god."

She could no longer contain her anger. "Get out of here, you fool! Get out, out all of you!"

Their eyes grew wide with fear. They turned and ran, falling over one another in an attempt to escape her harsh words and any curse or punishment that might follow.

After they had left, Hela fell back on the bed. Oh, what idiots her followers were, she thought. They still believed all the nonsense. She knew what the ceremony of the miracle was—Isis had raised her brother, Osiris, from the dead. He had survived just long enough to impregnate her. This miracle of fertilization guaranteed immortality to all those who believed in Isis.

Hela leaned over and touched her brother's shrouded body. She wished she did have the powers to perform such a miracle. To have Gravis back, she might even consent to an incestuous union with him. But she was not Isis, and Gravis was not Osiris. No amount of praying or plague or delusion could alter those facts.

"Holy One . . ."

She gritted her teeth at the hated and stupid salutation.

"You must try, Holy One," Ma-Set urged.

She stared grimly at him. "Why?" she asked.

"Because the plague has caused great misery. Your people are growing violent. Your followers are feeling unprotected. Because of Gravis's death, they are doubting your powers. They demand a miracle, and unless they get one, they will turn on you."

Hela laughed crazily. "Let them kill me. I'd be happy to join Gravis in the netherworld. Let those fools come to accept that I am a mere mortal, carried off from my home in the Great Sea."

"Holy One," said Ma-Set respectfully, "if something untoward happens to me, no one will fill my space as your protector. I wish long life for you and the child."

"The child? What child?" Hela shouted. And then she saw the little girl standing quietly behind the soldier, holding on to his leg. Tuk's eyes were wide and frightened. She had, Hela admitted, witnessed much death and misery for one so young. If Ma-Set died, there would be no one else to care for the girl. *Just as there would be no one else to care for me,* Hela realized.

She sighed, resigned. Her voice grew calm and weary. Yes, Ma-Set was right. She must try to perform the ceremony of the miracle. For the child's sake! Hela gave a sign of acquiescence to the faithful soldier, then covered her face with her linen shawl and rested her head on Gravis's chest.

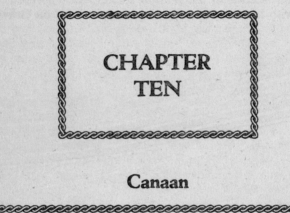

CHAPTER
TEN

Canaan

Miriam fled her brother's funeral and wept because of her father's behavior toward her. There had been a great feast set out, and Miriam was hungry and thirsty; but she would not dine with Gideon's mourners if it meant submitting to rejection and humiliation. She took the western path leading away from the burial rites.

She walked quickly toward the foothills and felt confident that she could gather wild berries and fruit there for her son, Jeb, who lay sleeping in her arms. Bless his little innocent heart, she thought, he was still oblivious to all the hatred and prejudice that existed in the world. What a good child he was, so placid and accepting.

As she walked, sadness overwhelmed her. Joash would never forgive her for having a child by a Bedouin, let alone without benefit of marriage. Her beloved Gideon was dead. Her Bedouin lover was in his netherworld, sent there by Gideon's own sword. She and her baby were alone —so totally alone that sometimes she felt as if she inhabited an empty land.

She was so lost in her reverie that she did not see the man who had stepped out of the underbrush and blocked her way. When she was almost upon him, she clutched her child more tightly to her bosom and turned to run. A powerful hand reached out and stopped her, then spun her around to face him.

"Miriam!" he said.

At the sound of her own name, Miriam tried to calm down. She studied his face. This huge and wild-looking stranger had long hair worn in the fashion of the hill people. His eyes were hard and cruel. But he looked oddly familiar, someone from her past.

"Don't you remember me?" the large man asked. His eyes bored into her.

"Abimelech? Is that you?"

Sudden pleasure flashed in his eyes. "Yes, it is I, your nephew."

Miriam smiled. Abimelech was one of Gideon's bastards, so technically, he was her nephew. She stared up at the fierce face. She had not seen him in many years, but he lived nowhere near Joash's village, and Abimelech was by reputation a recluse.

"I am happy to see you again, Nephew, and very glad that you are well; but I must not stay here. My child is hungry, and I have to find something for him to eat."

Something about the way Abimelech looked at her frightened Miriam and made her nervous. His mood had changed too drastically; it was not normal.

"Listen to me, Miriam," he said, one of his hands brushing against her cheek for a moment, then lifted away quickly as if the touch had burned him.

"I must go, Abimelech! My child is—"

"Your child is sleeping. Listen to me. I saw what happened to you at the funeral. I came here with the same purpose as your own—to reclaim my rightful place in the family. I am my father's heir. Like you, I was insulted and driven off. You and I are very close, Miriam. You and I are the true blood of Gideon. You and I were his beloveds." He clutched her hand and would not let her pull away. His voice was hushed, fervent. "Hear me, beautiful Miriam. For many years I have dreamed of you. No finer woman exists in all the lands that Yahweh promised to our people. Come with me now. Be my woman. I'll raise your child as my own."

Miriam, her heart pounding, backed away from him. Her hand slid from his grip. He was her nephew, for goodness sakes! His words were crazy. She hardly knew him . . . and what she did know, she did not like. He was said to be unstable and prone to unprovoked violence.

"I pledge to you my body and my sword," he vowed passionately, "and I shall lie with you until we are old."

She thought quickly. She had to get away from this man without infuriating him. "Abimelech, it is very kind of you to make such an offer. But as you well know, a union between an aunt and a nephew would be considered incestuous."

Abimelech narrowed his eyes, and he balled his huge, powerful hands into fists. "I care nothing for the rules of other men," he said to her. "Soon it shall be Abimelech who will write the rules in the land of Canaan."

What was he talking about? This hill shepherd, able to write laws? He truly was mad!

"Please, Nephew, let me go."

He stepped aside to let her pass, but she could feel the rage emanating in hot waves from his body. When she had gone a few feet past him, he called out, "Miriam!"

She stopped but did not turn.

"You stupid bitch," she heard him say. "You will regret the day you denied me your love! Soon Abimelech will rise above all beasts and men! You will curse yourself when you realize that you have denied King Abimelech his rightful pleasures of your body."

Frightened, she started to walk again, not replying, not turning back. She prayed that he would not follow. But he kept screaming after her. He shouted about his love for her, his desire for her, his claim that soon all men would bow their heads to him.

Miriam walked faster and faster and then began to run. Jeb started to wail, a protest at being jostled. Tears ran down her cheeks as she escaped the man. She ran until she was exhausted and fell to the side of the path. Then she looked back. The man was nowhere in sight. Her chest heaving, she kissed her child again and again. They were safe.

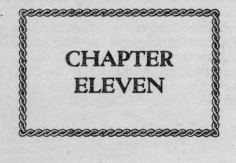

CHAPTER ELEVEN

Thrace

A cold wind whipped across the sun-drenched clearing. The elderly stranger, recovering from his beating, sat wrapped in blankets while carefully eating a bowlful of cooked grain. He favored his split lip and loosened teeth.

"We can't wait," Talus whispered excitedly to Theon. "We must go tonight."

Theon, however, remained silent and noncommittal as he watched the stranger. "Perhaps it would be better to wait another day," he finally told Talus. "I'm not sure our friend here would be able to make the long trek down the mountain to the secret tunnel."

In a fit of anger Talus broke the stick he held in his hand and flung it down on the ground. "No, Theon!" he erupted. "I can't wait any longer. This is the first luck we've had. We have to go tonight!"

Theon thought for a moment. "All right. If the old man thinks he'll be able to walk the distance, then we'll go tonight, Talus."

The younger man whooped with glee. Then he spread a blanket on the ground, laid out his short Greek sword and his daggers, sat down, and began to hone them with a stone.

Theon leaned back and watched him. Talus was brave and loyal and totally dedicated to restoring the legitimate fortunes of the Children of the Lion. His only fault was that he was too mercurial; his mood changes caused sudden loss of will, and there was no guarantee that even this one would last.

The stranger Circus finished the porridge and set the bowl on the ground.

"Feeling better?" Theon asked.

"Yes, thank you."

"Do you think you would be able to lead us to the cave tonight?"

"Definitely! I want to go as soon as possible, even if I have to crawl there."

Theon's brows came together as he studied the stranger. Circus appeared very shaky, and their path tonight would be a long, hard descent.

"See if you can stand by yourself," Theon suggested.

Circus nodded, took a deep breath, and struggled to his feet. It was a slow process, achieved with great difficulty. But at last he was up and standing alone. Talus cheered him.

"Now see if you can walk," Theon suggested.

Circus took three halting steps and then crashed to the ground in a heap. Theon and Talus rushed to the groaning man and carried him back to his blankets.

When he was settled, Circus looked crestfallen. "I'm sorry. And after all your kindness to me . . ."

"I think we should postpone our—" Theon began.

"No! There must be some way," Talus said.

"If both of you insist upon going tonight," Theon sug-

gested, "we'll have to rig a litter." He looked at Circus.
"Our shepherds will carry you down."

Talus nodded; Circus agreed. Then Talus rushed off to
make the preparations.

At dusk the expedition started out. First came Talus,
with a torch, then Theon, and Circus on a stretcher made
from tree limbs and covered with hide. Four shepherds
carried it. The two remaining shepherds took up the rear.
They descended cautiously and in silence. The night wind
whipped through their hair; the brambles cut at their flesh;
the hooting of the owls and the crying of the shrikes
haunted their imaginations.

As the men neared their destination, Theon told Talus
to extinguish the torch. The last thing he wanted to do was
attract patrols from the temple of Dionysus.

From time to time the small party stopped and rested.
Theon consulted often with Circus, to get their bearings.
They had covered more than a few miles. Each time they
started up again, Theon had to tell Talus to slow his pace.
The younger man was so eager, he was exhausting the en-
tire party.

"Theon!" It was Circus calling from the litter.

"Stop, Talus," Theon whispered, then went back to
where Circus lay.

The old man was clearly agitated. "We are very close
now," he said. "Ahead you will see two entwined olive
trees rent by lightning. Circle them until you come to an
odd outcrop of rock."

Theon nodded, then gave Talus the signal to continue.

Circus was right. Soon the group reached the strange
trees and then, circling them, saw the rocks that seemed to
have been thrust violently out of the ground.

"Bring me closer," Circus told the shepherds. Then he
showed them which rocks had to be removed to expose a
secret tunnel's access. It took hours of labor. The men used
makeshift hoists to roll back two of the large boulders. But
after they had done so, a small passageway became visible.

Theon and Talus exchanged glances. Taking Circus's stretcher through the tunnel would be difficult but necessary.

They entered the dark hole and moved very slowly, very tentatively into the underground abyss. The air was too foul to light torches so the men found their way by running their hands along the slimy walls.

The deeper they moved into the earth, the wider and the more navigable the passageway became. Minimal light came down through holes above the men. As their eyes became accustomed to the near darkness, they caught glimpses of the cave denizens. Massive, frightening bats with horrific squeezed skulls and glowing eyes appeared suddenly with a flurry of beating wings in front of their faces. Rats scurried under their feet. The Thracian shepherds chanted to ward off evil omens, and Theon angrily hissed at the men to shut up.

Their pace slowed as exhaustion and fouled air took their toll. Finally Theon called a halt and gave each man a small piece of goat's cheese and flat bread. Then he dipped a sea sponge into a jug of watered wine and allowed each man to suck the sponge once.

"Soon the passageway will widen," Circus promised. "And the air will be fresher."

They started up again and, indeed, within a few hundred yards, the passage did widen. At last the men found themselves in a large chamber with high walls.

"We seem to be in an abandoned silver mine," Theon whispered to Talus as they all stood in the center of the chamber. It was impossible to ascertain in the darkness just how deep the chamber ran in front of them.

"We'll keep to one wall and go slowly," Theon told the men.

They inched their way forward. The men stopped abruptly when a strange metallic sound clanked in the darkness of the far side of the chamber. And then, cutting through the air came a different sound—a woman's voice.

"How nice to see you again, my dear."

Theon and Talus, recognizing the voice immediately, froze with fear. It was Nuhara.

A second later the cave was flooded with the brilliant light of dozens of torches. Beside each torchbearer stood an archer. Arrows were notched in each man's bow, and the gleaming iron tips of the arrows pointed at the throats of Talus, Theon, Circus, and the shepherds.

Nuhara, resplendent in the elegant, rich robes of the high priestess, sauntered with studied nonchalance over to her husband. His body was caked with sweat and filth.

She looked at him for a moment as if she were studying a lamb at auction, as if she were evaluating the worth of his meat.

Then she reared back and spat into his face. "What a stupid, pathetic fool you are!"

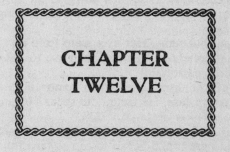

CHAPTER TWELVE

Kingdom of Babylon

"Who are you? What do you want? Leave us alone!" Luti's voice was high-pitched and frightened as she called out to the armed, fearsome-looking soldiers who had surrounded the family's oxcart.

There was no response. The soldiers sat on their massive horses and stared at her; their spears and swords glistened in the late afternoon sun.

Young Drak pressed against her, frightened. She put an arm around his shoulders and pulled him close. She could see Micah, near the ox, holding Seka in his arms. Her husband's eyes were wide with concern.

Then the front rank of the horses parted, and a solitary rider approached. Luti shrank back when she saw the tattoo of the evening star on his cheek. That mark could

mean only one thing: They were troopers of the cult of
Astarte, the goddess of the southern regions of Babylon.
The priests of this cult had branded her as a witch years
before and sentenced her to a traitor's death. The lucky
intervention of an old astrologer had saved her life. What,
she wondered, were these men doing so far north?

"Who are they?" Micah whispered, inching his way
closer to Luti.

She did not reply. Her eyes were fixed on the officer
with the tattoo. He had guided his horse to the ox, which
was standing placidly.

The officer dismounted, then removed a long spear
from its stirrup case. He tested the spear's balance in one
hand. The weapon quivered.

"No!" Drak suddenly screamed and broke loose from
his mother's grasp and began to run toward the ox.

But the child had not taken more than two steps when
the officer drove the spear through the beast's chest and
into its great heart. The ox knelt and died, gently, quietly—
its massive head coming to rest on its front legs as if in
sleep.

Sobbing, the boy sank down beside the fallen ox and
wrapped his arms around the beast's head.

At a signal from their leader all the soldiers dismounted and ran toward the cart.

They methodically destroyed the cart and its contents.
For a few seconds Micah and Luti watched helplessly.
Then Luti took Seka from Micah's arms. "Stop them,
Micah!" she pleaded.

He stared at the soldiers. His powerful arms and
shoulders, which had at one time made him the most
feared and bloodthirsty bandit in Canaan, trembled. His
dark visage, which had courageously stared death in the
eyes a thousand times, now seemed soft and unsure.

"Please, Micah," she begged him. "They are destroying all we own in the world."

But her husband was rooted to the ground. Her hatred for him in that moment was boundless. She had

pledged her eternal love to him, but now her eyes frantically searched for a weapon to drive into his heart so that he could never again betray his family and satisfy his absurd pledge of pacifism . . . his determination never to lift his hand in anger or hatred against his fellow man, no matter what the provocation.

Repulsed, she turned her face away and covered her eyes so that she would not see his weakness or the carnage wrought by the troops.

The soldiers broke the planks of the cart, destroyed the wheels, and hacked the axles into unusable pieces. They destroyed everything except for the bundle of items that Luti used for her prophecies.

"Why?" Luti demanded. "Why have you destroyed everything?"

The officer, saying nothing, waved one hand in the air. Two small shaggy ponies were led forward.

The soldiers grasped Luti's arms and lifted her and Seka onto one pony. Her ankles were tied together beneath the belly of the pony so that she could not dismount and run away. Micah and Drak were flung on the second pony and tied in a similar manner.

As they rode off surrounded by the armed escort, Luti turned her head around to stare at the gutted wagon, dead ox, and bits and pieces of pottery and fabric that littered the ground. Hot bitter tears squeezed from her eyes. Once again her world had collapsed. Once again she had lost everything. She turned back, covered Seka's little face with kisses and tears, and did not look back again.

CHAPTER THIRTEEN

Tyre

The whores sat silently on long benches in the dusty yard of The Nail as they ate their midmorning meal. The food, consisting of lumpy barley gruel with a few pieces of fruit and topped off by a spoonful of honey, was served in wooden bowls with wooden spoons.

The long benches were splintered and weatherworn. The whores all wore the same coarse garment—a simple, short shift fastened in the front by a single piece of rope so that the garment could be shed quickly.

The women were, for the most part, very young but looked very old. The Nail was the dregs—a brothel at the end of the line. It was a place for those who had nowhere else to go . . . or were too weak to fight . . . or were sent there in virtual slavery by overlords who were weary of them. The few attractive women in their prime, like Cotto, stood out from the crowd and were much sought out by the customers. Thus it was that the beautiful women died first from weariness, shame, disease, and beatings.

A high crumbling wall surrounded the yard. Escape was a possibility if one were strong enough, but the work had ravaged their bodies and destroyed their spirit. Their only desire was to die, not to escape and remember.

Cotto chewed slowly. The food was like ashes in her mouth. Her mouth was tender from a beating handed out for no reason other than the love of violence by a drunken Philistine seaman. While she ate, the owner had the whores' wine jugs refilled. He was generous with that commodity alone; it kept the girls subdued.

When Cotto finished her gruel, she walked to the large vat and flung her bowl and spoon into the murky water. Then she slowly climbed the stairs to her small cubicle.

The moment she entered, she grasped her wine jug and climbed into her hammock. Each room had a padded mat with pillows, but that was reserved for work. A beating awaited any whore who used the mat for sleeping. Hammocks, which could be rolled and unrolled, were the only beds allowed, unless the women wished to sleep on the stone floor.

Cotto took a deep swig of the wine and stared dully out the small window on the far side of her room. That window had become the center of her existence, for she could tell by the sunlight and the shadows when the sun approached the noon hour. She was safe until then. But the moment the sun was high in the sky, the sound of heavy footsteps would approach her room.

As the shadows lengthened, Cotto grew more anxious and drank more quickly. She wanted to be numbed by a stupor. Then she would not feel the shame and degradation that awaited her. Slowly, the wine took its effect.

Suddenly she heard footsteps thudding outside her

room. She moaned like a wounded animal. *No!* she thought. *It cannot be noon yet! Not yet!*

But a man had burst into her cubicle. He brutally ripped the wine jug from her hand and flung it against the far wall. Cotto cowered in the hammock and covered her face with her hands.

Then the visitor lifted one side of the hammock, and Cotto crashed to the floor. She opened her eyes and stared up at the brutal stranger.

Her heart beat fast when she realized who was standing there. It was none other than Navan.

"How do you like your new job?" he asked nastily. "Are the musicians congenial? Do you like your dancing partners?" He bent over her, and his lips curled into a smile. "Incredibly, you look as lovely as ever. But you stink like a drunken whore."

Gathering all her strength, Cotto wrapped her arms around Navan's leg. She wept and begged, "Please take me out of here! I can't stand it! I'll die here! What have I done to deserve such treatment? Please, Navan, I will do anything for you!"

Navan savagely kicked her away, then kicked her in the ribs twice for good measure. "Don't touch me, you filthy bitch!"

Cotto rolled around the floor in pain, whimpering and crying and pleading.

Then Navan barked, "Shut up. There is a way out of here. Listen carefully. Do you remember Purah? He was Gideon's servant. You made yourself available to him when he came to Tyre."

She nodded. A glimmer of hope shone in her eyes.

"Purah has been one of my spies for years. I have just received word from him. He's living in the city of Shechem. Dangerous new political forces are rising there in Canaan. I could use you there. It's your homeland. You understand the people there. If you want to get out of here, you will go to Shechem and contact Purah. He will let you stay in his house. I want you to use your erotic charms in my service

—to ferret out the offenders so they might be eliminated. Do you understand and agree to what I have told you?"

All she could do was nod. The pain and shame and degradation fell away from her. She was getting out of The Nail! She was going home to Canaan!

Then her voice returned. "Yes! Yes!" she screamed. "I will do anything!"

"If you fail in this," Navan warned, "or if you betray me with any of your filthy Israelite wiles, I will bring you back to Tyre and chain you to the wall here for as long as you live."

"I won't fail! I will do what you ask!"

He looked at her in disgust for a moment, then turned and strode out of the small room. His bodyguards passed him on the stairs. "Clean her up," he told them, "and then take her to the west gate."

CHAPTER
FOURTEEN

Egyptian Desert

Dawn rose brilliantly. The sun overwhelmed the night air, and its heat blistered the ugly ground. Inside the large tent, Hela dressed slowly. Her stomach was in a knot. She shrugged on the dark robes of mourning and removed all her jewelry and emblems.

Ma-Set came inside and stood behind her. "They are waiting for you, Holy One. All of your people are assembled."

Hela turned and looked at her protector. He was dressed in full regalia, in the uniform of what he had once been—a much-decorated chariot commander in the army of the pharaoh. His bronze breastplate shone like burnished jewels. His helmet was in the shape of a hawk, and fierce talons were etched into the flaps that shaded his eyes. He wore greaves of silver and high, beaded boots. At his side was the long, curved sword of the chariot corps, and his hand grasped a short spear with a gold-flecked point.

"Why have you dressed like this, Ma-Set?"

"In your honor, Holy One."

Bemused, she stared at him. Did he really believe that she could resurrect her brother? There was no way to tell.

Ma-Set stood beside the opening to the tent and bowed low. He was signaling her that it was time to leave.

"Let them wait!" she told him sharply.

Ma-Set bowed again and stood back.

This is madness, she thought, desperate. She felt alone, among dangerous, ignorant fools. For one bitter moment the memory surfaced of Gravis dying in her arms. She wrapped her arms around her chest and began to weep. Ma-Set moved toward her, but she stopped him with a quick gesture. She wanted no pity, and there could be no comfort. The center of her existence had been yanked from her. She knew her extraordinary powers were gone, never to return. She was like a thin branch, whipped by a storm wind.

Hela's eyes caught movement at the far side of the tent. It was Tuk, silent and removed but watching . . . always watching with her wide, unfathomable eyes. Hela averted her gaze. Why did the girl disturb her so? she wondered. What was wrong with the child anyway? Thus far she had not responded naturally to anything that had transpired. Hela felt sudden anger. How long could Tuk's strangeness be tolerated?

Hela took a step toward the five-year-old and shouted, "Don't you understand what has happened?"

But the child, eyes wide and impassive, merely looked at her.

"Don't you understand that I no longer care if I live or die? Don't you understand that my beloved brother has died, and now I'm all alone? Or that the woman taking care of you has died, and now you're alone?" She took

another quick step forward and raised her arm threateningly, as if she would strike the girl if Tuk did not speak. A
second later, Hela became ashamed and rushed over to the
child's side and consoled her. *Why do I seek this strange
child's pity,* she wondered, *while I spurn it from Ma-Set, who
truly loves me?*

"I'm sorry," Hela whispered into the child's ear, "I
didn't mean that. You're not alone. You can stay with me.
There is nothing to be frightened of. Ma-Set and I will take
care of you. Do you understand?"

But the child did not reply. She neither responded to
the kindly pressure of Hela's hand on her own arm nor
tried to pull away.

"Please, Holy One," Ma-Set implored. "We must go."

Hela stood and went to the tent flap. Yes, the soldier
was right; sounds of the restless crowd came through the
canvas walls. She would accept her destiny bravely. Whatever would happen was already written by the gods.

The moment Hela, followed by Ma-Set and Tuk,
stepped through the threshold of the tent, her eardrums
were almost shattered by an immense roar. Her followers
had lined up in columns, and the moment they saw her, the
throngs chanted: "Isis lives! Isis lives forever! Osiris will
rise again! Isis and Osiris!" They cheered and chanted, and
the very ground beneath Hela's feet shook. The woman
staggered slightly, and Ma-Set reached out with his strong
arm to steady her.

"Your brother is waiting for you on his bier," Ma-Set
said. "I'll help you get through the crowd."

Ma-Set cupped her elbow and slowly guided her
through the chanting masses, while Tuk walked in their
wake. The ranks parted to ease their way. As their goddess
approached the body, naked and perfumed on the bier,
Hela saw that a single branch of a willow had been placed
across his breast.

Seeing her twin lying there, naked and cold, caused
her to falter, and the ground seemed to tilt beneath her
feet. Her heart threatened to burst out of her chest, and

beads of perspiration slid down her face and down her sides until she was drenched. A whimper escaped her lips.

"Not much farther, Holy One," Ma-Set encouraged. "We're almost there. Take a deep breath."

She was about to say that she could not take another step . . . that it would be better to admit that she had no powers and let the people tear her limb from limb. But then Tuk moved in front of her, tugged on her robe, and looked up into her face. The black child was gazing at her intently, and the corners of her mouth were curled in contempt—a contempt for her weakness, Hela knew. She glared at Tuk and then walked forward, steadily now, one sure foot at a time.

The moment she reached Gravis, all chanting ceased. The crowd became respectfully silent. The quiet was so total, it was eerie.

Hela's vision was blurred by tears. Gravis was still, so very still. His beauty was undiminished in death. She reached out with both hands and touched her brother's face. The contact was so chilling and profound that a low moan escaped her throat. Many people in the crowd began to keen.

Hela took a deep breath and wondered for a moment if it might be possible to bring Gravis back from the dead. If wishing could make it so, then she might have a chance. Surely she had never wanted anything so much in her life. She and Gravis had been good and kind to others and had done enough of their own suffering to deserve a special favor from the gods. Perhaps? . . .

When the crowd realized that the ceremony was about to begin, all wailing stopped.

With her hands on her brother's face, Hela called out in a loud but quavering voice, "I, Hela, manifestation of Isis, call upon the spirits of the netherworld to release the soul of my brother from his captivity."

She did not know why she chose those particular words. In fact, she had no idea what she was doing. But for a heart-stopping moment, she thought she felt a twitch of life beneath her fingertips on Gravis's face. She stared down at him, but all she saw was the mask of death. It was no use. It was ridiculous for her even to hope.

Hela spun away from the body. The crowd expectantly stared at her. Their faces were ecstatic, hopeful. *You fools,* she thought. *You stupid fools. And I'm no better than you.*

Many of her adherents had fainted, overcome by the intensity of the emotional event, and she gazed down at their crumpled bodies. How could they have believed that she was a goddess? She had never claimed to be anything other than a woman. And now, because of her failure, her own life was forfeit.

I must try again, she thought, *for all these poor people who believe in me and for Ma-Set and Tuk.*

She turned back to her brother's body, lifted his hand, and pressed it against her lips. Then she gently set the hand on Gravis's breast and raised her arms again. "Hear me, my father, Ra, lord of the sun, lord of the heavens, lord of the earth and its dominions. This day give me the power to breathe life once again into the nostrils of my brother. Hear me, Ra, father of life and death! Bring this body once again into the realm of the living!"

The sincerity of her fervent plea could not be doubted. The masses were deeply affected by the woman's pain. Many more spectators fainted. Many wept. Others babbled and danced as if in the grip of magic.

Oh, please! Hela thought as she bent over the body once again and blew into her brother's nostrils. *Please, Gravis, come back to me. Love me enough to do what cannot be done!*

She stepped back and waited, her breath held, her head bowed. Nothing happened. Her brother was still dead. He would be dead forever. There would be no resurrection.

She threw out her hands to her worshipers in a gesture of defeat and despair. Then she closed her eyes and waited for what she knew must come next. The confused murmurs from the crowd rose up and surrounded her. The confusion turned to anger, then rage, and suddenly a clump of dirt hit the side of her face. Blood filled her mouth. And then a stone grazed a shoulder, and then more dirt. The crowd flung at their goddess whatever their hands could snatch. She had betrayed them! they screamed.

"Sham!"

"Fake!"

The cries surrounded her and were punctuated with sticks and mud and stones.

"Whore!"

A stone struck her in the mouth, and she reeled. She cried out for Ma-Set, but he was nowhere in sight. Tuk was at her side, standing calmly as the projectiles and curses rained down on them both.

I am going to die here, Hela thought, and fell to her knees waiting for the blows. She covered her head with her arms.

Through the multitude exploded a high-wheeled chariot, drawn by two magnificent horses. At the reins was Ma-Set.

Wild screams abruptly burst from the crowd. "Stop him! Stop him!" they shouted.

But he drove the chariot hard and without mercy through the people. Realizing his intent, the mob tried to stop the soldier. They threw themselves at him and at the horses. They tried everything. But Ma-Set was a genius with the reins, and his free hand wielded the short spear with telling effect.

Seeing his approach, Hela grasped the child in a tight embrace. As the terrifying sound of hoofbeats thundered in her ears, the woman was scooped up with a mighty sweep of Ma-Set's arm. Then he thrashed the horses and drove the chariot forward, toward the last ring of onlookers.

The chariot burst through the crowd's perimeter, scattering people before it. And then there was nothing but blessedly empty desert in front of them.

"I am taking you to the Sinai," he yelled at Hela. "We'll be safe there."

But Hela did not care about her own safety. She looked back, grief stricken that she was abandoning the body of her beloved Gravis to the crowd. The people would rip his corpse to pieces. She knew she could not let that happen! Struggling to find her balance in the swaying, speeding chariot, she tried to leap out, oblivious to the danger of the flashing wheels below.

While struggling to maintain control of the galloping horses, Ma-Set tried to restrain her. But Hela, becoming more and more violent, fought against his grasp.

"They'll defile his body!" she screamed at him. "We have to go back."

"Forgive me, Holy One," the old soldier yelled back. With full force he drove the blunt end of the spear shaft into the pit of her stomach.

The air exploded from her lungs, and she fell unconscious to the chariot floor.

CHAPTER FIFTEEN

Canaan

When Abimelech awoke at dawn, his powerful arms and huge balled fists were flailing at unseen enemies. Then he realized that he was alone. He had slept alone, and he had awoken alone. He had left the western road when it became dark, moved a few yards off, and gone to sleep. A shroudlike mist rolled in around him. Now, because of the mist, he could not see the road at all.

Hungry and thirsty, he cursed himself for not taking any food or wine from Gideon's burial banquet. He would have to kill for his breakfast—a hare or a partridge or perhaps a stray sheep. Yes, a sheep would be nice. From a distance of a hundred yards he could drive an arrow clear through a ram's body.

His hand reached out for the short, powerful bow that

lay on the ground. Abimelech fingered the bowstring. The secret of the bow's thrust was in the string, and his was made of braided leather, soaked in vinegar and shrunk dozens of times, then coated with linseed oil. He plucked it now, as if it were a musical instrument. The sound, high and taut, pleased Abimelech and brought to mind a runner about to leap or a leopard about to spring.

The morning fog began to roll away. He knew he should get moving, but instead he waited, sitting on the ground musing over his bow.

From behind him, in the heavy underbrush, the song of finches filled the air. The chirping annoyed him, and he spat on the ground, then rubbed the spittle into the earth with his bare foot. Then his mood lightened. Soon all of Canaan would sing like finches for him, he thought. He leaned back on his elbows and smiled. He was about to burst into legend as rapidly as the arrow leaves its bow. He was about to surge out of his isolation and loneliness and impotence to crush all those whom he despised. He grinned broadly as he relished the special vengeance he would wreak on Gideon's father and all those fools who had called him lowborn and spurned him as not being beloved of Yahweh or any other god.

Miriam came to Abimelech's mind, and the smile vanished. He had always adored her, but she, too, had rejected him and lied to him. Why? he wondered. It could not be because of their blood relationship. Surely it was better to lie with a nephew than with a Bedouin pig, and she had done that quickly enough, then delivered a son by him. No, Miriam scorned him because of the way he lived, what he thought, and how he looked. She, like the others, laughed at his dreams and considered him coarse. Well, she would regret it.

He bowed his head for a moment at the bitterness of her refusal. For so long he had craved to take her naked body in his arms. For so long, from afar, he had hidden outside her father's meager home or by the yard and caught glimpses of her sweetness as she dressed or bathed.

For so long, at night, his dreams had been flooded by the vision of her smooth, moist nakedness beside him, lying there hot and willing and open, always eager for him to slake his desire.

He jumped up with sudden frustration, shook the bow in the air, and howled. The finches burst from the grass and flew off. Yes, Abimelech vowed, all who had mistreated him would soon suffer his wrath and regret their treatment of him. He barked a laugh. His relatives thought Baal and Yahweh were powerful! His family burned their wretched little candles to the gods, and all for nothing. Soon they would grovel before a power that walked proudly in the form of a man—Abimelech the great, the invincible . . . the cruel.

He strode up the embankment to the road and walked toward home. As his muscles warmed, his gait quickened to an easy jog. When his hunter's ears caught the rustle of branches on the far side of the road, Abimelech immediately stopped and listened carefully. A friend or a foe could be hidden in the dense growth. Or it could be a meal.

Readying his weapons and slipping a small dagger between his teeth, he crept silently and swiftly into the underbrush. Even though he was a big man, he moved like a cat.

Hidden, he listened. The sound came again, closer now. He moved forward, every muscle tense. The brush thinned. Before him was a clearing, where a woman was gathering herbs. Near her, a baby lay on a blanket spread across the ground. As he watched, the woman straightened and revealed her profile. He froze and stared. It was Miriam.

Abimelech crouched and watched. She was so beautiful and graceful! Her body was so lush and strong! And she had been delivered to him. His breathing deepened as his gaze rested on the round softnesses of her hips and breasts. But she would never be his. The thought infuriated him. He could never win her love, no, but some dirty Bedouin—

Sweat stung his eyes. He would not wait! He could not

wait a second longer. He would take what he wanted, what he needed. Abimelech leaped into the clearing.

Miriam spun around and stared wide-eyed at him. Fright bleached her face. She forced a look of relief. "Oh, Abimelech! You scared me." She gave a little laugh. "At first I thought some dangerous stranger had found me."

He started toward her, his hands stretched out in front of him like a thirsty man going to water.

"What do you want, Nephew?" she asked, her eyes looking quickly at her child, then at Abimelech.

When he did not speak, she turned and ran, but he caught her in three steps and with one swipe of his mighty hand knocked her to the ground. He curled his fingers around her neckline and ripped her garment away.

"Stop that!" Miriam screamed and tried to cover her breasts with her hands.

He hit her hard again on the side of the head and straddled her on the ground. Then he pulled her robe off entirely and tossed the garment aside. For just a moment he sat still, breathing heavily, his eyes feasting on her breasts and stomach and beautifully formed thighs. He pried her knees apart. She pleaded with him and wept and then called out for mercy, but Abimelech, unhearing, jammed himself inside her and raped her savagely. He was oblivious to her screams, oblivious to the nails clawing his face as he drove himself inside her.

He raped her again and again. She was limp from the struggle, but he was like a ravaging beast in a pit.

Finally, when it was over, when he was too drained to rape her again, he righted his clothes and walked away toward the main road, leaving her naked and weeping in the clearing. The sounds of the crying child faded behind him.

When he reached the road he smiled slowly. The blood from his scratches was rolling down his face and into his mouth. He stuck out his tongue and savored the taste. It was sweet to him, like honey.

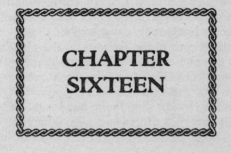

CHAPTER
SIXTEEN

Thrace

Theon closed his eyes. He could not stand to look at this evil, boastful woman who had once shared his bed, who had given birth to his children, whom he had once loved. He cringed when he heard her laugh again.

"Tell me, *Husband,* where has your wounded informer gone?"

He opened his eyes and stared around the cave. A lead weight settled in his stomach as the betrayal made itself clear. The stranger was indeed gone.

Nuhara laughed again. She was enjoying herself immensely. "Please explain to me, my dearest love, how such a weak old man could have escaped? Oh, you pathetic fool! How easy it was to trap you!"

Theon remained grimly silent, as did Talus and their

81

men. Nuhara, in her elaborate priestess gown, paced triumphantly in front of them, her eyes gleeful.

Then she walked up to one of Theon's shepherds and stared contemptuously at him. The man was trembling.

"Couldn't you have found better men, Husband, than these evil-smelling brutes? Did you really think these sorry shepherds would be victorious over me?"

Her voice rose in pitch as she spoke directly to Theon. "I and I alone control the treasure of the Children of the Lion. By my own stealth and cunning the riches were brought here from Home. I will multiply the fortunes, and I will send out the ships to find my poor lost Hela and Gravis. You could not save them, but I will, even if I have to scour all the lands of this earth. Look at you! The great and wise Theon trembling before the woman he used to scorn!"

Theon did not answer. He did not return her look.

Nuhara turned and pointed at another of Theon's allies. A second later the sickening sound of a shaft splintering bone and flesh echoed in the cave. The shepherd screamed and fell forward. A feathered arrow was buried in bubbling blood in the center of his spine.

Theon ran toward the fallen man. As he reached the hapless victim, he heard the whir of other shafts. Within seconds, all six Thracian shepherds had been murdered by Nuhara's archers. Theon staggered away. The cave had become a slaughterhouse. Those who had not been killed instantly writhed and rolled and screamed as their fingers futilely tried to pull the feathered death from their bodies.

"Why have you done this?" he screamed at Nuhara, his famous calmness shattered by the horror surrounding him.

Nuhara smiled. "Oh, does my poor darling hate the sight of blood? Isn't that sad?"

Nuhara walked past Theon and looked at Talus. His face was white from what he had seen.

"I am not finished yet," she promised, her gaze meeting his. Her laugh echoed and distorted as it spiraled up in the vaulted stone space.

Theon rushed between Nuhara and Talus. "Please," he said, "I beg you. Leave Talus alone. He can do you no harm."

She laughed again, and her men joined in the hilarity.

"You have killed enough, Nuhara," Theon said. "It is I, not Talus, who is your enemy."

"But I have many enemies, Husband," she replied airily.

"All he did was follow my orders." Theon stared at the carnage about him. The impaled shepherds were now dead. Their blood was beginning to clot. He could not bear the thought that his own stupidity had sent these men to their death and would soon destroy Talus. "Do you really need more blood, Nuhara? If so, then take my head."

"Are you begging me, Theon? Is the great Theon, the noble Theon, whining like a beaten dog?"

"I don't care what you call it. I will do anything to spare Talus's life."

She smiled at him wickedly and then sauntered over to Talus and looked him up and down. Grim-faced, Talus stared straight ahead.

Then she turned back to Theon and asked, "Will you really do anything to save this fool's life, Theon?"

"I told you I would."

"But the word *anything* covers such a large range of possibilities," Nuhara replied. For a moment she seemed lost in thought. As she wandered about the perimeter of the room, she daintily lifted her hem, making certain that the robe did not drag through Thracian blood that stained the ground.

The cave grew silent. Theon could hear the breathing of the archers as they remained on guard, their bows strung and arrows poised. The air began to grow fetid.

"Then I will give you a chance to save him," Nuhara said suddenly, folding her arms. "Tell me, Theon, about how many steps separate us right now, in this cave?"

"About twenty."

"Yes, I think you are right. Now I want you to get down on your hands and knees and crawl to me. Twenty times during that crawl I want you to stop and call out so that all may hear: 'All honor to Nuhara, high priestess of Dionysus.' "

"Don't, Theon!" Talus said. "Don't degrade yourself like that. I am ready to die."

Theon looked at Talus, then at Nuhara. All his life he had lived honorably. He had never begged or demeaned himself to gain advantage or favor. But what did high-sounding words such as *honor* and *bravery* mean if by simply groveling on the floor of this anonymous cave he could save his young friend's life?

Talus spoke again, with desperation. "Don't do it, Theon. You taught me to live with dignity and to face death stoically. I am prepared to do that. I would rather die than bring dishonor to you or to the Children of the Lion."

Nuhara called out, "Come, come, Theon. Time is a-wasting. Get down on your knees and crawl here. Once you reach me, and kiss my feet, I shall give Talus back his life."

Theon heard Talus's protests in his ears as he dropped to all fours. Sweat poured down his face and stung his eyes. At first the shame that welled up in him was almost overwhelming. But then he dismissed it, totally at peace with his decision.

He crawled one step, stopped, looked up, and cried out, "Honor to Nuhara, high priestess of Dionysus." Then he crawled another step, stopped, and called out the phrase again. Slowly, again and again, he diminished the distance between himself and a grinning Nuhara.

When he was only about three steps away from the feet that he was required to fall upon and kiss, Nuhara said, "Enough! Get up. It makes me sick to look at you."

Startled, confused, Theon stood. His hands and feet were blackened from the ground.

"You fool!" Nuhara said, incredulous. "Did you really

think I would kill Talus? Of course I wouldn't have. And I won't kill you, either."

Theon said nothing. He no longer knew how to respond to this woman's wickedness.

"I won't kill either of you because that would be painful to my beloved twins. You are their natural father; Talus is their treasured friend. In fact, I am going to send you to one of the most beautiful spots in Thrace—a resort where you and Talus can live out your lives in luxury. I am going to send you both to Traxis."

Theon and Talus stared at each other. Neither of them had heard of Traxis. Some of the archers, however, laughed out loud and then stifled their amusement when Nuhara glared at them.

"Yes, Theon, my dearest," Nuhara said, "I am going to send you to glorious Traxis, and you will thank me till your dying day."

She gestured, and Talus and Theon were bound and led back through the cave. As they walked together, in silence, they wondered about this strange place—this place called Traxis.

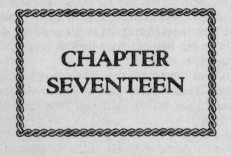

CHAPTER SEVENTEEN

Kingdom of Babylon

As the night wore on, the exhausted captives hunched over their shaggy ponies and tried to snatch some moments of sleep during the harsh ride. Their beasts rolled and jounced and staggered along, oblivious to the well-being of the riders who had been tied so unceremoniously to their backs.

Luti knew by the stars that their party was traveling south, but she had no idea where the soldiers might be taking her and her family. When the first rays of sunlight filtered through the night air, however, she began to identify familiar landmarks. It was only then that she realized they were heading on a direct course to Ur, her home city.

Soon it was fully morning. Riding along the riverbank, the captives passed the long, low storage huts and dormitories that characterized the southern river region. It was in these sheds that seeds and produce were kept, farm workers fed and housed, and records and tithes maintained. The mere sight of them caused memories to flood into Luti's consciousness. For years she had worked in the fields of the priests of Ur; then she had been accused of treason and taken away from the farmlands, to be sentenced to death. Her coworkers, trying to help Luti resist arrest, had been beaten, and some were killed. Luti shuddered, remembering. Why, she wondered, had she consistently drawn such misfortune into her life?

The soldiers pulled up in front of one of these huts, untied the family's bonds, and lifted the prisoners from their ponies. The group was shoved roughly inside, then pushed against a far wall. At a command from the leader, one captor handed Luti, Micah, and their son some peaches to slake their hunger and thirst. Luti crushed another into a pulp and fed it to Seka.

Then the soldiers vanished without a word of explanation, leaving the family alone in the dimness.

"Do you know where we are?" Micah asked.

Luti nodded. "We're on the northern outskirts of Ur. But look at the religious symbols on the walls here. This hut is owned by the priests of Astarte. We must be their prisoners."

"Why?" Drak asked, his eyes wide with fear. "What have we done?"

"I don't know," Luti told the boy. "I don't know what's going on. But let's try to stay calm. I am frightened, too, but we haven't broken any laws that I know of. This might all be a mistake."

Suddenly the hut's door swung open, and two men entered. The first was a short, heavyset man, dressed in the light yellow robes of the priesthood of Astarte. He carried the carved staff that symbolized the goddess's power. Behind him was a massive, well-armed man, grasping a double-bladed javelin at the ready. His face was cruelly disfigured, and he had only one eye.

Luti, trembling, held Seka tightly and put an arm around Drak's bony shoulders. But then the short man greeted them kindly, in a deep and soothing voice.

"My name is Akkad," he said. "I serve Astarte, goddess of the earth and below, begetter of fertility in flowers and man, the hope of the world." He stepped directly in front of Luti and addressed her. "Hear me, woman. Many years ago you performed nobly for our nation and our people. Once again, as great and darkening clouds now approach the kingdom of Babylon, we need your skills and bravery."

He paused, leaning on his staff. The mellow kindness suddenly vanished from his demeanor. He looked with shrewd hardness at Luti. "Listen closely! The Phoenicians and the Assyrians are planning a massive assault against us, supported by the evil cabal in Tyre. The Assyrians have threatened that once the conquest is complete, once they have crushed us, the Phoenicians will take control of all our lucrative trade routes across the great rivers. The Assyrians will make our lands their own, and our people will be their slaves."

Luti felt the fear in her heart harden into fury. She opened her mouth to speak, but the priest continued his exhortations.

"Hear me well, Luti! You must proceed to Tyre and as a prophetess insinuate yourself into the good graces of the powerful Navan. The Phoenicians depend upon bird omens to determine the sailing schedule of their fleet, so they will welcome an accurate soothsayer. Once ensconced in Navan's court, you will search out the date of the Assyrians' invasion and the direction from which the Phoenicians' attack will come. Armed with that information, we will be able to prepare for the attack and repulse it."

The priest then stepped back and waited for Luti's response. The huge armed man hovered close by his master, the javelin always ready, always threatening.

Luti barked out a bitter and contemptuous laugh. "This is the reason you destroyed my wagon and my livelihood and brutalized my family? This is the reason you threw us like bags of grain onto ponies and sent us riding through the night?"

She did not wait for an answer. She stepped forward toward the priest and stabbed a finger at his face. "Do you think I am such a fool as to trust the priests of Astarte ever again? Once, I risked my life to bring you a war chariot, so different and so powerful in design that it saved you from invasion, defeat, and slavery. And what was my reward? My houses and properties were seized because of groundless accusations made by an envious servant! My wealth was confiscated, and my life shattered. And all of this was done with the complicity of the priests of Astarte. I trust none of you! I will do nothing to save you!"

As she fell silent, her anger simmering, Luti felt exhausted from her long night of terror and the sudden cessation of fear.

"You're a very bitter woman," Akkad said.

"Wouldn't you be?" Luti demanded.

He shrugged with the philosophical calm common to holy men who realize that earthly events mean little in the infinite scheme of things.

"Many errors have been made, and we are sorry for all of them. Complete restitution will be made to you. All your lands and houses and possessions will be restored to you. Never again will you have to wander the kingdom in a broken-down wagon and wonder where your next meal will come from."

"Liar! Viper! I will never trust any of you again!" She turned her back on the priest. "I would rather live hand-to-mouth and depend upon myself than give over control of my life to such as you."

"That's your final answer, then?" the priest asked.

"That is my final answer," Luti replied.

Akkad waited for a moment, considering. He looked from Luti to Micah, then at the children. Finally he nodded to the armed man. A second later the large soldier moved with blinding and brutal speed.

He plucked the baby from her mother's arms and held the little one upside down by one ankle. Seka began to wail.

Luti leaped forward to rescue her child. She was met by the point of the javelin, which, before she pulled up short, pricked the skin at her throat, bringing forth blood. Horrified, she grasped her neck and turned toward her husband. But then she realized with disgust that, once again, there would be no help from him.

Seka shrieked louder, and Luti charged the armed man again. But once more the javelin stopped her. He used it as a club, hitting her on the side of the head and sending her sprawling. Agitated, Drak cried out. Still Micah did not move.

Then Akkad moved to stand over Luti. "If you refuse this mission, your baby dies now. If you accept this assignment, the child will be kept safe in the palace of Astarte and returned to you after the mission is completed. Make your decision now, Luti of Ur."

Seka's wailing rang in Luti's ears. "Don't kill my baby! I'll do whatever you want! Just don't hurt Seka!" Luti screamed those words again and again until her throat was too raw to utter another sound.

Then Luti stopped her ears with her fingers so she would not have to hear Seka's piteous cries as the child was carried from the hut.

CHAPTER EIGHTEEN

Sinai

Under the cover of darkness Ma-Set's chariot crossed the desolate Red Sea marshes, and when dawn broke the vehicle entered the vast and barren Sinai Desert. It was a difficult journey. The earth was hard and rock strewn. The distant mountains gleamed like burnished gold weapons, both threatening and dazzling. The sun was like scalding oil, taking the travelers' breath away, tormenting the soul, making the limbs feel like jelly.

For two days and nights Hela, overcome by deep depression, lay in the back of the chariot. Because her brother was dead, his body probably mutilated, she had abandoned all hope and become a limp, lifeless thing, taken care of by the soldier. Ma-Set kept her covered from the sun by day and from the cold wind at night. He caught tiny lizards and forced their entrails into her mouth to give

91

her a bit of sustenance. Tuk, on the other hand, needed no help or encouragement to eat the lizards.

It was thirst that broke Hela's depression, for when the need for water was great, the body triumphed over the mind. Feelings were of no importance next to the dreadful pain and fear of extreme thirst.

"Ma-Set! Ma-Set!" she rasped out on the third night in Sinai as the chariot rolled slowly across the darkened landscape. "I must have water! I must drink!"

The soldier stopped the horses and helped Hela from the vehicle. He settled her on the ground, wrapped his garment around her, and built a small fire. Next to her sat the wide-eyed, ever-silent Tuk.

"Holy One," Ma-Set said, "you must be strong and patient. I am always looking for the milk plants that live in the desert and yield good liquid when their stalks are cut. Many years ago I crossed this same terrain with my troop, and the plants were all around us. Alas, they seem no longer to grow wild in great abundance, but I will find some somewhere. I promise."

"Hurry, Ma-Set. My lips feel as if someone is pulling the skin off."

Neither the child nor the soldier complained about thirst. They were obviously suffering, too, but in brave silence.

Ma-Set told Hela not to be ashamed of her complaints, that he himself had experienced the incessant pain of thirst and knew how horrible it was. Long years as a soldier, however, brought about his stoicism.

But the young woman was not consoled. She stared balefully at the black child, whose courageous calm and easy adapting infuriated her. "And get that child away from me!" she ordered.

The faithful soldier, whispering comfort into the girl's ear, judiciously carried Tuk back to the chariot.

The small fire soon flickered and died. There was no kindling left. The only light the threesome would have in the future was provided by the moon and stars. Ma-Set watched Hela carefully as she sat huddled against the night's chill. None of them would last much longer, he knew. Five days were the usual limit for life without water, and they were all very close to that deadline.

There was something he could do to alleviate their thirst, but he was not yet ready to go to that extreme. He could begin to bleed the horses and drink the blood. That would provide nourishment—life- and strength-giving liquid. But that meant that the horses would be condemned to death, for the constant bleeding would sap their strength, and the cruel desert would finish them quickly. No, he was not yet desperate enough for that.

"Please, Ma-Set, bring the child back near me. I am sorry I acted so foolishly. It's just that her silence is sometimes hard to bear, and her behavior makes me see my own as lacking."

Ma-Set obeyed Hela's wishes with alacrity. He returned with the child, and Tuk sat down as if nothing had happened. The three travelers lay down, and soon they were all asleep. . . .

Hela dreamed easily in the darkness. Gravis and she were on the island Home and climbing a steep mountain path to bring food to Talus. They were laughing and calling to each other as they climbed. She felt wild and free, and her long golden hair flowed and rippled like a banner in the wind. As they reached the top of the mountain, Hela slipped—but Gravis's strong arm held her and pulled her up to the summit. She turned to thank her beloved brother, only to stare into his plague-scabbed face. . . .

Hela woke up, screaming.

"Holy One, be calm! I am here. You're all right!"

He anxiously stared down into Hela's wild eyes. His hand remained firmly on her shoulder as she regained control of herself. But then sadness overwhelmed the young woman. She lay sobbing on the ground. The sounds from deep in her throat were dry, harsh, brittle.

Ma-Set knew he could wait no longer. Hela must have something to drink. He returned to the chariot, untethered one of the horses, and forced it to kneel. He made a slit along the beast's neck with his dagger and collected the thin flow of blood into his helmet until it was half full. Next Ma-Set mixed some desert earth with his own spittle and covered the horse's wound so it would clot quickly.

He carried the helmet back to the campsite, helped Hela into a sitting position, and, while Tuk calmly looked on, guided her lips to the liquid.

Hela drank gratefully, gurgling and swallowing the life-giving blood until she almost choked. Ma-Set pulled the helmet away.

"More! Give me more!" she pleaded, the blood running down her chin.

"In a moment, Holy One. But you must drink slowly. Blood is heavy to digest, and I don't want you to become ill."

"Blood?" she cried out in horror, and covered her mouth with her hands. She gagged but managed not to vomit.

Ma-Set brought the helmet to Tuk. The young black girl drank steadily but sparingly.

"Ah, that's a smart girl," Ma-Set said, patting her on the head. He was growing very fond of her. Tuk was braver than any soldier he had ever known.

Hela reached out for more of the blood, and Ma-Set handed her the helmet. He was pleased that she had reconciled herself so quickly to the situation. She finished what was left. There was none for Ma-Set, but he had already decided not to drink until it was a last resort.

"Where are we headed?" Hela asked.

"To the great passes to the north and west, Holy One. Only there will we be truly safe, for only from that vantage can we see all around for miles. We'll camp on the slopes of the cliffs and be safe."

"How long till we get there?"

"A week perhaps. That is another reason why we must

drink the horses' blood very slowly. Each drop we take to sustain our lives destroys theirs."

Hela nodded in understanding. Then he saw her shudder. Fate was against them, and he and Hela knew it. If they survived to reach the passes, what then? Why were they fighting to stay alive when the future was so bleak? To subsist in the Sinai was like being dead . . . perhaps worse.

"Let's try to get some more sleep," he suggested, then reached out to check on his sword. He always set it within easy reach before he fell asleep.

"Ma-Set?"

"Yes, Holy One?"

"Thank you. You're a wonderful friend—brave and truthful and loyal."

"You are most welcome." He smiled, content, as he reached out to gather Tuk into his embrace. The girl's head fell against his shoulder. Her small, dimpled hand rested on his chest. . . .

Ma-Set and Tuk fell fast asleep. Hela, watching them, felt a great surge of warmth for the child and promised herself that in the morning she would show kindness toward her. The girl had suffered enough. It was not Tuk's fault that she was so strange. Circumstances had rendered her emotionless.

Hela fought to remain awake because she was reluctant to dream—afraid to see the plague-ravaged face of her beloved brother. But finally she could not battle against fatigue. She dreamed again, but this time it was a soothing and beautiful escape. She was in a strange land and in an otherworldly grove. About her were the most lovely of blossoming trees with enormous spreading boughs and leaves. Luscious fruit lay on the ground. She picked one up that was a glowing reddish orange and bit into it. How cool and sweet and juicy it was!

Then she walked on through fragrant air and came to a massive tree. It was almost entirely white, including the leaves and bark. As she came closer she saw that the mark of the Children of the Lion—the lion's paw print—was burned into its trunk. For a moment she was frightened, but then a mellifluous voice advised her to be calm, that there was nothing to fear from this strange tree.

From behind the trunk stepped little Tuk. But the girl was no longer silent. She spoke and laughed and whirled like a happy child. She skipped over to Hela, took the woman's hand into her own, and together they traced the design on the tree trunk. Just the touch of it infused her with great strength and a sense of well-being. . . .

Hela woke smiling. It was still dark, but clouds no longer obscured the light from the brilliant desert stars. She glanced at Tuk, who was asleep. Hela smiled at the child. Was Tuk dreaming the same dream? she wondered. Was Tuk dancing in that same lovely glade with the strange white tree and the mark of the lion's paw upon it? Hela recalled that Tuk had the clan's mark, but it was yellow.

She realized that Ma-Set had gotten up. She turned her head and found him sitting to her other side, wide awake and staring at her.

"Can't you sleep, my friend?" she whispered.

Ma-Set did not answer. Hela reached out to him.

The old man pitched forward against her. She stared down at the back of his head. It was covered with pulp and blood. Someone had murdered him!

Suddenly the night was lit by torches.

Hela could not scream. The horror of Ma-Set's murder made her mute. But her whole body trembled as long-haired naked demons emerged from the darkness. Their eyes were so full of hatred, the malevolent glow seemed to dim their own torches.

Silent, menacing, they stood surrounding her and Tuk. Hela could no longer bear it.

"Who are you?" she cried out. "Why have you killed my friend?"

CHAPTER
NINETEEN

Canaan

Abimelech entered the bustling city of Shechem two hours past dawn. He strode through the southern gate of the city to find that the narrow streets were already choked with people. He walked slowly, imperiously, his hands on his belted daggers, his lips curled in contempt at the mass of humanity surging back and forth in unrelenting waves.

Shechem, on the western edge of the Jordan Plain, had become the main commercial center of Canaan. Standing at the east-west crossroads, it was the focal point for caravans moving toward the wealthy cities of the Philistine League on the coast and those heading toward the important desert routes on the far side of the Jordan.

It was a rich and dangerous place. Each year thousands of young Israelites from all the tribes migrated there to seek their fortune. Most of them found nothing but violence and hunger. They joined deadly gangs, which preyed on affluent citizens and travelers. The violence on the streets of Shechem—the murders and robberies, the muggings and rapes—had become infamous throughout Canaan. Nonetheless, the country bumpkins continued to pour into the city—and many of them ended up as corpses. These unfortunates were collected daily at dawn by the so-called meat wagons, which removed the evidence in well-ordered stacks and dumped it outside the city walls in a mass burial pit.

But, ironically, it was the religious violence that made the city truly dangerous. Shechem had become the center of two rival faiths—those of Baal and Yahweh. Each religion maintained a central shrine in the city, staffed by priests and attended each day by fervent worshipers. These zealots, armed with sticks and rocks and swords, clashed constantly in the streets.

The Yahwehist cult was also plagued by internal violence. Each day wild-eyed, long-bearded men entered Shechem from the hill country and proclaimed themselves true prophets of Yahweh. They accused the priests of the Temple Mount of being charlatans; they claimed the mantle of Moses and predicted great horrors unless the Israelites returned to the simple precepts of the desert covenant; they condemned in fiery words the sexual depravity and larceny of the populace.

Shechem was indeed a boiling pot, almost beyond control, always spilling over. And Abimelech saw this clearly with every step he took through the city. It pleased him mightily, for it offered fertile ground to an ambitious man. When he reached the great square of Shechem, he purchased a cup of water and, sipping the warm, evil-tasting liquid, studied the terrain.

Directly in front of and above him was the great Temple Mount of Yahweh. There were nine landscaped levels, each one containing formal gardens and areas conducive to worship and meditation. The two highest levels contained the Holy of Holies, the Ark of the Covenant, and admittance to these terraces was restricted to high priests.

His gaze slid away from the Temple Mount to the ugly stone fortress, which anchored the eastern end of the square. Therein was the court of the elders of Shechem—and Abimelech's ultimate destination.

He stared down at his feet, covered with the filth of his long journey. The sight caused him to laugh out loud so uproariously that people looked his way in startlement and a covey of doves nearby took flight in a panic and circled up toward the highest ring of the Temple Mount. Abimelech's filthy feet made him happy. What other man had ever approached the court of elders of Shechem without sandals? None, he knew, for the elders, the city's rulers, would be insulted by such disrespect.

Abimelech did not care. His contempt for the elders was total. If they did not like the condition of his feet, he decided, then let the rulers wash them. Yes, he thought, let them bow down and wash his feet.

He strode into the fortress, identified himself as Abimelech the Israelite, son of Gideon. Because of his proud parentage—and in spite of his appearance—he was led immediately into the council chamber.

The fifteen elders were gathered inside. They lounged on assorted divans in the large spacious room, which was crisscrossed by light from high windows cut into the stone along all four walls. In one corner of the chamber was a series of low tables piled high with wine bowls and raisin cakes.

All members of the council looked up with interest as Abimelech was announced.

Zebul, the most high lord of Shechem, introduced himself. "Will you sit, Abimelech?" he inquired politely.

The elders wore long linen robes fastened by magnificently tooled leather belts. Zebul wore the same clothes as the others, but what distinguished this small, tough, gnarled old man were the unique designs of his robes. On his right breast was a hand holding two lightning bolts.

This was the symbol of the Baal cult. And over his left breast, over the heart, were the twin stone tablets of the Yahweh adherents.

"Sitting is for women," Abimelech replied, an insulting allusion to a bodily function since all the elders were sitting.

The council members whispered angrily among themselves.

Zebul took a deep breath and spoke again, with far less warmth. "Abimelech, we know who you are. Your father was a great commander, and your mother was a Shechemite. Through both lines, you are entitled to address us. Have your say. You requested this audience, and we will hear you out."

Abimelech made a great show of removing the powerful bow from his shoulder and the quiver of arrows from his back and setting them on the ground. Then he took off his belt daggers and placed them next to the bow.

His eyes sought out each of the elders in turn. Few of the men could meet and hold his fierce gaze. Finally he spoke. "You are all blind fools. Your city is being ripped apart by violence. Your women are being raped, and your children cut down. Your city has become the laughingstock of Canaan and the entire region around the Great Sea. Your gods are in hiding. Your world is collapsing, and yet you sit here sipping wine, eating raisin cakes, and talking about nothing."

The content and force of his words took the elders by surprise. At first there was total silence, and then the councilmen began to shout back at him, infuriated by his arrogance.

Zebul glared at his colleagues and held up his hand for their silence. Slowly the furor subsided, and Abimelech continued.

"You have eyes in your head, but you do not see. The seventy so-called sons of Gideon have brought chaos and ruin to all of Canaan. They have turned you into pathetic whores. They have mocked your gods and your values."

The youngest of the council, a nobleman called Gaal, shot out of his divan. He wore on his right hand the studded glove of a master swordsman. He was so angry that spittle flew from his mouth as he demanded, "Do we have to listen to this insolent fool tell us what we already know?"

Abimelech stared at the speaker, and retorted with sarcasm, "If you know it, why have you done nothing?"

No one answered—not even Gaal. The humiliated man sank back to his seat.

Abimelech moved closer to Zebul and addressed him directly. "I am here to save you," he said flatly.

Laughter greeted his statement. A voice called out, "Why you? Why not Moses?" Again more laughter.

Disgusted, Abimelech looked at the rulers, and their good humor faded. Then he spoke with confidence. "You will make me your king because I am the true son of Gideon. I am flesh of his flesh. My right arm is his right arm. And because of my blood ties, only I am beloved of Yahweh. Only I can save your miserable lives and fortunes."

The power of his words struck deep. They stared at one another, not knowing how to respond. Abimelech could tell by their expressions that they were wondering whether what he said was true.

Gently, tentatively, Zebul asked, "And if you would be our king, what benefits will accrue to your subjects?"

The councilmen leaned forward to hear his answer.

Abimelech picked up his bow, stood erect, and shook the fierce weapon in their faces. He spoke slowly, carefully. His words flowed in a deep, powerful, cadenced voice. "I will break the power of the seventy sons of Gideon. I will free the land from their extortion. I will return the produce they stole from the people, then break the strength of the bandit gangs throughout the land. I will rid Shechem of its lawless factions. I will force the religious cults to heed your civil laws. I will conquer all the remaining Canaanite cities, and in so doing I will turn you into men wealthy beyond your wildest dreams. Finally, I will reshape all of Canaan into the image that was given to me by the nobility of my blood, by the power of my bow, and by the face of Yahweh, which shines down upon me."

The elders stared in astonishment at this conceited stranger. They did not know how to react. His intentions were so bold and so audacious . . . and so desperately needed that they were stunned into confusion.

Then Gaal stood up and bowed sardonically to Abimelech. "Pray tell me, most revered *King* Abimelech. Are you going to accomplish all this by the power of the horse manure that seems to flow from your mouth in an enormous stream?"

Abimelech tensed. He knew that most of the elders were so desperate that they would take a chance on anyone, but this Gaal was becoming a problem. He studied the nobleman. While Gaal was obviously a formidable foe, there was no doubt in Abimelech's mind that he could obliterate the swordsman at a moment's notice. Now, however, was not the moment.

As a result Abimelech chose to ignore the insult. Instead he again addressed Zebul directly. "All I have promised I will accomplish before the great Harvest Festival. And all that I need to fulfill my promise are one thousand gold talents from the coffers of Shechem."

There was a loud groan from the assembled.

Abimelech frowned imperiously. Inwardly he was elated. Their reaction was a good sign. The elders were now thinking about the cost, as merchants do. But because they were mulling over the expense, they must believe that his plan was possible.

"That is a great deal of money," Zebul pointed out, and the other elders murmured agreement.

In answer, Abimelech grinned at them. They knew full well that if he could produce, their rewards would be great. They would be wealthy, powerful, politically secure.

"I don't know what to say," Zebul continued. "You

have arrived here so suddenly, and your claims are so ambitious."

Abimelech raised his voice in anger . . . but it was calculated to create an effect. "Do you doubt my strength? Do you doubt that this right arm contains the blood and sinews of the great Gideon, who destroyed the Bedouin armies?"

Then, before their astonished eyes, he fitted one arrow to the bow and let fly. Then another. And then yet another. Six arrows in a row were nocked and shot with peerless speed and strength.

The slack-jawed elders stared at the results. Each of the six loosed bolts had struck a wine jug on the six low tables across the room. Shattered pottery and splattered red wine covered the far wall and floor. Never had the men witnessed such accuracy.

The nobles stared at one another, and then all eyes rested on Zebul.

The most high lord of Shechem stood to bow formally to Abimelech. He said, "We will give you our answer within three days' time."

Abimelech, suppressing a smile, nodded, gathered his weapons, and left without another word.

Once inside the gates of Shechem, the donkey caravan was flanked by its own armed guards to protect the fine linen bolts fastened to the sides of the beasts. Thus defended against thieves, the caravan proceeded to the traditional watering place, the Well of Rachel, where the animals were refreshed and the drivers able to purchase fruit and flat bread from vendors.

Cotto sat easily on her donkey. She was smiling. True, the journey from Tyre had been long and arduous. Yes, this strange city seemed to be churning with danger and anger. But these unpleasantnesses were trivial when compared to the horrors of the brothel she had left.

The head drover swaggered over to her. "My orders are to drop you off at a street called Tamarisk, near the eastern wall. We will go directly there after filling our water jugs." He stared at her closely for a moment before turning away.

Cotto wondered what, if anything, he had been told about her. Did he know whence she had come and why she was in Canaan? Navan had obviously put her under the drover's protection because during the entire journey, the man had watched her carefully, allowing no one to approach her. He also gave her no opportunity to run away— but that had never been her intention.

She looked around the caravan. Knowing Navan as she did, Cotto assumed that others would be watching her. The Phoenician was a very careful man and trusted no one.

She heard the start-up call, and the drovers flashed their whips. As the caravan wound its way deeper into the city, Cotto remained alert. She listened carefully to all sounds. This was the first time that she had been in Shechem, and all the good feelings in her heart that had bloomed once she had crossed into her homeland now vanished. This mood swing was unexpected. After all, Shechem was primarily an Israelite city, and she was an Israelite. But, she admitted, it seemed to be a wholly different country—the rhythms were unfamiliar; the speech patterns were alien; the dangers were unknown and unpredictable.

The caravan passed through a seedy part of the town, and Cotto shivered when she saw brothel signs. Her heart went out to the girls and women trapped inside those walls. She thought about The Nail and prayed that all those who were still kept there would find a way out. Oddly, she could no longer recall the faces of her sister whores. But she could clearly recall the pain and degradation, and she had to work hard to drive those horrid memories away.

In an attempt to distract herself, Cotto ticked off all the facts that Navan's spy master had told her about Purah. Even though she had made love to the man, she had known nothing about him. Purah, a loyal servant for many years, had left Gideon's employ after the commander had begun to sink into debauchery. Using the money he obtained from the Phoenicians for spying and the gold earrings Gideon had given him after the victory against the Bedouins, Purah had purchased a small house in Shechem and was living a comfortable if simple life. But emotionally he was not doing very well.

The spy master had described Purah's current state of mind to her: "He is now depressed and reclusive. His unhappiness has been aggravated because Gideon's family did not invite him to the funeral. It was a great blow to Purah because he had been Gideon's closest companion in all the battles and his confidant during times of peace. Gideon had only one valet, and that was Purah. We no longer consider Purah a productive spy, but he is still on our payroll. He is highly dependable and may come in handy in the future. You will follow his orders explicitly."

Cotto chuckled to herself, remembering the one time she had met Purah. He had been entranced with her. But the sex he had requested was unimaginative. And then he had fallen fast asleep. Yet, she recalled, they had been at ease with each other. She had felt entirely safe in his company—perhaps because they were both traitors to their people, perhaps because he was so many years her senior.

The caravan veered sharply eastward, and Cotto came out of her thoughts. The travelers had entered a different part of Shechem with wide streets, lush trees, and fine houses with well-tended gardens.

The caravan stopped, and the head drover gestured to Cotto. He pointed to a small but well-maintained house in the cool shadows of a tamarisk tree.

She nodded, slid off her donkey, shouldered the possessions she had wrapped in a blanket, and walked toward the house. The caravan proceeded without her.

The home was set back from the street and surrounded by a large garden. The structure was made of good mud bricks, and Cotto guessed that they were washed frequently, for the bricks gleamed whitely in the sun.

She opened the gate's wooden latch and stepped onto

a crushed stone path, which led through the garden and to the house.

The young woman walked slowly, enjoying the sights and fresh green smell of the garden. Purah was growing food for himself: beans and lentils and peas, onions and leeks and melons and cucumber. Everything was lush and full and set in perfect rows without intruding weeds.

She caught glimpses along the far side of the house of a trellis laden with grapevines. She heard the bleating of a milk goat somewhere in the garden, but she could not see it.

"I've been expecting you!"

Embarrassed, Cotto whirled toward the voice.

The man was standing on the path. He must have been in the garden and stepped out just after she had passed. She stared at him. The sun was very bright, and it was hard to see. Yes, it was Purah. How he had aged since the year before! His hair was quite a bit grayer, and the lines around his eyes and mouth were much deeper. His body was thin, and his face was burned dark from working in the sun.

"Welcome, Cotto," he said genially. "I'm glad you're here. I fixed some refreshments for you. Are you thirsty? Hungry? Or would you rather rest? I'm sure you're exhausted."

She smiled gratefully at his rapid-fire concern for her comfort. "Yes, but more hungry than tired, thank you."

He took her bundle, and they walked inside the house together. The interior was clean and cool. A raised wooden platform for sleeping and storage had been built along one wall. A pit for the fire was dug near the two large open windows, allowing the smoke to exit. The roof was made of stout timber laid crosswise. Two large woven straw mats covered most of the floor.

Cotto sat down on a three-legged stool topped by a pillow. Purah, without any further conversation, brought her a bowl of fresh milk and some deliciously fresh grapes.

She ate quickly. "Are these from your garden?"

"Yes. I picked them this morning."

"They are wonderful."

Purah beamed and brought her some more. Then he sat cross-legged on the floor beside her stool.

"And how is your dancing career going?" he asked genially.

She flashed him a suspicious glance. Was he making fun of her? she wondered. Had he heard of the terrible brothel Navan had thrown her into? Then, looking at his ingenuous face, she relaxed. He might know all about The Nail, but he also seemed to be genuinely interested in her. Nonetheless, she decided not to discuss her prostitution until she was sure he already knew about it.

"I injured my foot some time ago, so I have been resting it," she lied.

"And that young man of yours—the one I heard came to Tyre with you. What became of him?"

His question crushed her. She bowed her head. How could she admit to anyone that she had betrayed Talus? As for where he might be now, she did not know. Dead, perhaps. Or enslaved, toiling in some foreign land and still mooning over the love they had once had.

"Please forgive me," Purah said into the silence. "I didn't mean to upset you."

She smiled wanly at him. "Oh, that's all right. I'm just tired, I guess."

"Then, you should rest. But first I must give you some information for your assignment." He brought her some more milk, then sat down again. She wondered if this was the way he used to sit beside the great Gideon after serving him food and drink.

"The Phoenicians," he began, "are committed to keeping the situation in Canaan as chaotic as it presently is. The seventy sons of Gideon have directed their violence from the Bedouins to their own people. They steal crops and women and gold whenever it suits them. They get drunk, then they kill and maim. There is no law to stop them, for they themselves are the law. The Phoenicians like it that way; they want a weak Canaan. If one strong leader with national aspirations were to emerge in Canaan, order would be restored. It is likely that the overland trade routes, and perhaps some of the sea routes from which the Phoenicians profit greatly, would be taxed heavily."

He paused and waited to see if she understood.

"Yes, Purah, I am already aware of all that. I also know that the Phoenicians are worried that if a unified Canaan emerged or even if the Israelites could form a loose association of the tribes, the Philistine League would reevaluate association with the Phoenicians. Navan would be ruined financially."

He smiled, satisfied. "You understand exactly. That is why the Phoenicians are concerned about Abimelech. They have been watching him for quite a while now, and recently he made his move. I've just had word that Abimelech was given an audience with the Shechem council of elders. Something is happening, but I don't know what it is yet. There is valid cause for concern, though. Many people call Abimelech a madman, and they may be correct. Unfortunately, he is a real son of Gideon and draws great status from that. The only other biological son, Jotham, is a weak child."

"Are the elders unhappy with the seventy sons?" Cotto asked.

"Very, and for many reasons. With so much violence in the area, the elders have been unable to provide their subjects with a sense of security or a stable economy. That makes the rulers' hold on power very tenuous."

Purah stood, walked to the window, and peered out. His movements, Cotto thought, were extraordinarily graceful for one his age. Several times he seemed on the verge of speaking again, but he always checked himself. For a moment, Cotto thought he was overcome by guilt. After all, they were both Israelites, calmly discussing the fate of their countrymen while betraying them, hoping their homeland would suffer continued violence and chaos. But then she realized his reluctance was based in something else—he was embarrassed for her. He could not bring himself to discuss the true nature of her mission: to make herself sexually desirable and available to Abimelech. Her goal was to be in his company often enough to learn his secrets, then report the information to Navan.

Cotto left her stool and moved close to her host. "Tell me, Purah, where I can meet Abimelech. Don't feel bad. I have agreed to do whatever is expected."

"Yes. Of course. I'm sorry. Abimelech is staying nearby, in a tent city called the Olive Branch. The best way to meet him is to disguise yourself as a wine seller. The man loves to drink. I have prepared several jugs of good wine for you to take along."

"I will go this evening," she said.

Purah looked at her tenderly, protectively. "You must be very careful, Cotto. They say that he is enormously strong and violent and cruel. For years he lived alone in the hill country, supporting himself by stealing and murdering and poaching. And there are horrible reports about the way he treats women." He paused and shook his head. "It is difficult for me to believe that Abimelech is a product of the seed of my beloved Gideon." There were tears in his eyes. "But some even say now that Gideon was a madman and a beast. Ach! Sometimes the world is too much for me to bear. I hate to send you to this man."

"Purah, rest easy." She put her hand on his cheek. "I have learned how to take care of myself."

All day Miriam had walked slowly, in agony. All day her ribs and back had ached. As if little Jeb somehow sensed her pain, he would not stop crying. His wailing rang in her ears until she could not stand it anymore. A thick wall descended in her mind and shut out all unpleasantness. She found a peaceful, quiet place in her mind and, liking it very much, stayed there. The madness was upon her.

When Miriam came upon a stream, she placed the baby on the ground and began to laugh. Then she cried out, "Come out of the water, Gideon. If you stay in too long, you'll drown."

But Gideon did not surface, so Miriam dove in and swam in the swiftly moving stream until she was exhausted. As she crawled, she called for her mother and father, but no one answered.

Suddenly she became aware of the cries of her child. She picked him up. "Who are you? Why are you crying?"

The child quieted when, at the orders of an unfamiliar voice echoing in her brain, she gave him her breast to suckle.

At sunset she dug herself a hole in the ground and like a beast huddled in it, holding the baby close. Every movement, every shadow, made her quake with fear. Every sound made her feel as if Abimelech was coming for her again, to ravage her and hurt her and break into her soft body with his crazed flesh.

Finally, near dawn, she fell asleep. Exhausted, she did not awaken until the sun was high. The moment she was fully conscious she stood up and whirled around and danced like a happy child.

She spoke to her baby. "Lie there, little one. I am going into the woods to find herbs and grasses so that Gideon and my parents can break their fast. We'll have eggs and those big brown mushrooms that my brother loves so much."

Miriam skipped off into the forest. In her mind she was twelve years old, and nothing in the world bothered her. But once she reached the lush meadow, she could not find the mushrooms she had known so intimately as a child. The delusion splintered, and she remembered for a moment who she was and what had happened to her. She ran, frantically calling out, looking for little Jeb. His wailing alerted her to his location.

Miriam lay down in the shade of a tree, and as her son nursed, she began to weep. Her grief was like a burning wound in her heart. Where was her beautiful Bedouin lover? Where was her beloved Gideon? Dead, both dead.

There was no one to hold her, no one to love her, no one to protect her.

When the baby was asleep, Miriam put him into his basket. Then she stood and pressed her face against the cool rough bark of the tree. It somehow comforted her. And then she touched the leaves from the low-hanging limbs, and they felt smooth, crisp, and good in her hand. But a moment later one of the tree limbs moved, and she thought she saw the brutal face of her pursuer, her violator. Picking up her child, she ran far from the tree until she was once again in an open field.

She whirled around, looking wildly about her. She needed help! She needed protection! He was tracking her! She knew it!

She held Jeb up, skyward, as if he were a sacrifice, and called out to the God of her people.

"Hear me, O Lord. Hear me, God of Abraham and Isaac and Jacob! Hear me, Yahweh, who brought us out of the Egyptian slave fields and gave us power through Moses and Joshua and Deborah and my brother Gideon! Give me a sign that You hear! Show me that Your strong right arm will be there for me, wherever I walk, whenever I need You."

But Yahweh did not reply. There was no sound, no sign. All was just as before. Her fear wound like a rope around her throat, constricting her breathing. Her heart beat frantically. That beast would violate her if he had the chance. He was coming . . . he was coming.

The unbearable fear caused madness to envelop her again. She lay her baby down and danced as she had as a child in the great autumn festivals, when all was peaceful. The face of her brother as a youngster filled her consciousness. The memories of their playing together with their small wooden toys filled her with joy. Around and around she danced, her lovely body like a leaf in the wind.

When she was tired she curled up in the grass and took her son in her arms. She told him about his father— how handsome he had been and how, at first, she had been frightened of him, even though he had been severely wounded. But then she had discovered that he was the kindest and most passionate of men.

Finally she slept. In the dead of night a sound disturbed her rest. He was stalking her! He was coming to hurt her again! She picked up her baby and fled through the woods. Her face was cut and slashed by the branches. Undergrowth snatched at her robes and tore at her sandals. She screamed at the wind, "Leave me! I am not Miriam! I am the witch of the desert. I live where the owl flies. Leave me alone, or I will poison you with red berries!"

She would not, could not, stop running now. Her fear fueled her madness, and her madness fueled her feet. She ran for hour after hour, calling out names and crying for help. She lost her sandals but had no recollection of doing so. Her feet were so lacerated that she left pools of blood on the ground.

She stopped at last at the sound of many voices. She fell to the ground and lay there, her child in her arms.

But the voices beckoned, so she crawled silently toward them, into the thick bushes ahead. Pulling apart the brambles, she found herself looking at the massive stone walls of a city. She knew it had to be Shechem.

Three families of beggars were camped there. She watched with interest as they squabbled among themselves. She saw them pick up their begging bowls, crutches, and eye patches and hobble toward the gate that led into the city.

She felt much safer. Nothing would happen to her when so many other people were around to come to her aid. She walked out of the wilderness and along the ridge that led to the city walls.

Outside Shechem were thousands of derelicts. The sick and the dying, thieves and beggars, whole families of lepers with bells of warning around their necks, bands of violent young men who had been driven from the city, old people who scavenged off the dead bodies that were dumped each morning into the communal grave . . . all made their home on the outskirts of the city and on the fringe of civilized survival.

Miriam came to a path and, holding the baby tightly, she herself entered that lunatic world. She stood calmly, staring at the walls of Shechem, smelling the food being cooked on the hundreds of fires, and listening placidly to the babble all around her.

PART
TWO

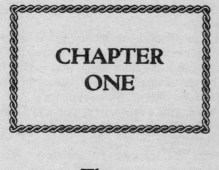

CHAPTER ONE

Thrace

Talus was crying out a name in his troubled sleep. His body thrashed around on the wagon floor in spite of the ropes securing both his hands and feet.

Theon, who lay wide awake next to him, could not at first make out what the young man was saying. But then it became clear to him: *Cotto*. Talus was calling out the name of the Israelite woman who had betrayed him.

Theon shook his head sadly. Talus was still in love with her. The only benefit of age, he realized wryly, was that he had learned not to love the woman bent on destroying him.

Theon shivered. It was dark and cold, and neither he nor Talus had been fed in the two days since they had started out. All they had been given was water, and that only when the ponies were given theirs. The wagon jounced once savagely and sent the two bound men careening to the far side. They crashed hard against the sideboard.

"Gods . . ." Talus moaned. He maneuvered himself into a seated position. "Not exactly the way I'd have chosen to be awakened. Are you all right, Theon?"

"Yes. How about you? I've been listening to your moans of love."

"I'm not surprised I was moaning," Talus replied, now trying to brace himself in the corner where the headboard met the sideboard, so that when the wagon lurched he would not be sent flying. "But are you sure I was moaning about love? More likely it was about food."

"The name you were calling out was Cotto," Theon told him gently. "Do you want to talk about her, Talus? I'd be glad to listen."

Talus did not respond immediately. When he did speak, his voice was sad and low. "She didn't care whether I lived or died after she betrayed me to Navan to save her own position in his court. In fact, she probably never thought that I'd be able to escape. But in spite of all that, and even though more than a year has passed since I last saw her, I still yearn to hold her and make love to her. I believe in my heart that she didn't know what she was doing, that it was all a mistake, that she still loves me as much as I love her."

"It is not unusual for the heart to lag behind the head," the older man soothed. "What you know intellectually is separate from what you feel."

They sat without speaking for a long while and listened to the wheels creaking and the ponies snorting. The vehicle was climbing higher and higher into the mountains, and the air was growing colder.

"I'm losing the feeling in my legs!" Talus cried out suddenly, obviously frightened.

"You're all right. They're just numb from the cold and the ropes. Wiggle your toes, Talus. Keep moving your toes. And your fingers."

Talus followed his friend's suggestion, and his panic subsided. "Do you have any idea where we are?"

"According to the stars we have been moving north and east. I don't think I've ever been in this area. Nothing seems familiar. It would appear very different by daylight, of course."

"Did you notice that the driver never speaks? He doesn't yell at us or at the ponies."

Theon shook his head indulgently. Talus's fears were taking control, and everything seemed menacing—the cold, the landscape, the driver's silence . . . His young friend missed the obvious fact that the driver was mute. Probably his tongue had been cut out, poor man. It was a common mutilation in the savage feuds that continually erupted between various mountain families in the Thracian interior.

"Why aren't there any guards to keep us from escaping in case we could loosen our bonds?"

"Because in this terrain we would be easy to track down."

The wagon took another sharp turn, but this time Theon and Talus were prepared. They braced themselves so that they were not thrown.

Suddenly Talus groaned.

"What is the matter?" Theon asked quickly. "Are you hurt?"

"No, I was just overwhelmed by the sadness of it all— how we, once one of the great families of the world, are now dispersed over the face of the earth and trying to destroy one another. The Children of the Lion will not survive this generation."

"You're talking nonsense, Talus."

"Am I?" he asked bitterly. "When I was a boy, I was told that the Children of the Lion were gifted armorers and artists. Our weapons were in tremendous demand, sought by kings and great warriors. Our gold and silver jewelry was sold dear in all the markets of the Great Sea. Everything we crafted was handed down in families for generations, treated like treasure. We changed history. Now look at us."

"All this shall pass. Families, like all else in life, have rhythms. They enjoy great luck and favor, then they endure times such as these. Think about Shobai, generations back, who enjoyed great wealth and power, only to end up as a blind slave chained to a wagon wheel in the desert sun."

"Do you really believe we can get our homeland back? But how? And if we could, then what? We would inherit a parched and ruined island, devastated by fire and theft."

Theon chuckled. "Oh, I'm sure we'd think of something to do with it." He paused a moment. "I think, Talus, that you have a very romantic view of our family. Your father was a great artisan in the working of metals and gold. But even he would have agreed that in recent generations, the strength of the Children of the Lion has rested in our financial and commercial empire. Many people say that our birthmark gives us mystical powers. I would be reluctant to disavow them of that notion. Of course, some of our cousins have dabbled in the black arts of the occult. A few have wrought terrible misery and pain. No, I feel confident that our family's high-masted ships, blown to the far corners of the earth, have made our family into a respectable cultural force."

Talus chuckled grimly in reply. "Well, right now, Theon, I would trade all of Nuhara's treasures for a bowl of hot pea soup with a large piece of fatty meat floating near the top."

As the wagon rolled on, Theon soothed Talus with more stories of the family—of the brave Hadad, the tragic Ben-Hadad, the beautiful warrior woman Teti, whose army guarded Egypt's trade routes, and her twin brother, Ketan. Talus was fascinated by everything he heard, even the stories Theon had told him before. Eventually the tales were completed. The night wind grew colder. The two kinsmen tried to keep the ropes that bound them from cutting off their circulation . . . tried to sleep. . . .

Dawn came suddenly to the high mountains. All was

dark, and then the sun was everywhere, white and blinding
and powerful. As Talus and Theon struggled to sit up, their
eyes were tearing in the light. As their vision adjusted, they
saw that the wagon had stopped beside several small
wooden sheds. The area was a flat plain, not very large,
and surrounded by foreboding mountain peaks.

"The wagon has stopped," Talus whispered.

The driver jumped down, walked to the back of the
wagon, and gestured that the two men should move toward
him. They inched to the edge, and the driver cut their
bonds with his knife.

Talus and Theon climbed off and, standing on wobbly
legs, rubbed their wrists and ankles. Then the driver
climbed up again behind his ponies, turned the wagon, and
started down the same path he had just ascended.

"Someone's coming," Talus whispered, inclining his
head toward a corridor in the nearest mountainside. Talus
looked to see four men emerge. They strode forward, then
halted about three feet away. The man in front was sandy
haired, dressed in a blue cloak, and looked like he was
from among the Sea Peoples. The three who followed at
his heels were obviously Thracians—small, powerfully built
men wearing skins.

"I am Ardenti," the leader said as his men moved
forward to flank the newcomers. "I am the administrator
of Traxis. And I want to welcome you to our . . . resort."

Theon and Talus exchanged a quick glance. In spite of
the unceremonious transit and delivery, Theon actually
harbored the hope that Traxis would not be so bad. "My
name is Theon, and my kinsman's name is—"

He never finished his sentence. And he never saw the
club that crashed down on the side of his face and sent him
sprawling. His mouth filled with blood, and pain shot up
and down his body. Dazed, he stared up at the smiling
Ardenti.

"Guests here have no names," the administrator said.
"Now get up."

Theon struggled to his feet with the help of a silent, shocked Talus.

For the first time, Theon caught a glimpse of the weapon that had struck him. It was a small, thick wooden club wrapped in rawhide. Each of the three Thracian guards had one.

"Your days will be most pleasant here," Ardenti went on, still smiling. "You may hike or bathe or hunt or play dice—whatever you like. And all during your stay here you will enjoy delectable food, superb wines, and the company of the most beautiful women in Thrace. But before you start your vacation, you must have something to eat. You are probably starving from the long trip." He snapped his fingers.

One of the Thracian guards ran to a shed, picked up a covered pail that was on the ground beside the door, and brought the bucket to Talus and Theon. He placed it on the ground in front of them and kicked off the lid.

"Eat as many as you want," Ardenti urged expansively.

Theon peered into the bucket. At first he thought he was still dazed from the club. But then he heard Talus gasp. Dozens of live mountain salamanders were inside the pail and crawling over one another.

"I can't do it," Talus whispered.

"You said in the cart that you were hungry," Theon said out of the corner of his mouth. "What's wrong with a little lizard?"

"I can't eat live things."

"It won't be alive the moment after you bite off its head," Theon said harshly. He had already felt the power of the Thracian weapon. He had no desire to be clubbed again. Eating a lizard was a small price to pay. He quickly reached into the pail, grasped one of the salamanders, killed it with his fingers, and swallowed it almost without chewing. Talus grimaced, then did the same, his face ashen.

Ardenti and the three guards watched impassively. It was impossible to know if this was a test, a torture, or an invitation. Next Talus and Theon were led across the small plain and through the mountain corridor. When they emerged from this high-walled path they found themselves staring into the deepest hole they had ever seen. It seemed to drop straight down for miles. The clanking of picks being driven into the mountainous sides echoed around them.

"A marble quarry . . ." Theon whispered to his young friend.

Along the walls hundreds and hundreds of men clung precariously to ropes and scaffolding as they wielded their tools against the rock. Theon staggered back as the impact of Nuhara's cruelty hit him with full force. At this moment he realized that in all likelihood he would not survive her ruthlessness.

"Follow me," ordered one of the three Thracian guards, and Talus and Theon walked behind him along the rim.

They had not gone three steps when they heard a bloodcurdling scream. They watched in horror as a man hurtled to his death far below. His screams quickly faded.

The guard shrugged. A small smile curled his thin lips. "Maybe he fell, maybe he jumped."

He led them to a large outcropping of rock manned by two other guests of Traxis, indicated that this was their workplace, then turned and walked away. A small Cretan thief named Lucien and a very big, very black-skinned murderer named Doro introduced themselves.

"We call that guard No Neck," Lucien said. "The other two are worse. One we call Crazy, and the other is known as Club. I'm sure you've already found out which one is Club."

Theon nodded grimly, and his hand went to the side of his head. His hair was sticky with blood.

"If you want to stay alive," Lucien continued, "then watch Doro and me very carefully. These cliffs are treacherous. In the long run, it really doesn't matter; no one lasts in this hole more than six months. You die of starvation, get beaten to death, fall, or jump."

Theon looked at his kinsman. Talus appeared to be in shock.

The small Cretan and the very large black man began to remove a slab of marble. It seemed an impossible feat with such primitive tools and rope pulleys—but they managed it: First they used wooden-handled saws to create a furrow about half an inch deep. Then they struck thick iron chisels with stout wooden mallets to open a wedge in the marble and break the marble along a seam. Finally, using two pulleys and nearly superhuman effort, they hoisted the huge slab up the mountainside and over the rim. In the process, the men raised themselves to the top of the quarry's lip.

Once the rock was delivered intact to the rim, Doro explained, shaggy mountain ponies hauled it away.

"If you miss the seam and the slab splinters, you're dead," Lucien warned. "Ardenti himself will kick you over the rim."

After Lucien and Doro had recovered their strength, they lowered themselves over the rim, again to cut more marble. "Pull on the rope when you're ready to come down," Lucien instructed. "And don't wait too long, because No Neck will be back to check up on you."

"I'm frightened, Theon," Talus quavered.

"So am I. But we don't have an option."

"For the first time in my life I feel that I am going to die soon," Talus whispered.

"No, Talus. You are wrong," Theon said in a strong, sure voice. He was lying but needed to fool Talus. Talus was still young; he had a chance to survive. "We are going to die someday, like all men, but it won't be here. Believe me, we will get out of this place. We will escape to see the restoration of the glory of our family. We will return the treasure to its—"

"Fantasy! Lies! Wishful thinking!" Talus shot back angrily. "We are finished, Theon! Accept it!"

"No! Please, Talus, now is not the time to despair. Now is when we need all of our strength."

"You made the same speech to me when we were in the mountains and fighting Nuhara. You told me that if I kept my faith in the future, we would triumph. Now look at us." A sound between a sob and a laugh escaped Talus's lips.

Theon did not answer. He stared out over the ledge and watched as Lucien and Doro dangled in space, a mere misstep away from plummeting to their death, always a single slip away from eternity. Acrid sweat slid down his skin in spite of the cold wind, and the taste of blood lingered as a bitter reminder in his mouth. He did not want to die here, the victim of brutal guards and a sadistic administrator. He had led too fine a life to sacrifice it to Traxis's lack of regard for the basic needs of humanity. He would choose survival as a rebellion against this mountaintop otherworld where there were no options. He clenched his fists suddenly. He *would* find an option!

He stared at Talus. The young man was pale, and his mouth hung slack. His eyes seemed dull. His will to live seemed to be dripping away, like water off a roof.

"Listen to me, Talus!" Theon said urgently, grasping the young man's shoulders and shaking him harshly, furiously, almost wanting to hurt him. "If you don't care about the Children of the Lion and if you don't care enough about yourself to stay alive and fighting, then what about the woman who loves you?"

"Who?"

"Why, Cotto."

Talus's eyes widened in disbelief, then he laughed in Theon's face.

"Even *I* don't believe my delusions, Theon. I love her, yes. But as for her love, well—"

"You don't know that. None of us knows. If you can survive this, Cotto may be at the end of the road, the prize you earn for enduring this nightmare. Maybe you'll find out that she's loved you all the while."

"What are you saying, Theon? First you tell me to be hardheaded and practical. Then you force-feed me my own delusions."

"To be honest," Theon confessed sadly, "your survival is my only concern. I will tell you whatever I have to."

"And why is that?" Talus demanded, disgusted. "Because you're a liar? Because the truth changes as effortlessly as the wind direction?"

"No, Talus. Because . . . you are a son to me."

Theon's admission embarrassed both men. Yet each knew it was true. The bond that had developed between them was the closest either had ever experienced.

The tears formed in Talus's eyes. He gripped Theon's forearms and squeezed in a gesture of masculine affection and affirmation. Then, without a word, he grabbed the rope and started to ease himself over the rim.

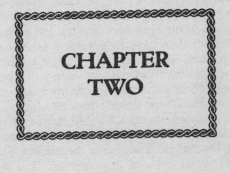

CHAPTER TWO

Sinai

The sun rose high in the sky, and blistered Hela's face. The corpse of Ma-Set was beginning to smell, and the skin across the features stretched tautly and resembled parchment. One of the two horses had collapsed and died. The other's connection to life was precarious.

Long-haired demons still surrounded the camp. *Why don't they come closer?* Hela thought. *Why don't they kill Tuk and me just like they killed Ma-Set?* She could not understand. Was this a sadistic game?

Tuk, who had been seated beside her, abruptly stood up and walked away.

"No, Tuk!" Hela cried out. "Don't go near them! They'll kill you!"

But Tuk was not walking toward the long-haired murderers. She was walking toward the horse that was still standing. In her hands she held Ma-Set's blade and helmet. Hela watched in horror and fascination as the child bled the horse, then returned with the precious fluid. It amazed Hela that a mere girl would undertake such a grim task. Tuk handed Hela the helmet, and she drank gratefully, keeping a wary eye on the murderers.

Hela had never seen such bizarre and primitive people. They seemed to have materialized from a place untouched by time. Their hair was long and matted. They were burned bronze from the sun. Men and women wore only the briefest of pure white garments made of coarsely woven linen. Had their crude weapons—slings and bone knives and wooden spears with flint tips—not proved so effective, they would be almost laughable. For the first time since the people had shown themselves, Hela could see their flocks of goats in the distance. They were obviously nomadic herders with few needs and fewer rules.

Hela tore her gaze away from the murderous strangers, and her eyes settled on the bloodied, contorted death mask of Ma-Set. She began to weep. First her beloved brother, now her faithful friend and protector. She closed her eyes tightly to shut out the glare of the desert sun and, more painful, the horrors of the world.

When Hela opened them again, she saw that Tuk had covered Ma-Set's face with a cloth. She reached out and touched the child in thanks. How odd it was; the child seemed to be taking care of her, the adult—the hapless, incapable adult.

The child stood to face her, then held out small, dark hands to Hela.

"You want me to stand up and go with you?" the woman asked.

Tuk nodded.

"What's the matter, child?"

Tuk was silent, so Hela, resigned, struggled to stand. Her whole body ached. She took a few tentative steps and grasped the child's chubby fingers. Tuk, tugging on Hela's hand, started to walk. She led Hela toward the savages.

"Stop, Tuk!" Hela cried. "Where do you think you're going?" She felt powerless to stop the child or to free her hand from Tuk's grip. Tuk was too powerful for her. Hela gave up the fight. They might as well die sooner than later.

When Tuk reached the savages, she veered sharply and stopped in front of a solitary young man who was hunkered down on the desert floor. His lean, well-muscled body was lightly coated with oil to fight the blistering sun.

The man rose to his full and impressive height, bowed, and said in a quiet voice, "I am Hosea, prince of the Nazirites."

Hela realized that Tuk must have identified their leader intuitively. She was also astonished at how courtly this murderer was.

"Who are you people?" Hela rasped through cracked lips. "Why have you attacked us?"

"We are Nazirites, true children of the one living God," Hosea said, as if that should explain everything.

"Which God?" Hela asked, confused.

"There is only one God. Yahweh."

"Then you are Israelites?"

"Yes, returned to the desert of Sinai to escape the abominations of Canaan. Here, in isolation, we can be pure. Here, in this hallowed place where Moses received the Word of Yahweh, we can remain a kingdom of priests and a holy nation." He smiled, showing teeth that were white and even. "We are seekers of the truth. The truth, you see, is always simple. People try to make it more complex than it is. We live with minimal possessions and ceremonies, so as to be at one with the truth. We do not cut our hair. We do not harm our bodies with unclean food. We do not insult our souls with perversions. We do not defile the living by having any contact with the dead."

He beckoned to one of his people, who hurried over with a small bowl of goat's milk. This, Hosea handed to Tuk. She drank a bit, then handed the bowl to Hela, who, in turn, drained the delicious milk to the last drop. Hela returned the bowl gratefully. Now she understood why the Nazirites had not approached her—any closeness to a corpse would be defiling, and she had been at Ma-Set's side.

"Why did you attack us, Prince? We meant you no harm."

"Because your companion was an Egyptian. We kill Egyptians on sight to avenge our people for the horrors the Egyptians wrought on us when we were slaves in their land."

"What do you propose to do with the child and me?" Hela asked.

"Do?" He looked startled. "We will do nothing. You are not Egyptians. We have no quarrel with you. Go in peace."

The long-haired man signaled to his band. They scurried around to get organized, then rounded up the goats. Hosea took the lead, and the group moved off.

"Wait!" Hela said, running after the prince and clutching his arm. "You can't just leave us here! We have no food or water."

Hosea stopped and looked down at Hela's hand. She quickly removed it from his arm. "You cannot join us," he told her. "You and the child are not Israelites. We must remain a pure people."

"How dare you! I am Hela, the seed of Isis," she screamed at him. "A hundred thousand people bowed down to me." Although she had spoken from desperation, the moment she uttered her words, she realized how pathetic they were. If she was the reincarnation of any god she would not have been at the threshold of death.

Hosea did not answer. He walked away quickly. She cried after him, "If you won't save me, then take the child. Please. I beg you."

But the long-haired Nazirites were swiftly fading from sight. Hela, still holding Tuk's hand, stumbled back to the remains of the camp and looked around. She had no alternative. She knew what to do—follow the Nazirites or perish.

"Bring the horse, Tuk," she said. "We're getting out of here. The Nazirites have food and water. We'll beg them to share with us."

But the second horse was already on its side and near death. It was not going anywhere.

Before Hela and Tuk started off, Hela knelt at Ma-Set's side. Her heart was heavy at abandoning him to the vultures. "Rest in peace, old soldier," she whispered into the desert wind. "We shall meet again."

Hour after hour they followed the tracks of the Nazirites and their flocks. When Hela fell, the child helped her up. Hela kept asking Tuk, "Do you see water yet? Do you see any trees with fruit?"

But there was neither. On they walked, across the parched stony ground.

"Look for a lizard, Tuk! Or for a plant! Keep your eyes open, Tuk!" she urged.

But the merciless land was barren.

Finally night came and provided a welcome cessation from heat and light. Hela lay down, breathing with difficulty. She loathed her pathetic helplessness. She realized that she possessed no skills to help her to survive. She did not know how to hunt or find water or preserve her own strength. She was no goddess; she was not even a grown woman. Despite her age and woman's body, she was a helpless child. The dreamless sleep of exhaustion finally stilled her self-recriminations.

The next morning the woman and girl started out again. Hela's throat was so parched that she could no longer speak. She assumed Tuk's throat was equally dry. Their feet bled.

Finally, late in the afternoon, they saw the Nazirite band setting up camp ahead. Hela wanted to run to them; but she was too weak, and her feet hurt too much. All she could do was put one foot in front of the other, and even this required every bit of her strength.

Suddenly, five big Nazirite men loomed up in front of her and Tuk. The strangers' faces were impassive; their long, matted hair looked dull, even in the long rays of the setting sun.

"Help us!" Hela begged in a cracked and almost silent voice.

The men flung their spears. Hela screamed soundlessly and wrapped her arms protectively around the child. She could see the arc of the weapons as the flint tips caught the rays of the sun. She turned and braced herself for the impact, the pain, the tearing of her body.

The five spear points dug into the earth inches from her body, a quivering fence separating her from the Nazirites' camp.

She understood the message: *Come any closer, and you will die.*

The Nazirites turned and rejoined the others. Hela, not to be repelled so easily, went after them. Let them kill her and Tuk if they wished, she thought defiantly. It was better to die by spears than from a slow and agonizing thirst.

They followed the five men at a distance. Almost crazed by heat and despair, Hela called out, "You will have to feed me or kill me. You will have to give me water or slit my throat."

She was too weak to catch up to the Nazirites. All she could do was follow them, trying to focus her bleary eyes on their dust.

Then, without warning, another spear was hurled. It came on a high trajectory, seemingly from out of the sun. The spear landed so close to Hela that she could feel the wind of its thrust. Something was attached to the shaft.

"See what it is, child."

Tuk removed the leather pouch attached to the wood just below the flint point. Inside was a chunk of moist goat's cheese.

They divided the offering and stuffed it into their mouths. Too soon it was consumed. It had not even dented their hunger, but it would be enough, perhaps, to keep them alive. And Hela knew that there would be more such gifts. She and Tuk would survive. The woman had suffered little adversity in her life on Home. In recent times, since her kidnapping, adversity was all she had known. Now, trembling, Hela began to weep. She understood the meaning of the Nazirite gift: *You have touched our hearts. We shall leave you food, but do not come close enough to defile us.*

Hela, now laughing as well as weeping, pulled Tuk to her breast. "Do you see, Tuk? We have become like pariahs. But the Nazirites will feed us on the outskirts of their camp. They will keep us alive."

The child, as usual, said nothing.

"But it is better, Tuk," Hela whispered, "to be a live jackal than a dead lion."

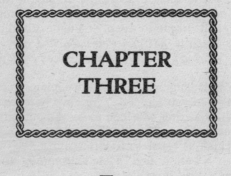

CHAPTER THREE

Tyre

The armed escort that had accompanied Luti, Micah, and Drak on their journey to Tyre left them at the eastern gates of that great city. The traveling had been arduous, but the priests of Astarte had supplied the group with the best food and finest mounts. Now the family was about to be left to fulfill the mission and save little Seka's life.

As the officer of the guard wheeled his mount around to head homeward, he said to Luti, "Navan holds court at the Palace of Weights and Measures in the port area." Then he and his men were gone.

The moment they were alone, Micah stretched hugely. "Let's get something to eat, then rest for a while before we get started. I'll look around for some quiet lodgings."

Luti turned on him in a fury. "How can you even think of resting? Our baby is being held hostage in Babylon!"

"Calm down, Luti. You won't accomplish anything if you're hysterical. Besides, you've been complaining about our poverty for a long time and treated me like garbage because I haven't brought any money into the family. Now, finally, you have a chance to become wealthy again. Enjoy it!"

"What will wealth mean if Seka is harmed?"

"Relax, will you? The priests will take good care of her. They're no fools. They need you, Luti."

But Luti had made up her mind. She would not take the time to pursue anything but the completion of her mission. She kicked her mount, and Micah and Drak followed her into and through the city, toward the Palace of Weights and Measures.

It was the custom of Phoenician noblemen to grant an audience to all those who requested one. But, perhaps because of the sojourners' strange Babylonian garb, the small family was kept waiting for hours in Navan's anteroom. Shopkeepers, ships' captains, drovers, and abandoned wives—all local residents, by their appearance—were called in immediately.

Finally, late in the afternoon, Luti, Micah, and Drak were ushered into the high chamber that held the official scales to standardize weights.

At the far end of the crowded, vaulted room, sat Navan. Dressed in formal high hat and long gown, he was obviously bored and weary from the long day spent hearing cases, schemes, and complaints.

Next to Navan was the old, wily adviser whom Luti had been schooled about by the Babylonian military. His name was Sutt, and behind him was the Egyptian astrologer called Zab—a man much admired by the Phoenician hierarchy. He was paid extravagantly for his services. Luti would have to be on her guard with him, for he would logically perceive her as a threat to his security.

Navan looked with disgust at the three travelers and commanded, "State your case quickly."

Luti stepped forward. Her palms were sweating. Navan was a very imposing figure. She knew that she could make no mistakes. "My lord Navan," she began, "I am Luti of Ur. And this is my husband, Micah, and my child Drak. We have traveled in haste to your court to offer our services."

Navan burst out laughing, and his whole court followed suit.

"Are you chimney sweepers?" Navan asked, then guffawed.

"No, my lord. I am a reader of bird omens. I can predict the future."

Now it was the Egyptian astrologer's turn to explode with laughter. Once he had restrained himself, he said to Navan, "My lord, she is one of those lunatics who shakes the dead bones of birds onto the ground and peers deeply into them. And when the bones and dried feathers don't work, she dips her nose into bird shit and sniffs out which way the wind is blowing."

Luti did not respond to the astrologer's insults. Insults were of no significance. Nor did the laughter erupting around her cause her discomfort. She had to concentrate on Navan. She had to tell him what he wanted and needed to hear. She realized, however, that her usual methods of reading bird omens would not be accepted as valid by the Phoenicians. They were too arrogant; they believed themselves to be scientists, men of reason.

When quiet was restored Luti said, "For men who are continually losing ships at sea because your astrologers cannot predict even the approach of hurricanes, your laughter is unseemly."

She had struck a raw nerve. There was a sharp intake of air as all eyes turned to Navan. It was well-known that the Phoenicians had just suffered a costly loss: a twelve-ship grain convoy, wrecked on the southern coastal reefs.

"And how do you predict the approach of the hurricanes?" Navan demanded, his eyes narrowing.

"Through the flight of the gull, my lord."

There was laughter again, but it was more subdued, more nervous.

"Are you as accurate as you are arrogant?" Navan asked.

"I am accurate, my lord," Luti answered flatly.

The aged adviser, Sutt, motioned with his hands. Navan, Sutt, and Zab drew close and began a whispered conversation.

Out of the corners of her eyes Luti caught sight of Micah's face. He seemed pale and agitated; he grasped Drak's hand tightly.

Navan stood up and addressed her. "You appear very confident of your powers."

"I am, my lord. I can be of great help to you."

Navan grinned nastily. "If you are so sure, then no doubt you would be willing to back up your claims with the lives of your loved ones. A kind of wager."

A shudder went through Luti's body, then she took a steadying breath. Seka was already being held at the point of a knife. Now even more was being demanded of the family. "I am very confident in my powers," she said firmly.

"Good. Bring the man and the boy."

Micah and Drak were pushed roughly out of the room. They descended a steep flight of stairs and went down a long, musty corridor. Luti, Navan, and his advisers followed, along with a contingent of armed guards.

They entered a dark chamber. Torches were lit and rammed into special holders in the walls. One flaming brand was used to ignite a large fire, which a guard fed with oil. It flared up.

"Tie them!" Navan ordered.

Luti watched in horror as their robes were ripped off and their wrists tied tightly with thongs. Micah and Drak were hoisted up on iron hooks and hung there, suspended six inches off the floor. Drak looked terrified, but he overlaid his fear with the courage of a man as he saw, then copied, his father's behavior. Luti bit her lip to avoid crying out. *I must be strong,* she thought. *I must see this through. If I weaken, we will all die.*

"Prepare the boot!" Navan ordered.

Luti watched in horror as one of the guards thrust a bronze replica of a boot into the flame and held it there with prongs until it was almost white hot.

"The man first!" Navan ordered, and two guards grabbed Micah's legs. He did not fight against them.

After removing the heated object with the prongs, the guard moved to slide it over Micah's foot. He held the boot just under Micah.

Drak began to wail now, thinking that after his father was burned, he might be next.

Luti fell to her knees. "Please!" she wept. "I'm telling the truth! I can read the omens and forecast the weather."

Navan looked at her for a long moment. Then he nodded to the guard, who set the boot on the stone floor. "You'd better be telling the truth," he warned. "Now you know what I'm capable of doing if you're lying." He turned again to the guard. "Cut down the boy," he ordered.

The soldier did so immediately, and Drak ran into the protection of his mother's embrace.

Then the Phoenician gestured again to the guard. He picked up the boot, which had cooled somewhat, with the prongs and in one quick motion brought the boot up to the sole of Micah's foot, burning him. It lasted only a second. Micah's screams rent the air.

"Enough for now," Navan said. Then he spoke directly to Luti. "The wager is on. Do your magic, woman. Tell me what the dawn will bring. If you are right, you and your family shall become treasured members of my court. If you are wrong, your husband and son will be tortured to death, then you and their corpses—what is left of them— shall be flung over the walls of Tyre."

*   *   *

Luti, standing on the balcony of the Palace of Weights and Measures, stared seaward. Behind her, Navan and his advisers, flanked by soldiers, waited expectantly.

The memory of Micah's screams still echoed in her ears, tormenting her. Why, she wondered, had Navan named such severe penalties for failure? Did he suspect that spies would try to infiltrate his circle and ferret out knowledge about the attack on Babylonia? She leaned against the stone wall and breathed deeply, afraid she might faint. Now the lives of her entire family depended upon her accuracy. Her eyes searched the horizon relentlessly. *Be strong!* she cautioned herself. *Be alert!*

Many shorebirds were wheeling around the port area. But she was looking only for one specific bird—the black-headed gull. Finally she spotted a flock of them hovering close to a berthed vessel. She watched carefully; black-headed gulls, she knew, were particularly adapted to the wind currents. If they flew high, it meant that a hard wind was coming. If they hovered low, then calm weather was approaching.

Today these gulls were wheeling high. But she needed more information. There was no margin for error. She watched them feed. What were they eating? Their choice seemed to be shellfish. That meant the birds were expecting high tides; they were harvesting before the tide covered the mollusks. That, Luti knew, meant rain.

She picked up a loose stone and flung it toward the gulls. They flew away . . . to the west. That meant the weather was coming from the east.

She turned to Navan and said confidently, "By dawn tomorrow, heavy rains and winds will hit your port area. The winds will be coming from the east. You will be able to send your ships out to sea, but the harbor will be treacherous for arrivals."

Navan seemed taken aback by her self-assurance and specific details.

"We shall see," he said. He turned to a soldier. "Take her to a room and place a guard by the door."

* * *

It was the longest night of Luti's life. Sleep was, of course, impossible. Her entire family was hostage, their freedom dependent upon the behavior of birds. Death and torture would engulf all of them unless her predictions were accurate. Anything could happen with the weather.

Each passing minute was a torment. She paced the room. Her body was drenched with sweat. Her fears rose up like demons in her breast to choke her. Finally, exhausted, she curled up on the floor under the window and fell into a troubled sleep. . . .

She woke with a start hours later, her heart pounding, as if from a horrific but realistic nightmare.

She stood up slowly and pressed her face against the cool stucco wall. It was still dark outside. But, thank the gods, tiny drops of rain had begun to fall. And she could hear the wind rising. Her joy was so great that she began to whirl about the room in a mad dance of victory.

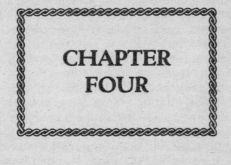

CHAPTER FOUR

Sinai

The woman and the child increased their pace as the sun moved low into the west. *We are like trained dogs,* Hela thought bitterly, *waiting for the scraps.*

The travelers' dehydrated bodies were like parched vines in the desert air. As Tuk and she struggled onward, keeping the dust cloud raised by the Nazirite band always in view, Hela marveled at—and was, at times, shamed by—the stoicism and stamina of the black child. No words of complaint or despair passed from her lips. There were no frowns. She shed no tears. Was the child biologically mute? Hela wondered, or had the hardships of her young life stunned her into silence? There had been no mother or father at the campsite where the plague had claimed Tuk's guardian, and this made Hela wonder whether Tuk had witnessed their death, too.

As they trudged on through the sunbaked wilderness, Hela wondered if Tuk actually comprehended their peril. Perhaps the girl was too young, or retarded. Still, she must feel the discomfort.

Hela could not answer the questions she continually posed to herself concerning this strange companion. And it did not really matter anymore. They would both live or die in this fearsome land, no matter how brave or how cowardly their behavior.

As the sun fell toward the horizon and the afternoon shadows lengthened, the young woman forced herself to move more quickly, anticipating the handout from the Nazirites. Their offering always came at day's end. Her mouth was parched, and her stomach contracted painfully at the very thought of the moist nutritious goat's cheese.

Then, as expected, out of the red glare of the setting sun, came the sound of the spear. Its point drove into the earth ten feet from Hela, and she ran wildly to unfasten the pouch that contained the food. The portion was always the same: enough to keep them alive but not enough for them to regain their strength fully.

After Tuk and Hela had eaten, they burrowed into the ground to wait the long hours before dawn, when their trek would begin again.

Hela woke with a start. In the darkness she could sense movement from very nearby. Tuk? No, the child was still asleep. Were the Nazirites coming to kill her?

Her eyes made friends with the darkness. Finally she could make out a figure . . . or was it a delusion? No. It was a man! Frightened for Tuk's safety, Hela moved toward the intruder, to confront him.

As she approached, trying to appear brave, the man took shape.

"Is that you, Hosea?" she asked, astonished.

"Yes," said the Nazirites' prince. "Are you and the child well?"

"We are surviving."

"I am sorry that we can't provide you with more food. But our own supply is sorely limited, and there are many other factors involved, which I must take under consideration."

Hela laughed bitterly. She understood exactly what Hosea meant: that many Nazirites did not want to feed them at all.

"But I have brought you something," the Nazirite said in a perkier voice, and he held out his hand.

Hela accepted the gifts. He had brought them cloths to put over their heads to protect their scalps and eyes, and a small swatch of linen wrapped around what felt to be a piece of clay.

"Pinch off small pieces of this special clay and work it between your palms," he explained. "Then rub the oily residue over the child's body and your own. The oil will protect you quite well from the sun."

Hela stared at the strange-looking, long-haired man. He seemed so primitive, but, in fact, was a gentle soul.

"This is very kind of you," Hela said. She was ready to turn back to Tuk, but she realized that Hosea had made no move to return to his own camp. "Is there something else, Prince?"

"You are very beautiful," he said softly.

"What?"

"You are very beautiful. Your hair is like beaten gold."

"Don't come too close," she warned bitterly. "I may defile you."

"Don't mock me."

"It is you, Hosea, who mocks *me* with all that nonsense about defilement."

"My people follow Yahweh," he said, then took a step forward. He was just inches away. His body was taut as a bowstring.

Hela began to tremble. "Please," she said, "go back to your people. I appreciate the kindness you've shown me, but—"

"I loved you the first moment I saw you," he whispered.

"Are you mad?" she asked. *Am I mad? Why don't I just run?*

His hand reached out and tentatively touched her face. Then he brought his hand down along her neck. It slipped inside her tunic, to circle her breast. His hands were rough and callused, but his touch was soft. She began to shake. The floodgates of her heart were bursting open, and all the horror and grief of the past year seemed to drive her forward into the stranger's arms.

Her lips feverishly sought his mouth. She wanted his love. She wanted to feel pleasure. She had known nothing but misery for so long. . . .

They fell to the ground together, and there, on the desert floor, he entered her. She felt a great surge of joy and strength. She cried out again and again as if every thrust of his body extirpated from her heart all the death and sadness she had experienced.

Then it was over. She watched dazed as his tall, lithe figure slipped away into the night. She lay there, confused but happy.

Hela and Tuk trudged onward. The woman had applied the oily clay Hosea had given her as a gift, and both travelers glistened from the substance and felt infinitely more comfortable. Hela had all but forgotten her weariness and her pain and even her perpetual hunger and thirst. Instead her mind was on Hosea. Would he visit her again? she wondered.

What had happened between them, she realized, was ridiculous. In a few nightmarish days she had gone from a virgin goddess to a common whore. But she could not stifle the desire to meet Hosea again . . . to feel his body again . . . to let herself go with abandon. The release and comfort he had brought her was overwhelming. This long-haired prince of the Nazirites had removed the death masks of Gravis and Ma-Set from her consciousness.

From time to time when she glanced down at Tuk, Hela wondered if the girl had heard or seen their lovemaking. There was no way to tell, although the child's exhaustion at day's end was so profound, she could have slept through anything.

Hela longed for the day to pass quickly. There would be the goat's milk cheese, then the cooling darkness, and finally, perhaps, the Nazirite in her arms.

On they walked. Their feet had become callused, so they no longer bled. And the cloth for their heads now shielded their eyes from the sun so that they were no longer at risk from the dreaded desert blindness.

As the afternoon shadows lengthened, the pair moved faster, decreasing the gap between themselves and the Nazirites. Hela's mouth began to anticipate the food. The sun dropped from the sky, but no food pouch was delivered. Hela's daydreams about her new lover paled before the growing realization that the food delivery was quite late.

The trekkers remained alert, their ears sensitive to the sound of the spear flying toward them. But that sound did not come. The food did not come. Hela panicked. What had gone wrong? Could Hosea have something to do with this? If so, how could he be so cruel?

Darkness slid over the desert. No spear had hurtled through the night. No food had come to them. Hela became hysterical, thinking that Hosea had been harmed by his people. Perhaps the Nazirites had discovered their prince's disappearance and followed him, to witness the tryst.

"We must go into their camp and search for food," she said to Tuk, "even if it means our lives."

They quietly approached the Nazirite campfires, which spread tongues of flame into the night air.

As Tuk and Hela came closer, sad, strange noises assaulted their ears. They had never heard such sounds in the night. First they heard the low, pathetic bleating of the goats. And then they heard human voices, people praying.

Hela stopped just outside the camp's perimeter. A horrible sight greeted her.

All of the goats were lying on their sides. The animals were still alive but too ill to stand. Their stomachs were distended, their breathing was labored, and their eyes rolled wildly about their sockets. The limbs alternately contracted and became loose. It was as if some murderer had run amok and smote every living member of the flock.

The scene reminded Hela of her own encampment after the plague had struck. She watched as the desperate Nazirites, Hosea among them, huddled in small groups, sending their prayers up to Yahweh. Their voices chanted and cried out their supplications.

Hosea, looking up and seeing her, immediately stepped from one of the groups and approached. His hands were held out in apology.

"Ah, Hela, I am sorry. I should have come to tell you what was happening, but I could not leave my people in this awful time."

"When did the plague strike?" she asked weakly.

"Just a few hours ago. The goats fell in their tracks."

Tuk disengaged her hand from Hela's and walked past Hosea into the Nazirite camp. Hela, meanwhile, hardly noticed. She stared up at her lover. Sadness overwhelmed her. She thought she had saved her life and found her first love. That was an absurd hope, she realized now. Her infatuation was born of desperation. It had all meant nothing.

Hela looked down and realized that Tuk had gone into the camp. "Come back!" she cried out. "They will kill you!"

But Tuk ignored her. In fact, she did not even approach the Nazirites. Instead she walked to the nearest goat, then knelt beside the sick animal.

"Don't get so close to them, Tuk!" Hela called out. "They are diseased!" But then, before Hela's startled eyes, the child leaned forward and kissed the goat on its nose.

A second later the beast scrambled to its feet, shook

itself, and trotted off as if it was perfectly well and had never been lying in a pitiful state near death.

Tuk moved to the next animal and repeated her actions.

Again and again the goats who were kissed by the child leaped to their feet, seemingly cured.

"What magic is this?" Hosea asked. "What is happening?"

Hela could not answer. Tuk was obviously a source of wondrous powers. The child was in touch with someone or something that was unseen, godly, and in possession of the most profound secrets of the natural world.

Hela watched in silent fascination as Tuk continued her work of healing. She remembered what her mother had told her many years before: that the lineage of the Children of the Lion included a secret, occult sect that had never been fully revealed . . . that had originated in the North and sent its tentacles throughout the known world. This branch sometimes acted for good but sometimes brought the powers of evil and darkness into focus.

Might Tuk be of that ilk when she got older? Hela shivered. She did not want to know.

The girl finished her work. The flock was up and grazing in the darkness. The child then simply wandered back to Hela and stood close by the woman's side, as if she had done nothing more than kiss the nose of a friendly goat.

Once the Nazirites realized that the child had performed a miraculous healing ritual, their prayers turned to celebration.

They accepted the visitors' presence among them wholeheartedly. They lifted the pair onto their shoulders and carried them in triumph about the camp. After Hela and Tuk were returned to their feet, the Nazirites fawned on them and sang songs for them and fed them and bathed their bodies.

Finally, Hosea lay before them a strange object of hammered gold.

"You and the child have saved our lives. We wish you to have our only earthly treasure."

"What is it?" Hela asked.

"The remains of the Golden Calf, which the Israelites worshiped in this wilderness while Moses was face-to-face with the Lord on Mount Sinai."

Hela was flabbergasted. Why would the Nazirites have preserved an item that symbolized the Israelites' lack of faith in Yahweh at a crucial period of their history? Perhaps, Hela thought, it had become holy to them because Moses himself had destroyed its form . . . transforming it, rendering it shapeless, in his rage, from a piece of sculpture to a lump of beaten gold.

She was about to refuse the generous offer. She was about to say that all Tuk and she wanted was to be allowed to travel with the Nazirites in safety and acceptance. She was about to whisper in Hosea's ear that all she wanted from him was night after night of lovemaking.

But then, suddenly, Tuk placed her right hand lightly on Hela's left hip. The child's touch seemed to jolt her. The woman felt renewed strength. Her view of the world was changed. She shuddered, and none of the words she had planned to speak came out of her mouth. Her lips became very dry. She stared at Hosea again. He no longer seemed desirable. She turned around, befuddled, and stared at the Nazirites and their now healthy flock.

I have been a fool, she realized. *I must take the gold. It represents escape, even freedom.*

If the Nazirites helped her to reach Gaza, she could use the gold to hire a ship to take her and Tuk north. There she could find out what really happened to her mother, Nuhara. She would be able to find out once and for all who among the Children of the Lion had escaped the conflagration on the island called Home.

Hela reached out for the lump of gold.

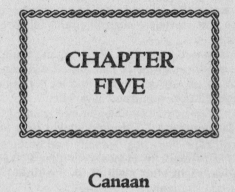

CHAPTER FIVE

Canaan

Cotto lay exhausted but satisfied on the mat in the open tent. As the night breeze fluttered the tent flaps, they sounded like waves washing up on the shore. Her ruse had worked perfectly. She had posed as a wine vendor, and this brute of a man, this Abimelech, had descended on her like a mongrel on a bitch in heat. Now he lay beside her.

In all of her sexual experience, including her time at The Nail in Tyre, she had never met a man so sexually insatiable as Abimelech. She felt as if she had been used by a whole battalion of soldiers. And throughout the night, as he was making love to her again and again, he kept calling her Miriam. Finally she asked who this Miriam was. But in response he raised one powerful hand in a threatening gesture, and she knew never to ask again.

Cotto glanced over at the man. He was asleep now, but she could see the tension in his face and body. Soon, she knew, he would awaken and want her again.

She stared at the wine jugs in the corner. She was thirsty and longed to drink something, but any movement on her part might disturb Abimelech's slumber. She realized that she would rather be deprived of wine, no matter how much she craved it, than bear the full brunt of his desire again.

At least you're freed from The Nail, she reminded herself. *At least you won't die in that locked and airless room.*

Cotto lay quietly on the mat and let her mind wander back to those brief, wondrous days when lovemaking was beautiful . . . when Talus and she had spent the night in soft and languorous love. He had sought only to give *her* pleasure.

The body beside her jerked violently, then sat up, his eyes blazing, a dagger in each hand. "Who are you?" he bellowed.

Cotto shrank back and began to identify herself. Then she realized that a man had slipped into the tent. Abimelech, in his sleep, had been more alert to danger than she had been awake. The newcomer stood quietly, nonthreateningly, however, framed by the moonlight.

"Sheath your daggers, Abimelech," the stranger whispered. "I come from Zebul, the most high lord of Shechem."

"Speak quickly then, before I lose my temper at your intrusion." He stood, jerked Cotto up by her hair, and pushed her into the corner, so her beauty and nakedness would be kept secret from the stranger.

It was too late, though.

The messenger's eyes swept appreciatively over her. "My apologies, Abimelech," the man said. "One hates to interrupt a feast when the dish is so delectable." At last he tore his eyes away and looked at the man from the hill country. "But Zebul and the council have ratified your plan. Gaal cast the lone vote against you, but he was shouted down. Zebul wants you to know that there will be no restrictions on your military action or decisions."

Abimelech nodded. "And the gold?"

"It will be delivered to you tomorrow morning at a place of your designation."

"Have it for me when the sun rises by the wall at the entrance to the Bloody Quarter."

Cotto could see that the stranger was stunned. Abimelech's desire was to receive the gold in what was commonly acknowledged as the most dangerous quarter of Shechem.

"You want the delivery there?" he asked. "The area is overrun by murderers and thieves."

"Deliver it there!" Abimelech ordered. "Now get out."

The messenger turned and left. Then Abimelech turned to Cotto. "You get out, too. Get back on the street where you belong."

Cotto moved sinuously to his side, then slid her slim, bare foot up the side of his leg as she pressed close and lipped his earlobe. "But you found me desirable, my lord," she whispered. "You told me so."

"And I may find you desirable again. But now—" He shoved her away.

Cotto could only obey. Her job was not to stand up to Abimelech but to maintain contact at any cost. She had already learned important information to be sent back to Navan, though, so she grabbed her clothes and her wine jug and slunk from the tent.

Abimelech strode into the Bloody Quarter the moment the sun began to rise. Instead of heading for the wall where the gold talents would be waiting for him, he entered the Alley of Pain—one of the most notorious nests of vipers, sharks, and aberrants in the Bloody Quarter, not to mention the entire city of Shechem. The alley was only three blocks long, snaking between rows of burned-out shells of houses that had long since been abandoned by law-abiding families. Only murderers, pimps, and others of their ilk now squatted among the ruins and planned their forays out of the Bloody Quarter and into the more affluent neighborhoods of the city.

From time to time, in response to public outrage, the lords of Shechem sent armed men into the Bloody Quarter in an attempt to extirpate the vermin with fire and sword. But the Bloody Quarter survived and even flourished. Many of the new arrivals to Shechem—the hungry and the adventurous—ended up there once all their other options had been exhausted. Anyone who had a knife and was not afraid to use it could find contacts and work in the Bloody Quarter—in the Alley of Pain in particular.

In minutes Abimelech found exactly who he was looking for—Menta, known in the alley as the king of thieves. Abimelech flung aside Menta's two burly bodyguards as if they were pieces of dried wood.

"Abimelech!" Menta shouted with glee after he recognized the powerful intruder as his old friend. "What are you doing here?"

The men grasped forearms, wrestled in jest for a moment, then leaned against a wall of a building bordering the alley.

Abimelech and Menta had been childhood companions. They had roamed Shechem together as young toughs. Now Abimelech got right to the point. "How would you like to have five hundred gold talents in your larcenous hands?" he asked.

Menta's eyes widened. He was a good thief, and he got a cut from many other thieves . . . but Abimelech was aware that five hundred gold talents was more money than Menta had ever seen in his lifetime—or even hoped to see. "Are you joking?" he asked. "How would we get our hands on such wealth?"

"It's already arranged. But I need one hundred armed men with good mounts. You can make your own deal with them, and the difference between what you pay them and the five hundred gold talents I'll give you will be yours to keep."

Even though they were old friends, Menta looked suspicious, obviously thinking that the task could be too easily accomplished for the money Abimelech was offering.

Menta stroked his short stubby beard. "Men are cheap in Shechem. You know that. I can get you a thousand in a few minutes—and all of them would slit their father's throat for a single copper coin."

"But I want ex-soldiers—men who can take orders and will fight to the death. They'll cost more. And I don't care what army they fought in."

"When do you need them?" Menta asked, his suspicions abating.

"Assembled and ready to move by sunset."

"Today?"

"Today."

"You have a deal, old friend."

Menta grinned.

Purah was working in his vegetable garden. When he saw Cotto, he dropped his tools and ran to her. The concern on his face helped her to feel better. She knew that he felt terrible about her consorting with Abimelech. *Too bad I don't get orders from him instead of Navan,* she thought, genuinely touched.

Purah offered her his arm, and together they walked into the house, where he offered her a delicious selection of fruits and cakes. As she ate, he walked around the house in an agitated fashion. He brought her wine. Then he took out a hammock. Then he put the hammock back into the chest. Then he took it out again, unfolded it, looked at it, then rolled it up and stuck it back into the chest.

"What is the matter, Purah?" she asked, concerned at his strange behavior.

He stopped and laughed out loud at himself. "I guess I am just becoming too old for this kind of work."

"You are *not* too old! You arranged the meeting perfectly. First he bought the wine, and then he bought me."

"Was he what you expected?" Purah asked delicately.

Cotto knew he was talking about Abimelech's sexual behavior, but she did not want to worry him any more than he already was. "He was what I expected. But, believe me, it could have been a great deal worse."

She saw him turn away and sigh with relief. *Does he look upon me as a daughter?* Cotto wondered. *What a nice man!*

"Can you stay for a while?" Purah asked. "Or do you have to get back to him?"

"I can stay here for as long as I like. Abimelech kicked me out of his bed."

Purah looked incredulous. "Why?"

She told him about the stranger who had appeared so suddenly and exactly what the message had been from the lords of Shechem. Then, word for word, she told Purah Abimelech's response.

The man's smile extended into his bright eyes. "This is very important news, Cotto! You have done excellent work. I must get your information to Navan as soon as possible. Abimelech is about to make his move.

"A thousand gold talents . . ." he mused, then whistled in astonishment. "You must rest while I hire someone to get your report to Navan. Rest! Bathe! Sleep! Drink some wine! I'll be back shortly."

As she heard the door shut behind her host, Cotto laughed indulgently, then sipped some of the cool, sweet wine. She bathed, then lay down on one of the pillows. She felt safe.

The Alley of Pain was choked with horses and armed men. Abimelech had hoisted himself up onto one of the crumbling walls to address his army.

He stared down over the throng. The men were all colors, shapes, and sizes. They were Israelites, Canaanites, Philistines, Sea Peoples, Egyptians, and Lebanese. Some carried swords and bows, some only bows, some spears and daggers. Seeing their weapons, Abimelech realized that he would have to make some adequate provisions for them before leaving Tyre—wooden clubs, perhaps, to supplement what they already had.

But in spite of their many differences, the men all shared three traits: They had once been soldiers; they had been on the losing side; and they had come to Shechem to sell their prowess with weapons and their propensity, often joy, for killing and maiming. Menta, he decided, had done a good job. He had recruited the scum of the earth.

Abimelech called out only twice for silence. His powerful, authoritative voice cut through the murmur. The gathering stared up at their new master.

"Today you are nothing," Abimelech began. "But I shall make you rich and powerful beyond your wildest dreams. Today you are standing in a stinking alley. A year from now you will all be with me in distant and exotic lands. Our coffers will be full, our horses the finest, our weapons the sharpest, our armor invincible. Our flag will be planted over countries and people who have not even heard of Shechem. But, first, tonight, we march north, to Ophrah. And this march, my comrades, will lead us to seventy men who now rest in the hospitality of Gideon's father, Joash, and Gideon's son, Jotham. These seventy men claim to rule our country."

He paused and then grinned wickedly. "Alas, the highest court in the land has condemned these imposters to death. Who is that highest court? I! Abimelech! The true son of Gideon! And so we go there, men, to carry out the sentence."

The gleam of his eyes and the wild promises of his speech brought cheers from the assembled troopers. Having been luckless for a long time, they were now caught up in the blood lust that Abimelech had loosed. Their desire to kill was never far from the surface anyway, and such was the level of their intelligence that any wild promises were easily believed.

War cry after war cry issued from their throats. Then they hurled themselves onto their mounts, which plunged and bucked and sidestepped furiously about in the cramped space. The men were no less patient than their horses in waiting for Abimelech to lead them north.

Cotto rolled over and sighed, resigned to getting no sleep tonight. Not ten feet from her was Purah, calling out her name again and again from his dreams.

She rose silently, found a blanket in the chest, and gently covered him. As she stood back and gazed fondly at her host, she realized that she had just done something she thought she had forgotten how to do—act with care and kindness for another person. She used to be a nice young woman. Even after her success as a dancer and the power she had over men because of her beauty shifted her preoccupation from others onto herself, she had continued to take food and supplies to her family. But when her fortunes dwindled, she thought of no one but herself. Now that had changed.

Why did Purah affect her in this way? she wondered, staring at him as he thrashed about. The dreams, whatever their content, still tormented him. He twisted and moaned and sweated and called her name.

Why did she feel such an affinity for him? Because he, too, was a traitor to his people? He, too, wrestled every day with his conscience . . . with memories of those he had betrayed and destroyed. He, too, probably lived with the omnipresent fear that they—or the many he would betray and destroy in the future—would come back seeking vengeance.

Was that it? Or was it something else? For a moment, as she watched the man's anguish, Cotto wanted very much to slip beneath the blanket with him . . . to allow him to console himself with her breasts . . . to give him her body totally, so that he might feel the strength of his maleness inside her.

These thoughts of love made her uncomfortable. She hurried back to her sleeping area. But all night long her musings were centered on this gentle man not ten feet from her.

* * *

For Joash, the father of Gideon, it was just another tedious visit by the seventy ex-soldiers who had served in his son's army and ruled the land that their leader had liberated. They always came during the first week of each month, on the holy day known as Rosh Chodesh, and they paid their respects to him with small gifts and sweets.

Then they always camped in the field where Gideon had smashed the sacred grove and idols of Baal. That was usually their last respectful gesture . . . before they got drunk and ransacked the countryside. For that reason Joash's entire village's residents made it their business to pack up their valuables and leave the area until the seventy sons had gone home again.

During the lengthy gift-giving ceremony, a weary Joash tried to keep his eyes open and tried to remember to thank individually and by name each of the seventy who pressed tributes upon him. The old man wished that he, like young Jotham, could have gone away.

Suddenly the line was filled with unfamiliar-looking faces. Joash was fairly certain that he had never seen them before. Were they new retainers of his guests? he wondered, or was old age playing another new trick on him.

The area was overwhelmed by chaos. Shouting, cursing men drew their swords on the sons, and the air was filled with the screams of the wounded and dying. The old man ducked the clash of weapons and was struck by falling bodies as he tried to escape.

A phalanx of horses ridden by ugly squat men charged into the melee. The attackers grasped large wooden clubs, which they swung with deadly effect in lazy circles, and crushed the injured beneath the hooves of their beasts.

The charge of these club-wielding men was so powerful, so unexpected, and so leveling that within moments the line in front of Joash was a shambles of broken bodies.

"All right, men! Good job!" a voice cried out. "You know what to do next!"

Joash turned and saw to his horror that Abimelech

was astride one of the mounts. The old man watched in a kind of dream state, unable to believe that what he was witnessing was actually happening.

Abimelech dismounted beside a large rock jutting up from the soil. At Abimelech's command, the first so-called son of Gideon was hooded, then dragged to the rock. His shoulders were held down by two men, and his screams muffled by the makeshift hood. His neck was bared, then Abimelech swung a huge two-edged sword and with a single massive blow beheaded the struggling victim. The blood and gore burst from the slain man like the gas from a bloated stomach and stained the rock.

One by one, the vanquished were dragged screaming to the rock and beheaded. As Abimelech's arms grew weary, his blows became less precise. He hacked away at his enemies, and the rock became a vast dripping horror of gore.

When the last of the seventy was beheaded, Abimelech, his body drenched with sweat and blood, turned to Joash. The old man was weeping.

"Neither you nor Jotham will die by my hands," Abimelech said in a booming voice. "You are both too pathetic to kill. Instead I will give you the great honor of being the first Israelites to bow low before a new king— King Abimelech of Canaan!"

was outside one of the rooms. The old man watched in a
... wide ... before he was

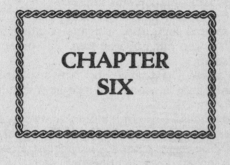

CHAPTER SIX

Thrace

"Hurry, Theon!" Lucien cried out. "Talus is threatening to kill himself."

Theon knew that Lucien was not exaggerating; the wily old criminal was wise to the ways of the quarry, and Talus had been morose for days. He let the basket fall back against the cliff, and he grabbed the rope to swing himself out over the abyss so that he had a clear view of the area.

"Where?" Theon asked desperately.

"Fourth ridge," Lucien said, pointing toward a spot high up on the face of the cliff wall—the north side of the quarry. Theon isolated the form of the black prisoner Doro, and past him was a figure leaning far out over the cliffs. *Talus!*

"He says he wants to die, Theon, and he may do it," Lucien cautioned.

As Theon began to climb, his limbs were infused with new strength—a gift of the knowledge that Talus was in mortal danger. He had known that Talus was weakening; the constant beatings and starvation were taking their toll. But he had not realized that the young man was in such despair that he would attempt suicide.

Now Theon could make out Doro clearly. The black man had spotted him, also, and was pointing frantically toward Talus, who hung by one arm. The other arm was waving in space.

From below, Doro called up, "It was sudden, Theon. He just threw away his tools and said he was going to kill himself."

Theon reached a spot not more than twenty feet from the younger man, and then he stopped. Talus looked out of control, as if he might jump at the slightest provocation.

Theon looked down, light-headed, then shut his eyes. If Talus let go, it would be a long, dizzying fall before the canyon floor claimed him. There was no reason for this kind of lunacy, he thought. Talus was strong and young. He could physically survive much more than he had endured up until now. Emotionally, however, Talus was without strength.

Theon called out, "Talus. It's me, Theon. What's going on?"

Talus did not answer. His face was expressionless, stupefied. His body spun slowly in the air, still anchored to the cliff by a few fingers on a piece of rope. The situation was chilling. Anything—a wrong word . . . a movement . . . a gust of wind—could send Talus to his death.

"Now is not the time, Talus! Things are starting to look up. There is a new escape plan, and the rumors are that rations are going to be increased."

Again Talus did not respond. But a grim smile seemed to dance at the corners of his pale lips as if he knew that Theon was lying without conscience.

Two specks appeared on the ridge high above them. It was Lucien and another prisoner. Lucien held something out in his hand and kept gesturing to Theon. Finally Theon understood Lucien's sign language: The object in his hand was a grappling rope. If Theon could keep Talus distracted and alive until Lucien got near enough to throw his rope from above . . . then there was a chance to save Talus's life.

"Talus! I heard some very strange news this morning."

Talus did not answer.

"About Cotto," Theon continued his fabrication. "A woman arrived on the coast about eight days ago. They said that she was a beautiful Israelite in the pay of the Phoenicians. They say she is searching for someone . . . an old lover. And she is determined to find him."

"Cotto? In Thrace?" Talus's voice cracked. His grip on the rope became more precarious.

"Yes, Talus! Cotto is in Thrace. To find you! And she will!"

From high above, Lucien flung the grappling rope, and his aim was true. It fastened around Talus's shoulders.

The young man was dragged unceremoniously straight up the face of the cliff. He hung limply from the rope, neither fighting to be freed of it nor protecting himself from being bumped and scraped against the cliff face. At last he was deposited on the ground.

Theon ran to Talus's side. Lucien moved away, to give them privacy.

"I'm sorry I lied to you about Cotto," Theon apologized, looking at his friend's lacerated back.

"I guess I would have done the same if the situation was reversed," Talus allowed.

"How are you?"

"Fair . . ."

"And your resolve?"

"What do you mean by that?"

"I mean am I going to have to keep my eyes on you twenty-four hours a day because at any moment you may decide to jump into eternity?"

Talus did not answer for a long time. Then, finally, he

said, "I can't be sure. One moment I feel that I can deal with what's happening, and the next moment I want to die. There is nothing here but cruelty and death. So I think, why go on?"

Theon nodded. He helped Talus to stand. The wind swirled around them. Below, they could hear their fellow prisoners working—the picks beating a tattoo against the cliff.

"I have a favor to ask of you."

"Ask."

"Back at our blankets, I have a thick piece of black marble, about twelve inches long and six inches around. I want you to carve something beautiful out of it."

Talus laughed humorlessly. "Please, Theon, don't baby me. You just want to keep me busy, so my thoughts won't go back to suicide."

"True, but that's only part of it. If you have inherited any of your father's genius in working materials, we may have a chance to survive this horror."

"No one survives Traxis!"

Theon merely raised his eyebrows in a questioning way. "Do you remember Troy?"

"Some. I was just a boy then. I do remember our escape from the burning city and the bloodshed."

"Think back, Talus. Do you remember the black ships?"

Talus started, and his sudden movement sent pain stabbing through his wounds. He stifled a yell. Obviously Theon's question had inspired a strong memory in him.

"Yes!" he replied, excited. "They lay in the harbor, huge and silent, like great spiders. Their sails were black, their planking was black, even the shields that hung along the sides were as black as night. They were the ships of Achilles's men."

"Well, then, carve a black ship out of the marble . . . a beautiful, delicate, savage ship of the sea. Make it as memorable and as elegant as the original."

"I will try," Talus said, with a resolve that brought some peace to Theon's heart.

In the weeks following Talus's suicide attempt, the prison-camp administration cut rations yet again and increased the severity of the beatings. Each week dozens of inmates, starved or insane, fell or leaped to their death.

Each night the exhausted prisoners wrapped themselves in thin blankets and crawled into crevices and onto ledges along the cliff to sleep. If they were lucky, they had enough twigs for a tiny fire to keep the frigid winds at bay. If they were very lucky they had enough moss and lizards to make a hot stew.

Lucien, Doro, and Talus huddled over a very low fire. They had no food at all.

"Where's Theon?" Lucien asked, his cheeks drawn tight across the bone, his eyes bulging in the age-old sign of starvation.

"He told me he'd be back shortly with something to eat," Talus answered.

None of them believed that Theon would return with a single morsel of food. When he did finally return to the fire, he was greeted with grunts. Theon stretched his hands over the flames.

"Nothing left to eat?" he asked.

"You talk as if we gorged ourselves and left nothing for you. Get it through your head, Theon. No one has eaten!"

Theon laughed. "But now you will."

He produced a thick chunk of cheese and a loaf of crusty bread. He held them near the fire for all to see. Then he dangled a heavy cluster of grapes before them.

Not a sound could be heard. No one around the fire dared even to stretch out a hand. It had to be a delusion. None of them had seen a single piece of fruit since entering the penal colony. These were fresh, ripe, pale grapes, obviously recently picked. They had to be a delusion.

Theon plucked one from the cluster and pushed it

into Lucien's mouth. Then he gave a grape to Doro and Talus. And he chewed one himself.

It was as if an enormous cloud of pleasure had suddenly covered them. They moaned as they chewed, reveling in the taste and texture. Then they shared the bread and cheese.

"How did you get everything?" Lucien wanted to know.

"Talus got them for us," Theon replied.

"Me?" Talus said. "I don't know anything about this."

"The guards sold your piece of marble carving to priests at the temple of Dionysus, then kept the money. In their desire for more sculptures to sell, No Neck and Crazy have given us food. And more food will be coming . . . as long as young Talus here exercises his muse."

Then, like a magician, Theon produced more bread and succulent grapes.

"Take these, Lucien," he said, "and distribute them among the other prisoners. Tell them that in the future no one can be concerned only for his own life. Our only chance for survival is in unity. Our only strength is in unity. Tell them that from now on, each of us must look after the others first."

Lucien nodded, gathered the food, and left the ledge cave to do Theon's bidding.

"Our only hope," Theon told Doro and Talus, "is to build an organization that will eventually rival the power of Traxis's administrative structure."

Then Theon grabbed Talus by the shoulder in a powerful, comradely grip. He looked the young man in the eyes, and his gaze burned as he said, "It is only your artistry, Talus, that can give us that hope."

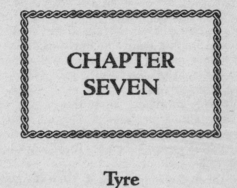

CHAPTER SEVEN

Tyre

They stood silently before Navan's palatial home. Every tree behind the garden wall was pruned with precision. The Sea Peoples guards patrolling the perimeter of the estate were perfectly turned out. Their bronze breastplates gleamed; their long golden hair matched the glint of their swords.

"Are you sure this is where you will work?" Micah asked Luti. His foot was swathed in bandages, and he leaned on crude crutches. His eyes were darkly rimmed—the pain of the burns on his sole kept him awake most of the night, every night.

"Yes," she replied. "I was told to report here. Navan does the real business out of this house, not the official buildings lining the port."

"Are you frightened?" Micah asked, reaching out to touch her shoulder.

"Only a fool wouldn't be," Luti retorted angrily, pulling away from him. "One mistake, and I'll never see my daughter again." She was furious with him, but she did not know why. *Maybe,* she thought, *I'm angry with the world and taking it out on poor Micah.* Realizing that this was no time for family squabbles, she kissed her husband, then Drak, quickly. She left them standing outside the gate.

After identifying herself to the guard, the man saluted smartly and ushered her through the gate. He motioned to Micah and Drak to come along, if they wished. The trio entered the large courtyard, where they looked around in astonishment. The grounds were littered with sleeping bodies—both men and women—who had obviously had too much to drink the night before. They slept with mouths agape and arms outstretched, and many snored loudly. Drak found it hilarious and had to stifle his giggles with both hands clamped over his mouth.

"The Phoenicians must throw great parties," Luti whispered wryly as the three of them tiptoed through. Among the exhausted revelers were broken wine jugs, the remains of meals, and discarded clothes. Dozens of brightly colored pillows were also scattered about. A few servants were beginning to clean up the mess, but they were moving very carefully so as not to disturb anyone.

When Luti and her family reached the high-vaulted corridor at the edge of the courtyard, the guard turned and looked at Micah. This, obviously, was where Luti was to take leave of them. She turned to Micah and said, "I have no idea what time I'll be finished. Stay with Drak and keep your eye on him." She turned to her son: "And you be good. No nonsense. Do you understand?"

He nodded silently.

Luti followed the guard down a corridor, then up narrow, twisting stone steps. At the landing the guard ushered her into a massive room crowded with people. A long desk had been placed by the windows. Navan was seated there, surrounded by advisers, including the wily old Sutt, whom she had met at the Palace of Weights and Measures.

"Don't get too interested. You won't be here that long."

Luti turned toward the voice. It was the Egyptian astrologer Zab.

"It is my unfortunate task," he continued, "to show you where and how you will work in the court of Navan." He led her to an alcove where several people stood hunched over high desks. Zab pointed at an unoccupied desk piled high with charts.

"Each morning," Zab explained, "you will report here and study the charts. They are compiled daily to give you the approximate location of all the ships either flying the Phoenician flag or under contract to the Phoenicians. You may do whatever you wish for the rest of the day—you can go out and stare at seagulls, or you can buy chicken eggs and break them over your head to see which way they drip. It doesn't really matter. But each evening before you go home Navan expects to have accurate weather reports and warnings concerning any sector and any fleet. Understood?" Without waiting for an answer, he turned and walked away.

Micah and Drak watched and waited while Luti vanished down the long, dark corridor. Only then did they begin their walk back through the littered courtyard and out of Navan's property. Micah was feeling very uneasy. "We'll have a lot of good times together here, Drak," he said, forcing optimism into his tone. "You'll see. We have a whole new city—a whole new world—to explore."

The boy looked doubtful. "But isn't there some way we can help?"

"Yes. By staying out of your mother's way. Unfortunately, Drak, neither of us knows how to tell the future from bird omens. We'll just—"

Micah staggered from a blow to the back of his head. His crutches went flying. Drak rushed to help him. Micah brought his hand to his head where the blow had struck. His hand, hair, and robes were stained by a dark pulpy substance. He stared down. At his feet was a melon rind. He realized what had happened: Someone had thrown a melon at him—a rotten ripe melon.

Infuriated, he crouched down like the Micah of old—the assassin, the feared avenger—ready to kill, his body taut, his senses keen. Then peals of laughter sounded from behind him. He looked over his shoulder. A woman, not more than a few feet from him, was laughing so hard that tears came to her eyes. She was naked from the waist up, and her luxurious black hair flowed around her beautiful face, over her shoulders, and far down her back. One of her breasts was painted, he noticed immediately, and one of her eyes and one of her shoulders. In fact, half her body was painted, but not divided down the middle. It was a random, asymmetrical ornamentation. All she wore on the lower portion of her body was a silken wrap.

"I really am sorry," the woman said when she had regained her faculties. She bent to pick up his crutches and brought them to him. "I don't know what got into me. I couldn't resist hitting you in the head with a melon." She giggled, then regained control. Laughter still shone in her eyes. "You just looked so stupid standing there, in your strange costume, lecturing to your son. You looked so stupid and so serious at the same time that I had to hit you with a melon. I hope you understand." And then she broke into peals of laughter again.

Micah grabbed the crutches from her, gestured to Drak, and started to walk away. *Stupid bitch*, he thought, *humiliating me in front of my boy!*

"Wait!" the woman said. "Please!"

Micah hesitated, disgusted. But he did not want to draw attention to himself by ignoring her and causing her to make a scene. The woman was trouble. He wanted to get out of there and take Drak back to their small house in the port area.

"Where are you from?" the woman asked, circling him, with a smile on her face.

"Babylon," Micah replied icily.

"For a moment, when you crouched like that, I thought you were going to kill me," she admitted. "Lucky for me that . . . umm—" She nodded at his bandaged foot.

Two years ago I would have killed her, Micah thought, but he said nothing.

"Will you accept my apology?"

He nodded and started to walk away, but again she ran in front of him, blocking his path. He stopped. "Drak, wait for me at the gate." The boy nodded and obeyed.

Then the woman, after unwrapping her garment from her waist, used it to wipe the pulp off his face and robes. Her nakedness unnerved him, and he was glad he had sent Drak ahead. Her beautifully formed breasts brushed against his arm. He could feel her nipples against his flesh. He stared straight ahead, not breathing.

"There!" She stepped back. Her eyes were both mocking and friendly. "Now you look like a worthy representative of the kingdom of Babylon!"

Micah felt uncomfortable. He had never encountered such strange behavior before . . . and it was especially disorienting because she was so young and beautiful. She acted as if she owned the world, as if everything was her due, as if she could play with other people without regard for their feelings.

"Why have you come to Tyre?" she asked, retying her garment, this time covering her breasts.

"My wife is in the employ of Navan."

Her eyebrows shot up. "Ah ha. Then no doubt you are living not far from here. Am I correct?"

"Yes. I am going home now with my son."

"I will take you there in my litter. It is the least I can do. Come along!"

It was useless to protest. Micah followed. At the gate was an elaborate curtained litter carried by four big-boned, burly bearers. Drak was much taken by the beautiful woman and her attendants. Micah had to give the boy a harsh look to get him to stop staring.

"My name is Riza," she said once they were comfortably seated in the vehicle. Micah sat beside her, Drak across from them. "And I must warn you that everyone considers me to be very wicked." She laughed lightly at her own characterization.

When Drak confided that they were newly arrived in Tyre, the young Phoenician woman drew back the curtains and cheerfully pointed out dozens of streets and alleys and homes along their route. Here was where a famous Phoenician was assassinated, and there was where so and so was seduced. Her enthusiasm was infectious, and her sense of humor was irresistible. Micah and Drak began to laugh and lean forward, anticipating the next stop in this tour of celebrity and crime.

From time to time Riza leaned against Micah and remained pressed against him for several seconds. Once he saw that Drak seemed not to notice, he found himself longing for it to happen. The closeness of her made his head swim. She wore a beautiful scent, and her voice was one moment velvet and the next moment pitched high in laughter.

He closed his eyes, ashamed. The strength of his desire for her grieved and embarrassed him. While Luti was trying to save their daughter's life, he was falling under the spell of a temptress.

But it had been so long since he had laughed! So long since Luti had looked at him with anything but a dour expression. So long since he had felt like making love to her! He frowned, looking down at his bandaged foot. That had been Luti's fault.

They stopped in front of the small modest rental house. The litter was set down, and Micah started to climb out.

"Wait a minute," Riza said. She took hold of Drak's arm. "How old are you, young man?"

"Twelve," the child replied.

"Well then," said Riza, "you're old enough to stay home alone for a few hours, aren't you?" She turned to Micah. "And you, my new friend, can come with me."

"I can't," Micah said quickly. "I promised my wife that I'd look after him."

"And so you shall. But not for the next few hours." She turned to Drak. "Are you afraid to stay alone?"

Drak, in a huff, said, "I like to stay alone. I'm not afraid of anything."

Micah smiled at the childish bravado. He remembered that when he was not much older than his son, he ran away from home. A few years later he ran away again, to join Joshua's army.

Drak jumped down from the carriage and ran into the house. Micah sat uncomfortably. "I shouldn't be doing this," he said to Riza.

"Life is short, and the afternoon is long," she told him. Suddenly she leaned forward and put her hand inside his robes, to roam over the hard muscles of his chest. "Don't fight destiny."

"What destiny are you speaking of?" he managed to say.

"Why, our own! First, I woke up and saw you in Navan's courtyard. Second, I hit you with a melon. Third, we became friends." She paused. "Would you like to become lovers?" she asked in a low voice.

Micah did not answer. He sat back against the pillows, and Riza gave her servants the signal to go. *Forgive me, Luti,* he said to himself as the vehicle was raised, then carried down the street. But although he was apologizing, all he really felt was a sense of excited anticipation. He had spent years feeling dead inside. Now it was as if he was back again in the Wilderness of Judea, about to raid a convoy. Those had been the days of violence and death. Why, then, did this strange young woman arouse those long buried feelings?

* * *

Luti walked slowly along the shoreline. She had spent the morning at her new desk and studied the charts provided for her. The sheer magnitude of the Phoenicians' shipping activity had amazed her. Theirs was such a small country! Yet these people had virtually cornered the market on the shipment of food and raw materials. Their ships plied all the waters of the earth. Their captains and sailors were sought after by all the kingdoms to the north, east, and south. No wonder they needed weather predictors and cared little of the source or the cost.

The sun had vanished behind early afternoon clouds, and a brisk wind was blowing in off the water. She looked up. There were few birds in the air and no gulls. Some terns were walking along the water's edge. She did not know whether the birds' absence meant anything beyond the fact that there were too few to provide her with an accurate reading. Luti moved toward the port area, where the ships were docked. Surely more birds would be there, feasting on the ships' garbage.

As she walked, her thoughts meandered back to the charts. The same people who drew the shipping notations with such skill must, she assumed, also draw up the strategy charts for the Phoenician-backed Assyrian invasion of her country. In fact, the charts were probably kept in the same place that the commercial shipping charts were stored—somewhere in Navan's estate. All she had to do was find out where.

All! She laughed bitterly to herself at her optimism. Here she was—only one day into her mission—thinking that she would be able to flee Tyre on the second day, with all the secret data to save her daughter and restore her wealth. As if the secret information would fall into her hands like a ripe plum from a tree!

She was so deep in thought that she did not notice the man standing in her path along the beach until she crashed right into him. She stumbled backward. "I'm so sorry!" she said, horrified. "I wasn't watching where I was going. Are you all right?"

"Fine, fine," the fellow said, laughing. "I admire your ability to concentrate."

Luti could tell by the man's long robe and high hat that he was of the Phoenician nobility. He was not much taller than she, stocky, and of middle age with powerful hands and arms, and gentle gray eyes. A deeply furrowed brow gave the impression that he had many worries, but dimpled cheeks balanced the impression of woe.

"My name is Traggo," the stranger said, then bowed low and elegantly. "I saw you at your desk this morning."

Luti, astonished, stepped back. She did not remember ever seeing him. Was he spying on her? Had he been waiting for her, to threaten her?

Reacting to her expression, he explained quickly, "I also spend my mornings in Navan's chambers, you see. I am in charge of the ships' stores—a very boring position, believe me. But I've always been fascinated by people with magical powers who can peer deeply into the natural world and uncover its secrets."

"I am no magician," Luti said defensively.

Traggo bowed low again, this time in sincere apology. "I have offended you. Forgive me. I meant your wondrous ability to read the flight of birds."

Luti smiled. He had charmed her. "Well then," she said, "if you wish to walk with me, I will teach you some things."

Luti started off again, beckoning Traggo to join her. As they moved toward the port area, Luti pointed out various birds and identified them. Once in a while she told the Phoenician an interesting fact about an individual bird's mating or nesting or migratory habits.

"How could so young a woman have learned so much bird lore?" he asked.

"I don't honestly know," she admitted. "But in Ur, from the first moment I could talk and walk, I sensed that birds were my special friends. It was evident to me that they wanted to share their secrets with me as much as I wanted to share them."

Luti and Traggo stood for a moment in silence, looking out across the water. "Whenever a bird was taken by a hunter," she continued, "I would feel its pain." She smiled wanly. "So it's not always a blessing."

"I know what you mean," Traggo said quietly. "I saw how Zab treated you, and I felt your misery. I want you to know that not all of Navan's courtiers are barbarians."

For a moment Luti felt protected, secure. It was as if the man's gray gaze had enveloped her and given her a cushion against the world. She smiled gratefully at him. A *whir* of wings intruded and broke the spell of the moment. Overhead flew a pair of black-headed gulls past them.

Luti, flustered, moved away. "I have to go now. I have to work. I have to study the gulls."

She walked away quickly, not looking back, and then felt the need to run.

Micah stared down at the handsome slave who was waiting calmly. The boy had long black hair and olive skin. The muscles of his body were fine and sinuous, almost sculpted.

Micah was fascinated. All day long Riza had shown him the hidden wonders of Tyre: She had taken him to exotic gardens, opulent brothels, transvestite bars, and artists' studios. In a few short hours she had shown him the magnificence that the new Phoenician wealth had made possible. Much of life here was perverse and ugly, but some of it was exquisite. All of it was charged with an energy that he had never encountered before.

Finally she had brought him to this small amphitheater on the southern outskirts of the city. The seats were packed with wealthy, casually dressed men and women who sipped wine from jeweled goblets.

"Watch," Riza said. "Soon three small jars will be brought in and put on that tiny table in front of the slave."

Micah nodded. He did not know what exactly was about to happen, but because of the sort of day he had spent with Riza, he felt certain the slave would do something bizarre. As the three jars were placed in front of the boy, the crowd exploded with applause.

"Do you want to place a bet?" Riza asked, her eyes glittering with excitement. She leaned over and tightly grabbed his arm, pressing it against her breasts.

"On what?"

"The spiders' stratagem."

"What are you talking about?"

"It's a game. Why do you think I brought you here?" She threw her lovely head back and laughed. "What do you think is happening? Why are all these people here? It's a game."

As Micah watched, the slave picked up one of the jars. The crowd began to shout out their bets, and a man sitting on the side marked down each wager. The slave smiled bravely as he opened the jar, turned it upside down, and shook the contents onto the palm of his hand. A small spider tumbled out. The people in the amphitheater became silent.

"Do you see now, Micah?" Riza whispered. "Of the three spiders in the jars, only one is poisonous. Its bite means death. Would you have bet on the first one?"

"I-I don't know."

The slave boy winced as the spider bit into his palm.

"We'll know in a moment," Riza whispered.

The calm on the boy's beautiful face vanished. In its place came terror, and beads of perspiration slid down his forehead. Micah could not stand to watch the child's suffering. If this spider was poisonous, he would suffer terribly, then die. He realized that the slave was only a little older than Drak. How tragic to sacrifice such a young life, so full of promise, so a few wealthy Phoenicians could win a little money.

Without uttering a word, Micah picked up his crutches and left the amphitheater as quickly as he could manage. Outside, he gulped deep breaths of air. He wanted to go home. He stopped within an adjoining orchard filled with small fruit trees and vines. There, in the peaceful, fragrant environment, he caught his breath. He simply could not tolerate brutality of any sort—against any creature, human or otherwise—for any reason. He heard footsteps crunching on leaves and snapping twigs. He turned to see Riza.

"I didn't know you were so squeamish," she taunted.

Micah moved away from her. She closed the gap between them. "What is the matter with you, Micah? Are you ill?"

"No. I'm confused. I don't know why I'm here." He heaved a deep breath. "I don't even know why I let you lead me around by the nose all day or why I'm fascinated by all those strange places you took me to. I don't know why I left my son alone so I could be with you. I don't know who you are or what you're after."

His sudden admission embarrassed him. He turned away from the woman.

"I know why you're feeling that way," she said gently.

He exploded angrily. "You know? What do you know? You know *nothing* about me! You don't know who I am or where I came from or why I'm here. You know nothing!"

"Come on," she said, holding out a slender hand. "I'll show you why all this is happening. Let me show you rather than tell you. You'll feel better, I promise."

He stared at her hand. It had tattoos spiraling up her fingers. He found them indescribably repulsive. "Where do you want to take me this time? An execution?"

She smiled indulgently. "You are beginning to taste freedom, Micah," she told him. "It can be painful. You crave freedom. You desire abandon. You need to experience the very best and the very worst my city can offer. You are in a prison, and you need to break out—no matter what the danger, no matter how high the cost. Otherwise your spirit will wither and you will die. That is what I saw in you the moment I flung the melon—it was your desperation. Follow me, Micah, before it's too late for you."

Numbly, he nodded his assent. He knew she was right.

He had lost his manhood, the wildness of his true nature, when he settled down with Luti.

She led him slowly through the orchard until they reached a natural bower formed by low, branching olive trees against the perimeter wall of the enclosure. She turned to face him and began to unwrap her silken garment. Her bright eyes, so full of life and mischief, never left his. He watched her, entranced, mute. When she was naked, she raised her arms and turned slowly, a full circle.

He stared at her magnificent body, the full breasts, the taut, flawless skin, the small, rounded buttocks, the delicate curved thighs. She took his crutches and set them on the ground, then she lay down on the lush green grass and held her hands up to him.

Micah lowered himself carefully beside her. On hands and knees, he kissed her nipples and then gently bit the sweet and tender pit of her stomach. His body was trembling, his mind racing. He had never been unfaithful to Luti. Never! Tears welled up in his eyes. He knew he should stand up . . . he knew he should run away. But the effort and cost would have been too great. Instead he stretched out beside this strange young woman who was both a gift and a curse, and his eyes, hands, and mouth feasted upon her. He was sucked into the whirlwind of love.

"Where is your father?" Luti asked Drak. She had studied the gulls all afternoon, then made her report to Navan. It had been a long, tension-filled day, and she was not happy that Micah was not there to greet her.

Drak told her of the melon incident and how Micah had left him home, gone off with the painted woman, and not returned.

Luti sank down wearily. A dull fury burned in her heart. How she longed to be back in Babylon! How she yearned to hold her daughter again! She was fully aware that this mission would be difficult. And Micah's irresponsibility and uncooperativeness were making everything harder. It infuriated her that he had left Drak alone so soon after their arrival. Tyre was too big and too dangerous a city to let him fend for himself. Boys could get into trouble easily. Although Drak seemed perfectly fine about his time alone, Luti cringed to think what might have happened if he had needed help. They knew no one in the area yet. What would Drak have done?

On the walk home from Navan's estate, she had purchased some milk and bread and three small plums. Now mother and son shared the meal in silence.

"When do you think Daddy will be back?" Drak asked at last.

"Oh, soon enough," Luti replied nonchalantly. She did not want Drak to know how angry she was. But her concern was growing, also. On crutches, Micah would make an easy target for thugs. Where *was* he?

"Can I go with you in the morning?" Drak asked.

Poor thing doesn't want to be alone again.

"Not tomorrow, dear. Maybe in a few days. Let me get settled there first. I don't want to stand out in Navan's court. I just want to remain invisible."

Drak sulked. Quickly she said, "Do me a favor, honey. Go out and fill the water jugs from the well. Your father can't do it until his foot heals."

The boy was not thrilled, but he obeyed. Luti sat down on a mat, leaned her back against a wall, and closed her eyes. She thought for a moment about her day, and the kindly Phoenician, Traggo, came to mind. She smiled as she remembered their conversation. It had been the one bright point in an otherwise stressful day. She had felt surprisingly at ease in his company. He had wanted to know about her gift. How odd, she thought, that most people assumed that someone who reads bird omens must be a witch or a magician. She supposed there were mystical elements in the art; but for the most part she considered herself to be just naturally observant of behavior patterns. Unlike most people, who never noticed their environment, she maintained an openness to the natural world, a strong belief that birds and humans shared a kinship. They were touched by the same air currents, part of the same food chain, influenced by the same patterns of life and death and love. She leaned her head back against the wall and closed her eyes. She felt her mind slowing down. She was so tired. . . .

Luti woke with a start. The unfamiliar dwelling frightened her. Then she remembered where she was. Across the room, Drak lay sleeping.

Moonlight flooded the small room, casting odd shadows on the walls. She sat up quickly. Someone was standing outside the house! She could see the dark, motionless shape through the window.

Luti crawled silently along the floor and picked up a clay pot. She would use it as a weapon if necessary. Battling her fear, she slipped out the door and confronted the intruder. Then she noticed the crutches. Relief weakened her legs.

"Micah!" she cried out. "Where have you been?" Then she lowered her voice so as not to awaken Drak. "Why are you standing here? Come in."

He shook his head.

"Can't you speak?" she asked.

"I'm not staying," he said flatly. "I just came for a change of clothes."

She was staggered by his words. For a moment she felt sick as the meaning sank in. Then she felt like slamming the clay pot over his head. At last she realized that she must maintain control. Everything was collapsing around her. She did not have the luxury of falling apart with it; she had Drak and her assignment to take care of. Luti forced herself to speak in a very low, calm voice, almost as if Micah were a child.

"I don't know what's come over you, Micah. Drak told me that you met a woman and went off with her." She paused to regain her composure, which was fading under her hurt and anger. "I don't really care how stupid you acted today. But if you in any way threaten the success of what I need to accomplish here, I swear I will haunt you the rest of your days. Tell me, Micah: Do you truly understand what is at stake? Do you? Our *child*? Our *baby*? Seka."

"Oh, Luti! I'm so ashamed." His voice was constricted, his words were a mere croaking sound. He stared at her as if he wanted to say more, but he did not speak again. He walked past her, into the house, and came back out after a few minutes with a small bundle of clothes. He paused and looked over her shoulder. Keeping his eyes averted, he mumbled something. She could not understand what he was saying. *Is this the way he's getting back at me?* she wondered, a lead weight in her gut. *Is he paying me back for all the times I felt frustrated by his inability to contribute money to the family? By his refusal to be a man?*

Finally he said something she could hear: "I can't stop what I'm doing. Please understand. It's my survival, Luti. The whole thing has overpowered me."

He looked around wildly as if the right words to explain might be written for him on the side of the house. Then he dropped his crutches and lunged at her, grabbing her harshly, pulling her to him in an embrace. He kissed her again and again like a desperate man.

She twisted away from him, and her anger erupted. She glared at him for a moment, then slapped him across the face with all the strength betrayal can give. Then she slapped him again. "You bastard," she seethed. "Get out of my sight."

He turned, snatched up his bundle and crutches, and left.

For the next three days she saw Micah briefly. She could not believe that he had the audacity to come by the house; but he did, in the late evening or the early morning, to pick up a few more of his belongings, then leave moments later. He would skulk out, saying nothing, not even to Drak. Luti gave much thought to barring him from the house but could not come to a decision. At last she asked Drak's opinion, and the child felt strongly that his father should be allowed to come in without restrictions. It would be easier for his father to come back home to stay, Drak reasoned, if he had been allowed uninterrupted access to the house.

Luti was not sure she would ever allow Micah back into their lives on a permanent basis, but she would not tell that to Drak. Life had a way of turning things around, even hard and fast decisions. Besides, the child had enough to cope with already.

Luti kept an iron control on herself, acting as if nothing had happened. She arrived at Navan's court on time each morning, studied the shipping charts, then walked to the water to study the gulls. Then, after making her weather predictions, she went home, exhausted from coping, to feed Drak and spend the evening with him.

On the fourth day after Micah's departure, her anxiety became so strong that she felt incapacitated. She broke out in a cold sweat, her heart leaped and jumped in her chest, and the floor seemed to tilt beneath her feet. She left her charts and walked unsteadily to the adjoining courtyard and lay down.

Luti chose a place near one of the lovely sunken pools because it reminded her of Ur. She closed her eyes and, concentrating on her breathing, tried to relax.

"Drink this."

Startled by the voice, she tried to sit up but could not. Dizziness forced her back onto the cool tiles. Traggo was kneeling beside her. He held a small, exquisitely carved bowl.

"I—I just needed a rest." It was a lame explanation, and she knew it.

"Please, stay where you are. Try to drink this. It will make you feel better."

He held the bowl and put a supporting hand under

her shoulders. She drank gratefully. He had brought her peach nectar.

"Thank you very much," she whispered, and he lowered her head gently.

"I've been watching you for the last few days," he said, "and I must admit, you have me worried. Obviously something is bothering you. Can I help?"

Luti closed her eyes. She had to be careful. She was a spy and could trust no one. But this man was an oasis of caring, and her burdens were too great for one person to carry. She had to confide in him and opted for honesty—as far as it went.

"My husband has become infatuated with a Phoenician woman," she said simply.

"Ah," Traggo replied sympathetically. "He will come to his senses soon. It is almost to be expected in Tyre. He is probably acting like a child let loose in a store full of sweets."

"Perhaps," she allowed. "But it's my son, Drak, I'm worried about. He's only twelve, and I have to leave him alone all day."

Traggo nodded with understanding. "May I offer a plan?"

"Of course."

"Because I am in charge of ships' stores for the port, I must go aboard all the ships and inspect their cargo. Boys usually love ships. Perhaps your son would enjoy accompanying me?"

"He would love it!" Luti blurted. "He dreams of great ships and adventures at sea! But I couldn't—"

"Then it's settled," Traggo said. "If you think you'll be all right, I will leave now, pick him up at your house, and take him with me. Then I will deliver him home, safe and sound, in a few hours."

Luti was silent for a moment. Her breathing had slowed. The squeezing sensation in her chest had faded. She started to sit up, and Traggo took hold of her elbow and helped her. She trailed her fingers in the still pond, then turned to the Phoenician. "Why are you being so kind to me?" she asked bluntly.

The question seemed to embarrass him. "Please believe me when I tell you that I have no hidden nefarious motives. Let's just say it's because we both need a good friend in a difficult world."

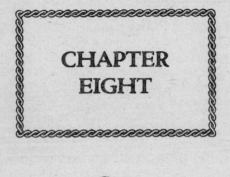

CHAPTER EIGHT

Gaza

The three travelers climbed the rise. A panoramic sweep of magnificent blue opened before them.

"The Great Sea!" Hosea the Nazirite happily called out to Hela. She was walking a short distance behind her lover and holding Tuk's hand. Something at his feet caught his attention. "Look there!"

"What do you see?" Hela asked.

Hosea dropped the sack that contained the gold. He pointed at a stone embedded in the ground. He beckoned them to come over, and when they joined him, he was already brushing away the soil to expose the rock fully. "Do you see the markings? It means that north of here all land is under the control of the Philistine League. The city you seek—Gaza—is just beyond the next rise, where the swampland begins to firm."

Hela took a deep breath of relief and happiness. They had reached their destination.

"I must leave you two here," he said. "I must return to my people."

"We are forever in your debt for guiding us here, Hosea," Hela replied. "And for . . . other things." She smiled at him.

Understanding that she was referring to their night of shared pleasure, he grinned back at her. "My services as a guide and even this gold are paltry things compared to what the child did for us. Her miraculous healing of our flock saved the Nazirites from destruction." He tickled the silent black child under her chin. "She is truly a daughter of Yahweh."

Tuk neither pulled back nor rewarded his affection with a smile.

Hela did not respond, either. There was no doubt that Tuk had powers beyond her comprehension. But a child of Yahweh? Hardly. If Tuk had been a child of blessings, why had she not brought her guardian back to life after the plague stole the breath from her body? Why had she not used her considerable powers to bring Gravis, or any of the other victims of the epidemic, to life? Why goats? The whole thing was infuriating to Hela. Infuriating and disgusting.

Hosea dropped abruptly to one knee, as if he had been felled by a blow. Hela knelt beside him and put her hand on his shoulder. But he held up his own hand to signify that he was all right.

"Sorry," he said. "I just became weak for a moment. Memories are sometimes like weapons."

"What memories?" The moment she spoke, she knew exactly what he was talking about. Blushing, she turned her face away from him.

"I was thinking of that one night, Hela," he whispered. "The memory of that night in the desert when we made love is always with me. It burns in my breast. All during this long journey I have wanted to touch you, to love you, but I knew it wouldn't be right. I need to return to my people, and you need to leave me here for the great task that awaits you." He paused and touched her once, on the thigh, then drew back his hand as if her flesh was fire. "If I made love to you again, I'd never be able to leave you."

"It was not fated for us," Hela whispered.

"No," he agreed sadly. "But one day you might hear my God calling you. When you reach out for our God, perhaps you will stop whatever you are doing, in whatever distant land you inhabit, and think of me with longing and affection. If you decide to return to the purity of the desert, Hela, come to me, for I shall be waiting—I and my people."

A tear rolled down her face. She took his hand and held it to her cheek. "Hosea, I respect your faith and the faith of your people, and I'll think of you every day until I die. But I can never worship any god—not yours, not the god of the Egyptians. I've seen too much pain."

He was silent for a long moment, then said, "Well, let's not talk of the future." He stood and gathered her into his arms. They kissed softly, then parted. Hosea shouldered his meager possessions. "Be careful. Go with Yahweh. May His protection always follow you." Then he walked away, his back proud and erect.

Hela watched as he receded into the distance.

The city of Gaza was divided into two separate entities, attached by a long and treacherous causeway. The old city—the port area—contained hundreds of rotting wooden sheds that sank deeper into the marsh each year. The new city was the residential area, with many brightly painted and scrubbed houses and shops of all kinds.

Hela and Tuk entered the new city. It was a brisk morning. People were out and about, looking clean and well dressed and friendly. Hela sought out and found the name of a well-regarded smith who specialized in gold. His name was Aoka, and he seemed utterly surprised but mightily pleased to be visited in his shop by a tall and beautiful blond-haired woman . . . no matter how miserably she was dressed or that she was accompanied by a child as dark complected as the woman was fair. His astonishment was heightened when she opened the sack and showed him the considerable shattered remains of the golden calf.

"Please melt down the gold and recast it in the form of three-ounce medallions," she requested.

The burly smith did not reply. He slowly removed his thick leather apron and his leather hat with the protective visor. Wary, he peered at the heap of gold. Next he ran his fingers along the metal, and then touched the gold with his tongue.

"This is Egyptian gold," he said. "I haven't seen such quality and purity in years."

Hela did not reply. She knew the smith was right—it had to be Egyptian gold, for when the Israelites created their blasphemous golden calf in the desert, it had to be made from gold they had brought with them out of Egyptian bondage.

"What did you say you want? Five-ounce medallions?"

"Three," Hela corrected him.

"Why?" Aoka asked.

"To carry it easier."

"If it was my gold, I'd bury it."

"But it isn't your gold," she said, trying to sound affable. "Now how much will you charge me and how long will it take?" Hela asked.

"Twenty ounces for me, and it'll take two days."

Hela shook her head.

"Too much. Too long." She started to wrap the gold as if to leave.

"Wait! Don't be too hasty," the smith pleaded.

They bargained for a while and settled on nine ounces for Aoka, and the entire job was to be finished by sunset.

As Aoka began to work the metal, Hela said, "There is something else I need."

"My blood?" the smith retorted. He was not happy about the woman's ability to negotiate.

She laughed. "No. I want the name of someone who knows all about the ships in the harbor . . . someone to whom sailors confide . . . someone who can give me information about events in the Great Sea."

"With the gold you have, lady, you can get any information you want."

"I don't have time to shop around. And I need someone whose information I can trust."

Aoka began to pace, drinking from time to time from a small squat beer jug. Its neck was covered with a patch of leather with small holes punched in it, allowing the liquid to pass through but not the residue of hops. He offered some of the famous Philistine beer to Hela, but she refused.

"There is such a man in the old city. His name is Pleon. He's been a sailmaker in Gaza all his long life. And the word is that he knows just about everything there is to know, legal and illegal, regarding all ships entering and exiting the harbor."

"Where can I find him?"

"Along the southern strand. He has an enormous wooden shed. You can't miss it. Sails are spread out over the planks."

Hela walked outside with Tuk to wait the long hours while Aoka worked the shattered idol into manageable and identical gold medallions.

As they waited, Hela watched the people walking in the street. She was suddenly overcome by a great sadness. If only Gravis were still alive and with her! How he would have loved the strange sights and sounds of a new land! How he would have laughed and enjoyed the long bargaining session between herself and the smith! How he would have thrown himself with passion into her quest to find out what happened to the survivors of Home, whoever they were! She wept bitter tears, her right hand holding Tuk's tightly.

Pleon the sailmaker's tent was massive, with cloth sides that could be raised or lowered. Through the open sides, one could watch the ships move in and out of the port below.

The finished sails, either newly made or repaired, had been rolled and piled in the center of the tent so that the old man seemed to be ensconced in a temple of canvas.

Hela entered with Tuk in tow. The sailmaker had fallen asleep at his workbench. Large sheets of canvas covered the table in front of him and spilled over onto the ground. His needles had fallen to the floor, and he was snoring loudly.

Hela tiptoed around and picked up the dropped needles, then placed them on the man's workbench. The movement woke him, and he stared dumbly at the two newcomers. His eyes darted around, as if he was making sure he had all his belongings.

"Are you Pleon?" she asked.

"Yes. Who are you?" he finally demanded in a gruff voice.

"Do you think we're thieves?" Hela asked sardonically.

"Only three kinds of women wander around the port of Gaza—whores, thieves, and fools. Take your pick."

Hela grinned in spite of herself. The old man was certainly unusual. She removed one medallion of gold from her purse and plunked it into an empty wooden bowl with a small bit of soup in the bottom. The coin splashed and then fell still.

The old man fished it out, bit it, and then stuck it in a small purse he half sat on.

"Do you like gold?" Hela asked.

"It's what feeds me. A man's got to live."

"With three of these coins you won't have to eat soup anymore. You can eat the choicest cuts of meat and wash them down with the best wine. With three of these you can go north, where it's cooler, rent a villa along the beach, and fish or just sit in the fresh air for a few years."

The old man listened to Hela and nodded as she described how the gold medallions would improve his life. "And why are you so generous, young lady? Are you a lost relative of mine?"

"No. The smith named Aoka told me that you might sell me some information."

"Why? Why should I even talk to you?"

"Because, you grumpy old man, talking to me is the only way you're going to get more of this." Hela set two more gold medallions on the table.

Pleon began to scoop up the medallions, but Hela put her hand on his wrist and stopped him. "Not just yet, my friend."

"Where did you get this gold?" he asked, suspicious.

"That's none of your business."

He thought for a moment, then laughed. Hela was surprised by what a nice sound it was. "You're right. What do I care where you got it?"

"Do you want it?" she asked.

He stared at her, then at Tuk. Finally, his eyes dancing, he nodded.

"I want it."

"Good," Hela said. "It shall be yours. All I need is information about the island called Home. It used to be headquarters for a great shipping emp—"

"I know what it is," he interrupted. "For the Children of the Lion. The first island known as Home was wiped off the face of the earth years ago by a volcanic eruption. Everyone knows that. The second Home was destroyed by an invasion. Where have you been living? In a cave?"

Hela turned. She raised her long garment until the old man could see the mark of the Children of the Lion on her buttocks. Then she dropped the garment quickly.

He was clearly astonished. "You were on Home?"

"Yes," she whispered.

"Then you already know what happened! You could probably tell me a thing or two. What kind of information are you seeking?"

"My brother and I survived. I want to know who else survived."

He glanced once at Tuk, probably weighing whether or not what he would have to say would give the child nightmares.

Hela nodded to him to feel free to speak.

"It was a terrible thing," he said. "A terrible slaughter. You and your brother were among the few survivors."

Her heart leaped in her breast. The old man had used the word *few*.

"Tell me!" she cried out. "Who else survived?"

"There are rumors, bits of information, a few drunken songs—all from sailors talking in bars. You understand?"

"Yes—so there might be exaggerations and distortions. I don't care. I want any information you have! Tell me, and the gold is yours."

"Calm yourself," the old man said, and got slowly off his bench and gestured at Hela to sit down.

She did, then looked up at Pleon expectantly.

"Khalkeus of Gournia is reported to have survived," he began. "And his daughter."

Hela burst into tears. Her mother and grandfather were alive! They were alive!

"Where? Do you know where they are?"

"Thrace."

"Thrace? Why there?"

He shrugged. "I don't know. Thrace is a wild, dangerous country, far beyond the Great Sea. And it is ruled by a cruel and violent god named Dionysus."

"The gold is yours!" Hela said, leaping off the bench and handing the medallions to the man.

He looked down at the three coins in his palm. His

fingers curled closed around his bright and secure future. When he looked at Hela, gratitude shone in his eyes.

"There is another rumor," he said quietly.

"What? Tell me."

"That the son-in-law of Khalkeus also survived."

"No—my father is dead! He was drowned years ago, when I was a child." She sank back onto the bench and said quietly, "I can barely remember him. He was a wonderful father, though. He was very good to us."

"Then I feel I have given you something as meaningful as you've given me," the old man told her. "His death was mistakenly reported. He survived the storm at sea that was said to have taken him. I remember because his name, Theon, rhymed with mine, Pleon."

"And is he also in Thrace?"

"That I can't say. I heard Theon was among those attacking Home."

"How can that be?" Hela cried out.

"I don't know. I don't know where he is now, where he came from, or what he was doing on or near Home when it was invaded. All I know is that he survived."

Hela began to pace in the tent. The old man and Tuk watched her.

"I think I may go to Babylon and meet some pretty girls, just like you," Pleon said to Tuk, then winked at her.

Suddenly Hela stopped pacing and stood before him. "Tell me one other thing, old man."

"If I can."

"Where can I get a ship to Thrace?"

"You can't. I told you, Thrace is a primitive country. No one goes there. But there is a ship leaving tonight for Crete. Once in Crete you may have better luck getting to Thrace; many Cretans have relatives there."

"What's the name of the ship?" Hela asked.

"*Thresher.* She'll leave sometime after midnight, depending upon the tide."

"I want you to know how much I appreciate what you told me." Hela placed an affectionate hand on Pleon's shoulder. "I lost my brother and a close friend recently. I thought I was alone in this world. You've given me back a family."

"You paid for it, young lady," he said, laughing.

She took Tuk by the hand and hurried from the tent. It was almost dark.

She walked down to the harbor and found the ship called the *Thresher*. It was a single-masted bark with the high deck common to all the Greek ships. The master was delighted to sell her two passages, but he warned Hela that the accommodations were primitive. In case of a storm the berths would probably be flooded and remain that way until the ship reached Crete.

When Hela was not discouraged by the warning, the captain told her to be aboard with the girl by midnight at the latest, for the bark would be towed for about half a mile by picket boats with rowers to set the bark on the tide.

"I'm starved," Hela said to Tuk as they left the ship. "And you must be hungry, too. We'll get some food, then find new clothes. These rags deserve to be thrown away."

As usual, the child did not deny nor confirm Hela's statement. The woman walked quickly, half pulling Tuk along the muddy wooden planks that functioned as sidewalks in the old city of Gaza. Her thoughts were racing with excitement. The good news about her parents and grandfather and her impending adventure were beyond her wildest dreams. What little she had learned of Thrace seemed foreboding, but the place could not be any worse than others she had seen or the experiences she had suffered during the past year.

In retrospect, Hela felt proud of herself. She had endured hardship, survived a plague, and withstood hostile attack. Not only was she taking care of herself, she was responsible for a child's well-being. Not bad, she thought, considering how inadequately she had been prepared for any sort of life in the outside world.

Hela smelled fat sizzling. She followed the tantalizing aroma, which brought her to a food vendor peering out from his murky shed. The man sold small chunks of lamb seared over a smoky fire pit, and stewed peas, which were spooned over the meat after it was placed in a palm leaf. His coals glowed redly in the deep dusk. Hela bought two leaves—one for herself and one for Tuk—and the two travelers stood outside the vendor's shack and wolfed down the delicious food.

After they had finished, Hela purchased another leaf of lamb and peas, which she and Tuk shared. The woman chuckled, watching the youngster eat carefully, fastidiously, almost like a little princess. Hela was grateful that the girl seemed to need little sleep and less food. As that thought occurred, she admitted to herself that Tuk's good health was not entirely attributed to the care given her. In fact, the relationship was fairly balanced, with Tuk being entirely self-sufficient. As for the black child's evident occult powers, perhaps Tuk had been the one taking care of Hela! Guilt and self-doubt rippled through the woman. Perhaps she had not progressed at all! Well, she could not be bothered with that now. They had a long and dangerous journey ahead of them, and if Tuk had been intervening in her behalf, then fine! Fortunately, the child had not exhibited any evil tendencies. All her actions, as inexplicable as they were, seemed to point to a good heart.

Hela smiled affectionately as the girl popped the last piece of seared lamb into her mouth. One thing was certain; it was Tuk who had saved them in Sinai. It had been her curing of the Nazirite flock that allowed them to get this far. Impulsively, she reached out and stroked the child's face. Tuk stared blankly at her.

"One day you will speak to me, won't you?" Hela asked. "Let's find some clothes. We have hours to spare, and I want to look nice when I find my mother."

Together, woman and girl walked the streets of old Gaza. The night air was damp, and the fog was beginning to roll in. The area was alive with activity. Vendors displayed their wares in booths or on blankets spread on the ground. Raucous music and laughter filtered into the darkness from inside the many crowded inns. Lovers walked arm in arm, their heads tilted together, touching. Sailors weaved and staggered down the plank walkways to the harbor. Musicians played their instruments and gratefully accepted copper coins from passersby.

At last Hela found a merchant with fine linen robes and sashes and headwraps that came in child and adult proportions. She purchased three changes of clothes for her and Tuk.

After paying for the goods, Hela said, "Well, we better get back to the ship. I don't want to be on the streets by the waterfront too late at night."

They walked quickly toward the pier until they saw the tall mast of the *Thresher,* illuminated by moonlight, looming in the distance. Hela stopped. "It's a lovely sight, Tuk, isn't it? Our ticket to freedom and family." Holding the child's hand tightly, she began to run toward the ship. It had been so long since she had felt joyful or optimistic.

Their path was blocked by three men who slipped like ghosts out of the darkness. But these were not apparitions, and each one held a short Philistine sword.

"You know what we want," one of them said in a low voice.

Hela dropped the bundle of clothes and stepped back, clutching the purse in her garment. Fate was too cruel. She was so close to the ship, so very close. Her heart beat furiously, and she felt dizzy with fear. Who had betrayed her, the smith or the sailmaker? More likely the smith—or that these thieves had watched her pay for the clothes. What did it matter? These men wanted her gold, and if she lost it, she would also surrender her chance to find her family. Grasping Tuk's hand, Hela wheeled and started to run, but the three assailants had anticipated that. They surrounded her quickly, cutting off all means of escape.

One of the men approached Hela, his sword pointed at her throat.

"The gold," he said.

"No!" she screamed, looking with fear-dilated eyes at

Tuk. Why wasn't the girl using her powers to foil the robbery?

In a flash the tip of his sword pressed against the skin of her throat, and a tiny drop of blood stained the blade. Then, inexplicably, the force behind the sword point was lost. Hela, expecting to die, stared wide-eyed at her assailant. A hole had appeared in the center of the man's forehead, as if impacted by a stone flung from a sling.

A second later a horrible roar was heard, and a man leaped between Hela and the two remaining thieves. A dagger flashed in her savior's hand. Screams of pain surrounded her, and she clamped her hands over her ears and squeezed her eyes shut. Then an eerie silence descended. Tuk stood behind her, and the girl's thin arms were wrapped around one of Hela's legs. Hela, shaking violently, forced herself to open her eyes.

Four bodies lay twisted on the ground. The man who had come to her aid had stabbed both swordsmen through the neck. They lay dead and bleeding. Sadly, the mysterious protector had been gutted with one of the swords. He, too, was dead.

As bitterness rose to the back of her mouth, nearly choking her, Hela bent to see the man's face. She staggered back and threw her hands up in horror. Hosea!

"Oh, Tuk . . ." she moaned, then fell to her knees beside her lover's body.

He had followed her! Why? To go with her to Thrace? But how could he have even thought of leaving his God and his people?

She picked up his limp hand, pressed it against her face, and wept without restraint. She closed her eyes and rocked back and forth with grief.

Hela felt a tap on her shoulder. It was Tuk, and she brought the child into her embrace. But the girl was not looking for comfort; she was pointing to the mast of the *Thresher,* still visible in the distance.

"You're right," Hela told her. "We've got to get to the

ship now if we want to leave." A spasm of grief shook her; Hosea's ultimate sacrifice made it possible.

Regret enveloped her. After all he had done, she felt sick about leaving his body here in the street. At the very least he should be returned to his people for honor and burial. But she had no choice; the thieves' attack had proved that she had to get herself and the girl out of Gaza.

She dropped his hand, scooped up the bundle of clothing, and stood up. She was unsteady on her feet.

Once again Tuk pointed toward the vessel.

Dazed, Hela allowed herself to be led to the *Thresher*.

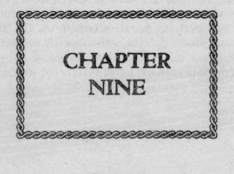

CHAPTER NINE

Canaan

The news spread swiftly throughout the land: The seventy so-called sons of Gideon had been slain by the deceased commander's bastard son, Abimelech. Each hard-riding messenger conveyed the details of unparalleled cruelty and assured the horrified listeners that he had added no embellishment or exaggeration. All seventy *had* been beheaded on a single stone. It was a deed of awesome impiety.

No one who heard the tale could do other than shiver with revulsion at the barbarity one man had shown to his rivals. No one at all mourned the seventy themselves; but even the foulest criminal deserved to be executed at a cleansed and consecrated site.

"Who is this Abimelech?" people asked.

It was said that he had proclaimed himself king of the Israelites. It was said that he was a madman who could barely speak coherently. It was said that he had lived for many years as a hermit in the hill country.

The seventy sons of Gideon had stolen the farmers' crops and their gold and their women. But that was to be expected; those in power always took advantage of their position. Would Abimelech be any different? The Israelites waited, fearful of this monster who had the audacity to proclaim himself king . . . terrified of this ogre who, totally oblivious to or unmindful of the creedal commands of Yahweh, had slaughtered his enemies. If he increased the amount of the people's tributes to him, they would have no choice but to pay. If he wanted their young boys as well as their gold and daughters, the Israelites would have no choice but to obey.

Morning had broken, painting the sky with peach and gold. Nahum, headman of the village of Ai, north of Jerusalem, and an elder of the tribe of Benjamin, was drawing water from the communal well when he saw three horsemen riding toward him. Curious, he hurried out to the road to meet them. They pulled their horses up beside him and slid from their saddles.

"Greetings," said Nahum, his hand raised. "And welcome to Ai."

"Water the horses and rub them down," one of the strangers ordered gruffly. He was a large, burly man with a dark beard. He carried only a bow on his back and a dagger at his belt. The other two were more heavily armed, carrying clubs tied to their wrists and long swords in scabbards on their backs.

The headman stared at the arrogant visitor as if he were mad. Then he softened his expression. These men were strangers and could not know his status. He chuckled genially at the man's error. "I am Nahum, the *headman* of Ai," he explained. "I do not water the horses of strangers. I do not water any horses."

The bearded stranger reached out and grasped Nahum's shoulder with a grip so powerful and painful that the harmless headman sank slowly to the ground. He twisted and writhed to escape from the terrible vise, but his contortions were in vain.

"And I am Abimelech, king of Canaan, lord of all the Israelite tribes—including yours, you accursed Benjaminite. You will do whatever I ask, or you will die right here, right now."

Nahum trembled and wept. He begged for forgiveness. He quavered. He said he had no idea. He lost control of his bladder.

"Let me call the people, my lord," he begged. "Let me give them a chance to honor the new king of Canaan."

Abimelech released his grip and stepped back. Nahum scrambled to his feet and ran to the village well, over which hung the massive ram's horn. His robes, soaked down the front, flapped around his ankles.

He lifted the ram's horn off its hook, shook it twice, and then brought it to his lips. He filled his lungs, then tried to blow. But the sound was weak and pathetic. Nahum closed his eyes and tried to compose himself. He was still quivering from the shock of his ordeal. One cannot truly blow the great ram's horn while trembling. One has to be calm and totally focused and in control of every muscle.

He breathed deeply again and again, then wriggled his toes and fingers. He rolled the shoulder that had been crushed by the powerful grip of the king. Now, that was better. He would try again. He ran his tongue around his lips, filled his lungs, then threw his whole body and soul into the horn. Out came that terrible and beautiful sound that signaled to all Israelites that they must assemble quickly—that some danger or promise was imminent. Then he whipped off his robes and poured water over himself from the well's bucket. Better to stand in a drenched loincloth than to let the people see that he had wet himself. Lastly, he poured water over his robes, in a heap at his feet.

From all corners of the village of Ai, the people ran to the well in response to the horn. As they gathered, Nahum called out: "We are honored! We are honored! The great king Abimelech has come to us! Bow low and worship him, the beloved of Yahweh."

Many of the villagers, hearing the news, turned and hurried back to their humble homes. They gathered food-stuffs and jewelry and baskets and wine and fruit and even a baby goat or two. Then they hurried to the square, to pay homage to the three strangers, one of whom had to be the king. They placed the treasures at the men's feet. Nahum, meanwhile, scurried back to his own home and quickly changed into his best robes. He grabbed his finest posses-sion, an intricately carved wooden box, then ran back to the square.

All the people had assembled. A mound of treasures had grown in front of Abimelech. The headman added his own offering to the top of the pile.

Then Nahum strode to the fore and bowed low. "I speak for all the people of Ai, King Abimelech. Our trea-sures are yours. We are at your service. I beg you, O com-passionate one, that you leave us only something to eat, for we are many."

It was exactly the same speech he had made on occa-sion when any of the seventy sons of Gideon visited Ai to loot it.

Abimelech smiled benevolently. Then he circled the mound, inspecting the treasures that the villagers had pro-vided so quickly. The villagers held their collective breath, awaiting his reaction. After completing the full circle, he faced the assemblage, smiled again, and raised his arms.

"Let me show you what the king of Canaan thinks of your generosity," he called out. He signaled to his two troopers. They walked to the pile, opened their garments, and urinated on the offerings.

The villagers muttered in astonishment, then fell into frightened silence.

Nahum stepped forward. He could not remember ever wanting less to do something. But he took his responsibility as headman seriously. He had enjoyed the status and rewards of his position, and he was willing to accept the unpleasant aspects, too. "I am sorry, my lord, that our efforts displease you. But we are a poor village. We cannot give you what we do not have."

A blow from Abimelech's fist sent the headman to the ground. His jaw was broken, and blood poured from his nose and mouth.

Abimelech again motioned to his two troopers. Swinging their clubs, they entered the crowd of villagers. The people screamed and ducked and tried to ward off the blows. All the young men were ordered to line up in front of Abimelech. Once they had, they were ordered to their knees.

The king said to them, "You are now Israelite soldiers in the New Army of Canaan." He grinned wickedly. "Your term of enlistment is until death. Now get up and follow me."

Menta, the prince of thieves, watched the torches being lit and the wine jugs being filled. He felt satisfied; his childhood friend, Abimelech, was returning to Shechem. He was due to reach the city within the hour, and Menta was making certain that the reception in the Bloody Quarter's Alley of Pain would please the new king.

With his oldest friend as absolute ruler, Menta knew there was no telling how far his own star would rise. Abimelech would remember always that he, the trustworthy Menta, had provided the first of the new army's soldiers. Perhaps the onetime prince of thieves would become the prince of Shechem? . . .

All the preparations were complete. The only task that remained was to assemble the musicians: cymbal players, flutists, and drummers. But now that Menta had a purse filled with gold talents, all that was very manageable. Anything could be bought in Shechem—anything.

Menta walked around, drained another jug of wine, then went to lie down on some thick cushions out of the way of the main activity. There was plenty of time before Abimelech was expected to return. . . . Plenty of time . . . his eyes grew heavy. . . . He dozed. . . .

It was the sound of a cymbal that woke him. He sat up, confused at first. Then he became oriented. Musicians had arrived and were practicing at the entrance to the Alley of Pain. Crowds had assembled in the Bloody Quarter and were growing ever larger. Yes, this would be a great homecoming given for the new king of Canaan by his old friends!

Menta lay back down on the pillows to wait. Although he was not entirely sure about how long he had slept, he reckoned that not much time had passed. Abimelech was probably still some twenty miles from the city, and his approach would be hindered by the crowds lining the roads.

By quietly passing through a rear gate into the city, Abimelech had avoided the mobs and was standing in the shadows not more than twenty yards from his old friend. Behind the king stood twelve heavily armed troopers. He was enraged to see that Menta had gone back to the cushions. This was no time to rest! There was never time to rest.

By the blazing torches that had been lighted for his entrance into Shechem, Abimelech carefully drew his bow and nocked a jagged-edged arrow. The first bolt shattered Menta's larynx. The second arrow broke through flesh and shoulder blade to pin him to the pillows. The final arrow drove into his rib cage and pierced his heart. Menta convulsed wildly, his eyes staring, and then died without knowing who killed him.

"Form your column now!" Abimelech told his troopers. His mission was clear: to clear the rabble from the city, using any means necessary. The troopers knew their job.

They formed a fighting column: one club-wielding man front and back; one more on either side; and within that square, eight swordsmen. There were many such columns of soldiers, and other troopers had already taken up positions to prevent the victims from fleeing. The murdering began so silently that the musicians, unaware of what was happening, did not skip a single beat of their gay song.

Led by the king, the "clean up" of Shechem began. Every known thief, arsonist, and pimp in the Bloody Quarter was dispatched by club or sword. Blood ran in the gutters, the currents like small rivers.

Soon the screams of the wounded and the dying were like alien hymns to the gods of the night—pathetic and mysterious and in a language that few could understand. But the killing did not stop; it was citywide. After the Bloody Quarter, Abimelech and his execution squads visited the precincts of Baal and the Temple Mount of Yahweh. Anyone found with a weapon—sword, dagger, sling, bow—was put to death instantly.

When the sun rose the extent of the slaughter became fully evident.

Many more columns, all under orders from Abimelech, had entered Shechem that night. Although the elders had made it clear that Abimelech would dispose of only the criminal elements, the soldiers had gone after the beggars and homeless and lunatics who chose to remain within the city walls rather than live on the hillsides surrounding the city. Hundreds were slaughtered, then their bodies were stacked and set afire.

By midmorning an eerie silence descended over Shechem. The uninformed might have mistaken the silence for blessed peace. But the absence of sound was based in the citizens' horror. What had their elders commissioned Abimelech to accomplish? And if people had been murdered not for their lawlessness but for having been deserted by luck and the Fates, then who would be the next to die?

*   *   *

The moment Abimelech entered the chambers, the lords of Shechem cast all decorum to the wind. They began to chant his name, and a few of them even attempted victory dances, whirling about the massive room, their garments billowing. Although they had not been informed of his intentions, he had been promised a free hand militarily. To a man the elders had known doubt when the extent of the massacre became apparent; but aside from Gaal, who was appalled, the feeling had not lasted long. After all, Abimelech had done them a service they had not had the guts to perform.

Abimelech did not even acknowledge their lavish praise. His garments were streaked with blood, and his arrows still flecked with gore. He strode to where Zebul, the most high lord of Shechem, sat.

"Welcome!" Zebul enthused. "Welcome! A thousand welcomes and the blessing of Yahweh on you, King Abimelech."

Abimelech did not reply. He turned and, with the light of triumph in his eyes, looked at the celebrating elders. "Hear me!" he bellowed.

Silence quickly asserted itself.

"I have destroyed the seventy sons of Gideon, who have plundered our land. In the great city of Shechem I have put to the sword all those elements who brought disrepute to your name. But that is only the beginning. Young Israelites from all over Canaan are flocking to the banners of their new king. They carry sharp weapons, and their hearts are fearless. Soon we shall march to the east and west, south and north. The Philistines, Amorites, and Egyptians will all feel our might. The Canaanites who have obstructed the will of Yahweh will be dealt with once and for all. My mighty armies will rise up like the blades of grass over the lands. Soon Damascus, Tyre, and even Thebez will tremble before our will. The tribes will be reunited! The land will flow with milk and honey! The power of Yahweh will be known over all the world! All this I promise you."

And then, without another word, he strode out of the chambers.

"This madman will lead us all to ruin," Gaal said into the void.

Zebul laughed indulgently, as if humoring a child. "If I remember correctly, Gaal, you cast the lone vote against giving Abimelech the money. Maybe you are just being a bad loser. Come now, my friend! The man has accomplished what he promised he'd do. I encourage you to take a walk through the city. He's removed all the unsavory elements."

Gaal was unconvinced. "It is one thing to murder thieves, Zebul. It is another to take on the military forces of our neighbors. How can you stomach his hypocrisy? This man does not speak for Yahweh. This man is evil incarnate."

Zebul just clucked at the younger nobleman's misgivings and gave him a fatherly pat on the back.

Cotto stood trembling in the center of the tattered tent. Why had Abimelech not moved his headquarters, she wondered, now that he was king of Canaan? All the Israelites bowed low to him. He could requisition any grand house he chose. Instead, when he had summoned her, it was to the same old tent where she had first sold him wine, then herself.

She started to undress, but he told her no. Their foreplay had begun with his telling her with an almost joyous blood lust of the murders of the former rulers, the innocent villagers, and the underbelly of Shechem. The stark details in which he took such obvious pleasure were almost too much for her to bear. And while he spoke of these triumphs, his hands roamed over her body and under her robe.

Suddenly he ordered her to take off her clothes.

She stripped naked where she stood. He circled her,

staring at her body. Cotto kept her eyes to the front and tried not to shake. Her fear of this brutal man was beginning to know no bounds.

He walked close to her, reached out and twisted one of her nipples until she cried out with pain. Eyes burning, he stepped back. "What kind of whore are you?" he asked angrily. "A thousand dirty farmers have probably already kissed your breasts dry. And yet you whimper when the king of Canaan, the beloved of Yahweh, touches you?"

"I am not a whore," she told him.

He laughed. "Then what are you?"

"A wine vendor."

This struck him very funny. "Ah, so you're a wine vendor! No doubt a seller of fine wines? A woman who knows how to judge the best fruit of the vine?" He ripped away the bloody skins that covered him, flung his weapons to a corner of the tent, then picked up one of the wine jugs she had brought with her this night.

He opened the jug with his powerful hands and poured the wine all over his head and down his nakedness. "Come here, then, my beautiful vendor, and tell me the quality of this wine."

Cotto grimaced.

"Lick it off me, bitch! Start at my feet!"

She thought about running from the tent. This man was too frightening. But there was no escape. If she did not fulfill her mission for Navan, he would kill her. And if she did not do as Abimelech insisted, she would die right now.

Shame, fear, and revulsion made her feel weak. The brute grabbed the back of her neck and shoved her to the ground. She crawled to him and licked the wine from his toes. He laughed and cursed her and mocked her.

"Is it good? Is it sweet?"

Then he savaged her until she cried out. His powerful thrusts were like a battering ram's, forcing the breath from her body, crumbling her defenses. He drove deep into her flesh until she felt she was being ripped apart.

At the moment of release, as he reached the crescendo of his passion, he called out, "Miriam! Miriam!" And then he surged into Cotto so forcefully that she raked her fingernails down his back. She wanted to hurt him; he seemed not to notice any pain.

It was over quickly. Abimelech fell into a deep sleep, and she lay weeping on the ground. She calmed herself, made sure he would not be disturbed by her movements; then she dressed and ran from the tent.

Purah was waiting for her by the gate of his lovely little home. The moment he saw her, he knew that she had suffered terribly. He could say nothing; his breaking heart no doubt stole his words. He took her slowly into the small house and onto a prepared bed. She walked like an old and brittle woman. Inside, he sponged away the filth and residue of the night, then covered her with a blanket.

"It was very bad, Purah," she whispered. Tears squeezed from the corners of her eyes.

"Yes, I know, dear. Be quiet now and rest. You're safe here."

He brought her some cold clear juice in a bowl and held it for her as she sipped.

"He's a madman."

"So I have heard, my dear."

Cotto watched the calm sad face of her friend as she drank the cool juice. He was the only one she trusted. He was the only one who gave her the strength to continue. He was the only one who did not expect anything from her in return.

Feeling better now, she made her report. She told Purah the substance of Abimelech's monologue about his brutal murders and other atrocities. Evidently Purah's good sense dictated that he not interrupt. She did need to get it all out of her system without a pause. When she had finished, she began to weep anew. Purah tried to comfort her, but she cried out in despair, "I am being forced to pay for all of my crimes—for my arrogance and conceit, my dishonesty and greed. Oh, Purah, whatever led us to betray our own people? How did we end up like this?"

The man gently stroked her arm. "It's futile to look back on the past," he said. "Fate has not been kind to us, but then fate has no compassion."

"Is there any hope for us? Any future? How can we survive? How can we learn to live? I used to think I could get away with anything because my beauty would carry me through. Now I know that that's not true."

He shook his head but did not answer. *Is he trying to spare me from his own despair?* she wondered. She lay back, closed her eyes, and relaxed into the pleasant sensation of his work-hardened hands stroking her arm. She sighed. Ah, Purah was such a good, remarkable man. Suddenly her eyes flew open as she realized that in her own strange way, she loved him. Because she did not understand what that would mean for either of them, the idea frightened her, and she rolled onto her side, away from him, and buried her face in a pillow.

Multitudes of homeless people lived a precarious existence on the hillside outside the walls of Shechem. In spite of their starvation and tattered garments, they were feeling as if their luck might be taking a turn for the better. If they had chosen to live in the streets and alleys of the city instead of on its neighboring hills, they would have been massacred by Abimelech's fierce army. A close call with death reminded even the lowliest beggar how good life was. Today they were awakened by three shattering blasts of the ram's horn. The sound always meant that some important person was exiting the city—and that could mean coins flung in their direction if they lined the road and cheered.

In anticipation, the crowd surged toward the high gates of Shechem. Miriam and her child were carried along by the wave of humanity. Her life had dissolved into a landscape of shadows. Everything about her was slow—the way she walked, the way she spoke . . . on those few occasions when she did speak. Those who slept near her on the hillside considered her a hopelessly deranged woman but for the way she cared for her son. They gave her food and tried to help her in any way they could.

The ram's horn sounded again, three more times, and then came the deep rumble of the massive skin drums stretched wide on their frames. The huge bronze buttressed wooden gates of Shechem slowly opened. The crowd on the hillside began to cheer—but their shouts were choked back when, a moment later, the new king of Canaan came into view, riding on a magnificent bay horse between twenty-four mounted spearmen.

The people of the hills knew full well what Abimelech had wrought inside the city. The beggars retreated, fearful —and with good reason—that this man was leaving the city in order to slaughter them.

Only Miriam did not shrink back. She stared openmouthed at the oncoming horsemen. Her body became rigid, and she trembled so violently that she pressed her son tightly to her breasts lest she drop him accidentally.

As Abimelech's face came into clear view, for the first time since the rape Miriam reexperienced every moment of the horror. She looked around wildly, as if she had been asleep and had suddenly recovered consciousness.

He came closer on his prancing horse. Her terror and loathing of this man returned in full force. As much as she wanted to run and hide, she could not move.

But then, in the place of her fear came a surge of power. She was abruptly beyond all earthly trepidations. An awesome strength flowed through her, as if it had been building quietly and unnoticed during her madness and only now was expressing itself.

The king was coming closer. His sweeping eyes caught her face and recognized her. She could see that without a doubt. He shouted her name and pulled back on his horse's reins. The bay horse neighed and reared, and the king was nearly thrown. Chaos erupted on the hillside as the homeless ran to hide.

Miriam laughed and ran, also. But while her companions' flight was fueled by panic, hers was a light and easy gait, as if she were a very young girl again. And instead of putting distance between herself and the armed troopers, she ran toward them.

The wind blew through her long, matted hair, lifting it from her face and shoulders. She felt a mantle of spirit enveloping her. Many years, once before, she had experienced this—in the green fields of home. She had been alone, and she had cried with joy because the love of Yahweh had visited her. Today Yahweh had come to her again. On she ran through the mounted spearmen and disappeared into the city of Shechem itself.

"Stop her!" Abimelech screamed to his mounted troops. "Stop her!"

All wheeled at once. Horses and riders became entangled and made no progress. Abimelech, also trapped among the plunging steeds, risked being trampled by leaping down from his horse and running back into the city. He was sure the woman was Miriam. He had longed for her. He had dreamed about her. He craved and needed her. She invaded both his waking hours and his sleeping state.

He elbowed past people and shoved them roughly out of his path. "Miriam! Miriam!" Which way had she gone? His desperation increased as he lost sight of her swift-running form. Behind him came the shouts of his bodyguard, now attempting to catch up.

The king turned on him in a rage. "Did you see that woman?" he demanded.

The soldier took an involuntary step back, then squared his shoulders and jutted out his chin. "No, Sire!"

Abimelech stabbed the man in the chest with his finger. "Find her! A citywide search! Don't come back until you have her with you—alive!"

*　　*　　*

Miriam, breath coming in harsh rasps, reached the Temple Mount and began to climb the levels. Her legs ached like fire. Her child was restless. But she could not stop. She knew for a certainty what her destination was, even though she had never been here before. When she reached the highest level, the sanctuary that held the Holy of Holies, the Ark of the Covenant, she stopped. She stood with her toes touching the border of well-manicured grass. No woman could move beyond this point except on penalty of death.

Everything around her had grown eerily quiet. Only her baby's cries could be heard. She soothed and rocked Jeb. When he was quiet, Miriam sank to her knees and prayed that her life be spared. She begged God to spare the life of her son. She implored the One God to serve up to Abimelech exactly what his action had earned.

"Who are you?"

Miriam turned toward the voice. A man was standing not more than three feet away. He looked at her with compassion and confusion. She did not answer.

"There is no reason to be frightened," the stranger said. "I am Gaal, son of Ebed."

She regarded him calmly.

"Can you hear?" he asked.

But still she did not speak, and her silence obviously annoyed him. "Speak, woman. I promise I will not harm you. I might even be able to give you some help." He stepped forward and grasped her by the shoulders.

An instant later he pulled back his hands as if he had touched fire. His eyes grew wide with wonderment, and he stared at his tingling hand.

Miriam smiled. She understood what was happening. Because the strength of Yahweh had infiltrated her, the man beside her could not touch her without feeling the force. He would not be angry that she was trespassing. He would understand.

She spoke confidently to him. "You must help me. A terrible evil has been loosed on the children of Abraham and Isaac and Jacob. I will stop this man, but I'll need time. You will resist Abimelech, engage him in battle. That will give me the hours I'll need. I don't know how it will go for you, or even whether or not you'll survive. But draw strength from the knowledge that you do Yahweh's work and that Abimelech will not survive!"

She stepped back. Gaal nodded, his eyes wide and unblinking. Then, without saying a word, he turned and ran down the Temple Mount. She watched him go.

How tired she was! And yet, how fulfilled! Her time in Shechem was past, she realized. She must leave this city of blood and death. Wrapping her shawl around her head to shadow her face, she descended the mount. She would head toward Thebez and seek sanctuary there.

As she turned a corner, she saw Abimelech. Miriam ducked into a doorway, and the king wandered by, screaming hoarsely, "I shall find you, Miriam! You shall be my queen!"

PART THREE

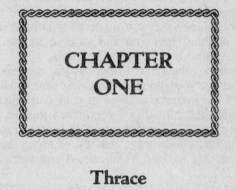

CHAPTER ONE

Thrace

Fresh-cut flowers, brought down at great expense from the mountains, surrounded the ornate marble bier on which the body of Khalkeus of Gournia lay. His soul had departed twelve hours before. Incense torches burned at the four corners of the bier, and from outside the site, beyond the low wall that surrounded the mausoleum, a dirge was played. Khalkeus had died a devoted believer in Dionysus, and all believers were accompanied to the netherworld by music.

The burial would be at noon the next day, and Nuhara, bowed by the weight of her grief, had ordered that a great event be held in honor of her beloved father.

Now, bereft, she stood motionless, staring through swollen, red-rimmed eyes at Khalkeus's face. He was the only man she had ever loved or respected.

Nuhara leaned over the bier and touched the face of the old pirate. She blew her nose, wiped her eyes, then managed a thin, watery smile. "Well, there's nothing keeping me here any longer, Father. It's time for me to do what we discussed so often—resurrecting the fortunes of the Children of the Lion in some other land. I promise you that a great fleet will soon control the seas, and every ship will fly the banner that you made so famous and feared."

She stopped speaking and whirled at the sound of footsteps behind her. It was Hipparchia.

"My lady," the servant said, "as you requested, I have had dinner for you and the high priest sent to Heraclitus's chambers. He awaits you there at your convenience."

"Good. Tell him that I regret not joining him right away, but . . . um, I feel the need to be alone for a while. Tell him to eat without me, that I'll be along later."

Hipparchia nodded, then turned and started to walk away.

"Wait, girl—deliver the message quickly, then return here immediately. Understand?"

The servant nodded and left.

Nuhara turned back to her father's body. "That takes care of Heraclitus. He'll wait for me in bed for hours, the fool." She grasped Khalkeus's stiff hand and pressed it against her face. Her voice was husky with promise. "Theon and the rest of our enemies will be dead soon. I promise you, Father, that I'll kill and kill again until our empire is reestablished. A new and greater Home will rise from the waves. And I'll find your beloved grandchildren, to live out their days by my side."

Nuhara gently set down the hand and, chewing on a cuticle, began to pace in front of the bier until Hipparchia returned. Nuhara ordered the servant to pack some warm clothes because she would be taking a journey into the mountains.

"When, my lady?" the servant asked.

"Now, you idiot."

"But your father's burial—"

"I know very well when it is scheduled. Now go . . . unless you'd care to accompany him?"

"No, my lady," said Hipparchia.

"Pack the gold bracelets from my bureau," she called at Hipparchia's quickly retreating back. "And your clothes, too. You're coming with me."

Brambles whipped the women's ankles and arms as they made their laborious ascent into the wild Thracian mountains north of the temple of Dionysus.

"This is dangerous, my lady," Hipparchia quavered as she struggled to break a path. "Perhaps I should return and bring back some of the temple guards?"

"You are a stupid girl. Who in these mountains would dare to touch me? I am in the service of Dionysus. Every peasant in the mountain knows that he and his family would be torn to pieces by the maenads if I came to any harm."

They struggled on. The air was growing thinner, and the sun was slipping away. Warmth left the day, to be replaced by a chilling mist. The servant was out of breath and drained of strength.

"Please, my lady," she implored. "Tell me where we are going."

"To see the green woman."

The girl stopped dead in her tracks, then sank to the ground. Her scratched and dirt-streaked face grew pale with terror. "But she is a witch!"

"And so am I." Nuhara's laughter at her own joke resonated through the woods. "Now get up."

Reluctantly, fearing the wrath of her mistress more than that of the legendary green woman, Hipparchia climbed to her feet and struggled onward.

It was pitch dark when they finally reached the rocky clearing that was their destination. In the center was the small and dilapidated thatched hut of the green woman. Tethered around the shack were goats and yellow-haired dogs with dull eyes and prominent ribs. Beside the door was an ancient rusted bell mounted on a tripod.

When Nuhara rang the bell, the dogs set up a terrible howl. The priestess took several gold bracelets from Hipparchia's bundle, then ordered her servant to wait outside while she walked boldly into the hut.

The interior was thick with aromatic smoke from several small pit fires. Over each dancing flame was a small black kettle, in which herbs and other plants were being reduced in an unknown liquid to yield their vital substances. Heavy iron pokers lay near each kettle, to stir up the brews and the embers.

The green woman looked up at Nuhara. The old witch was stooped with age, but her skin was fresh and wrinkle free, and her long hair was exceedingly black and lustrous. The few teeth she had were an old woman's, rotted and discolored. Her nose and earlobes were elongated, as was often the case with the elderly. Her tattered clothes were stained by many a brew, and she was barefoot. Like her hair, her feet looked like a young woman's. They were slender and without calluses, and the nails reminded Nuhara of small, perfectly formed pink seashells.

"What do you want? Why have you disturbed my peace in the night?" the green woman demanded in a low, rich voice.

"Your fame is widespread," Nuhara began, "and I have traveled far to seek out your wisdom."

"I spit on your flattery. Can you pay?"

Nuhara smiled. "With gold," she said, and dangled one of the gold bracelets above the flame. Hanging from the chain were faceted crystals, and the brilliant refracted rays sent dancing spots of color around the smoky hut.

The witch snatched the bracelet from Nuhara's fingertips. "Then be quick about it. What do you need?"

"A potion," Nuhara said.

The green woman laughed with great amusement, then stopped abruptly. "You appear young enough to snare a man without any potions."

"I do not want a love potion," Nuhara replied calmly.

"What then? Are you ailing?"

"No. I want a hate potion."

The green woman appeared startled. Then she thought for a moment. "Every emotion can be evoked from the green world," she conceded. "Hate also. But before I give you what you request, you must explain yourself."

"Why?"

"For my amusement," the green woman replied. "Do you want your potion or not?"

Nuhara shrugged, resigned. "Imagine two lovers. Their passion for each other is great. They think about each other constantly, almost to the exclusion of all else. They yearn to touch and kiss and join. They want to lose themselves in each other's eyes and embrace. I want a potion that will quickly turn the eros of one lover into hatred. And just as a moment before her fingers were gently stroking the flesh of her beloved, now those fingers will choke the life out of him."

The witch's eyes glittered in the firelight. "Yes! Yes! I know what you mean! An interesting concept. A challenge! I'm sure it can be done."

The green woman vanished into the shadows. Nuhara strained to see what the woman was doing, but her efforts were futile. She had to take the chance that the green woman's attention was fully consumed by her herbal preparations. Quickly Nuhara bent and snatched up the nearest iron poker. This she hid behind her, one end on the dirt floor, the other at an angle leaning against the back of her thigh. When the witch returned, she showed Nuhara the contents of one hand: several withered little mushroom caps. "These are called dark star mushrooms." Then she opened her other hand. On the palm was a small leather pouch. "This is filled with the powder made from the dark star. Just dissolve it in liquid."

Nuhara took the pouch into her hand. "Any liquid?"

"Yes."

Nuhara thrust the pouch into her garment. Her smile showed her small, even teeth as she held out two more gold bracelets to the green woman. But when the woman reached for her payment, Nuhara let the bracelets fall to the ground.

Cursing, the witch bent to pick them up. Nuhara reached behind her for the poker and smashed it over the head of the old woman. She cried out once and then collapsed. The priestess hit her twice more, just to be sure the deed was done.

Then Nuhara used the poker to pull several burning embers from the blazing fire pits. These she scattered against the walls of the hut. Finally, after retrieving her bracelets, she walked hurriedly from the hut as the walls ignited.

"What has happened? Where is the green woman?" Hipparchia asked, close at her mistress's heels.

Nuhara said nothing as she left the clearing.

"The woman will die in there, my lady!" Hipparchia shouted.

Nuhara turned on her. "Shut up! You saw nothing. You know nothing."

"Can we go home now?" Hipparchia, trembling violently, hugged herself.

"Not yet. We are going to the village of Three Gorges, just west of here, to hire men and mounts."

"Why?"

"For the god Dionysus," Nuhara replied.

That was not much of an explanation, but servants deserved no better, and Nuhara's nerves were still on edge from her murder of the witch. Hipparchia was lucky, the priestess decided, that she did not suffer the same fate as the green woman for asking her infernal questions. At least the hiring of men and mounts would pose no problem. She increased her pace under the light of the moon toward the village. Time was getting short.

*　　*　　*

Nuhara and Hipparchia returned to the temple precincts just before dawn. Hipparchia immediately fell into a dead sleep at her usual place, a small padded mat at the foot of Nuhara's bed.

The priestess waited until she was certain the girl was sleeping, then she slipped out of her chambers and down to the large temple cellar where the ceremonial wine vats were stored. She walked quickly, quietly from one barrel to another until she came at last to the one with a yellow paint slash across its front. This was the barrel with the new wine. It would be tapped during the funeral of her father.

She raised the lid and emptied the entire contents of the pouch she had received from the green woman into the wine. Then she hurried back to her chambers, washed, and fell into a peaceful, untroubled sleep.

The funereal ceremonies commenced at high noon. Big-boned, muscular slaves carried the bier containing the body of Khalkeus of Gournia into the main rotunda of the temple. Their expressions were appropriately somber as they set down their burden and then stepped back and away. Slave children came forward then, to cover the corpse with delicate freshly cut herbs and wildflowers. The scent of violets and thyme wafted across the room, masking the vague unpleasantness of flesh beginning to rot.

Heraclitus wore his most magnificent, gold-shot robes, and the elite temple guard standing at attention around him wore their dress helmets—brilliant bronze coverings with scenes of Dionysus and the nymphs etched into the metal. Atop each helmet swayed an exceedingly rare bird-of-paradise feather, imported from the East and used only when a truly great man had died. These feathers would be destroyed at day's end.

Nuhara was dressed simply, in the robes of mourning, as was her servant Hipparchia. They both stood off to one side. It was the way of Dionysian funerals that the truly bereaved must only watch, not participate.

The drum roll introduced the ceremony, then the tambourines joined in. Heraclitus raised a long bejeweled knife with a blade that had been honed to maximum sharpness. Slowly the high priest brought the blade down over the bier. As the observers held their breath, he sliced the thigh of the corpse.

The crowd gasped and then applauded. This incision signified the beginning of Khalkeus's journey to life everlasting in the vineyards of Dionysus, for the legend had it that the god was reborn again and again from a cut in the thigh of his goddess mother, Semele.

A long column of maenads snaked into the rotunda to perform the circling ceremony. How beautiful these young devotees of Dionysus were! Each one was naked except for the rope of grapevines that was twisted above one shoulder. The vines were laden with lush clusters of grapes and dark, shiny leaves. Each maenad had dyed her lips, nipples, and toenails purple.

The moment they closed the circle around the bier and the high priest, the women's undulating bodies kept tempo with the drums and tambourines. A servant came forward holding a golden cup. As each maenad passed him, he offered her a drink of new wine. When she had drained the cup, the servant refilled it from the cask with a yellow slash.

Faster and faster the music played, urging the beauties on. The women thrust out their hips and moved sensuously, erotically, spreading their legs and knees wide as they sidestepped around the corpse. They thrust their breasts toward Khalkeus's face as they circled him. They cried out praise and poems of love. They fondled themselves and fell to the marble floor, then writhed like maddened succubae. All of it was for Khalkeus, so his soul would know that those who believe in Dionysus will enter a vineyard where love is always present.

Of the many participants, slaves, guards, priests, and observers, only Nuhara was not beating her hands and stomping her feet in time with the music. In spite of the inspiring unfolding of events in front of her, only Nuhara was not moved by the maenads' stunning performance.

She waited . . . her narrowed eyes moving from one ecstatic woman to the next . . . watching for some sign that the dark star had begun its cruel effect.

Suddenly one of the maenads hesitated as she approached the corpse. She seemed confused, unsure. She drew herself up to full height, raised her hands high over her head, and spun around in place. The dark hair under her lovely arms glistened with sweat. Then she changed direction and twirled several more revolutions, stopped, and ran toward Heraclitus.

From deep in her throat came a scream so horrid, so animallike, that all the musical instruments were silenced.

The woman viciously attacked the high priest before he could think to defend himself. The force of her charge propelled her into the air, then onto his chest, and bore them both to the hard floor. The air exploded from his lungs as he took the full impact of her weight. Her teeth fastened on his Adam's apple and held on as he thrashed desperately to rid himself of this madwoman who was ripping his very life out through his throat.

Shock paralyzed everyone. No one moved except the two combatants.

As the high priest's heels pounded the floor in a dance of death, another maenad leaped upon one of the temple guards. She, too, sank her teeth into the man's unprotected throat as she wrapped her legs around his waist. Within seconds the entire temple was consumed in a maelstrom of terror and blood. The maenads had gone collectively mad, attacking every male in their view.

Nuhara smiled wolfishly. "Come quickly," she said to Hipparchia.

The two women fled the bloodbath and ran to a grove of olive trees close by the main path. A contingent of temple guards ran past them, toward the chaos.

The high priestess and her servant found the drovers and their sturdy mules waiting, as instructed, in the grove.

Nuhara led her hirelings down a steep trail and to a dense clump of scrub and bushes. She ordered one of the men to clear the vegetation, and his so doing revealed the mouth of a cave. Again Nuhara led the way, followed by men and beasts, deeper into the bowels of the earth. The air grew thick with the stink of bat dung. But the deeper the group traveled, the wider grew Nuhara's smile. Soon the workers behind her would be loading their mules with the great treasure of the Children of the Lion. Then they would transport it to the harbor, where five swift ships waited. Yes, she almost danced because the game was won.

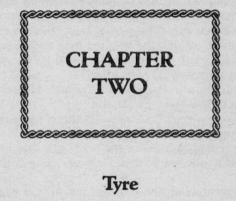

CHAPTER TWO

Tyre

Standing behind her desk, Luti pored over the latest shipping charts and, from time to time, stared out the high window. She did not need the gift of supernatural vision to confirm that the rain was coming down hard and the wind was up. That was very bad news, for it meant she would not be able to spend the afternoon studying the gulls. She would have to spend the entire day at her desk.

"I'm afraid your boy will have to stay home today."

Luti smiled. Just the sound of Traggo's voice made her feel good. She turned and looked up at him. "Maybe a day away from the ships will be good for him. He hasn't stopped talking about everything he has seen." Impulsively she reached out and grasped the man's hand. "I can't thank you enough, Traggo. Drak has been transformed."

He laughed warmly and squeezed her hand. Then they moved apart, self-conscious. "I assure you, Luti, I am enjoying it more than he. Conducting inspections used to be a boring job! But in the company of such an eager young companion as Drak, the hours go quickly. He notices and remarks upon everything—the sails, the weapons, the clothes of the sailors, the way the men speak, everything! That child is alert and intelligent. He'll go far in this life. You must be a very good mother."

"And you are a wonderful friend." Her eyes shone with sincere gratitude. "To both of us."

Traggo lowered his voice. "Is there any change with Micah?" he asked, concerned.

"No. He spends all of his time with that Phoenician woman. His foot has healed. He's not using crutches anymore."

Traggo nodded, then looked toward the window. He and Luti were quiet. There seemed to be nothing to say . . . and yet there was a great deal left unsaid. "A dreary day," he commented at last.

"Just a taste of the rainy season to come," Luti replied.

He nodded. "You know, Luti, Navan is very happy with your work, particularly that regarding the southern routes. He keeps track of everyone's weather predictions, as I'm sure you know. Yours have been accurate over eighty percent of the time on those routes—and almost seventy percent of the time on the other routes. A very impressive record."

Luti was surprised to feel herself blushing at the praise. "Well," she said, shrugging, "we magicians are very powerful. We have all hocus-pocus in our bags."

Traggo laughed at her joke. They had spent enough time together for him to know that the basis of her work was close observation of animal behavior. "Your magic has stolen my heart," he confessed quietly.

She leaned forward, intending to kiss him on the cheek, then pulled back suddenly, before she did so. It would have been a stupid thing to do in public. She was growing to love him, too. He had saved her life. She would have gone mad without his support. But anyone who saw her kiss him would assume she was sleeping with the Phoenician nobleman, and that was not the case . . . yet.

"Will you be going to the shore today?" he asked quickly.

She was grateful to him for pretending not to notice her near breach of etiquette. "Not in this kind of rain. It would be a waste of time. The gulls will seek shelter."

"Then let me show you the bottom floors of Navan's house. This estate was planned and built by architects and engineers brought here from Damascus. I assure you a tour will be most interesting."

"I'd love it," she said with alacrity. She set the charts neatly aside.

Traggo led her out, past the interested eyes of her coworkers, and then down a long narrow flight of stone stairs.

"Are we beneath ground level?" Luti asked, astonished by the length of the hallway they had reached.

"Yes. But notice that the air quality is unusually good. The Damascene engineers knew how to create ventilation from the outside garden through a series of pipes."

The woman and her guide walked past dozens of small rooms that led off the subterranean hallway. Burly Sea Peoples guards lined the hallway every twenty feet. As Traggo approached them, the big-boned men saluted smartly with their ferocious-looking swords and kept their pale eyes straight ahead.

"This is where you will find the people who protect the Phoenician wealth—lawyers, tax specialists, scribes, and analysts of all kinds."

They kept walking slowly.

"And here is a room I'm sure you have no desire to visit." The nobleman pointed to a large area, where dozens of people in neat rows hunkered down in front of low writing tables. Bottles of ink and writing quills were on the floor by their side.

"It is where those charts you study each day are made," Traggo explained.

Luti's heart lurched, then began to race. This was the bit of luck she had been praying for.

"Oh, I'd love to see how they work!" she exclaimed.

Traggo's face registered momentary surprise. "Well, then, let's go in."

Inside, the cartographers were so absorbed in their work, which required precision, that not a single glance came the visitors' way.

As Luti and Traggo walked slowly and quietly about the room, the woman let her eyes wander. She noticed that the far end of the area contained a single recess where two low tables had been set apart from all the others. No one was working at these desks. Luti casually worked her way closer to the recess and noticed that several rolled charts leaned against the tables.

Ribbons had been tied around the charts. They were pale blue and yellow—the royal colors of the kingdom of Babylon! Why would Babylon's royal colors be tied around scrolls in a Phoenician's workroom, she wondered. Was it merely coincidence or were these the prize she had been sent to find? She knew she had to find out. But how?

"Come, Luti," Traggo said, touching her elbow. "There is much more to see."

"But I love to watch these people work!" Luti replied with enthusiasm. "Their concentration! The steadiness of their hands! I would love to stay a bit longer. But I feel a little cold. Maybe it's the dampness. . . ." She hugged herself for warmth.

"Would you like me to go upstairs and get your cloak?"

"Oh, would you?" she asked gratefully. "I left it folded up, under my desk."

The ruse worked. Traggo, always the perfect gentleman, left to get her cloak. Admittedly, she felt a twinge of guilt, but nothing and no one would stand in the way of her saving her daughter's life. Luti saw that as Traggo left, one of the scribes noticed him and bowed deeply. Because Traggo was very high up in the Phoenician hierarchy, the scribes, by association, would consider her to be a person of importance. Luti knew that that could work to her advantage. But first she would have to assume the behavior appropriate to officialdom.

The moment Traggo left the room, Luti strode boldly to the recess and removed the charts with the ribbons. She confidently unrolled them and read them.

In front of her eyes were the logistical plans for the Assyrian invasion of Babylon. Military and financial backing, provided by the Phoenicians, was detailed.

Her mind soaked up the notations: Thirty-four warships would be sent to Antioch. Seventeen of the vessels would carry milled grain, fruit, and almonds. Another seventeen ships would carry disassembled flat-bottomed riverboats. At Antioch the convoy would be met by twelve hundred wagons, which would transport the supplies and boats to Ashur, on the Tigris.

Luti's excitement was so intense that she could barely stand. Her clothes were wet with sweat.

It was obvious from the plans what was going to happen: The Phoenicians would meet the Assyrian army at Ashur and supply them with food and boats. The attack on Babylon, to the south, would be mounted by the Assyrians, who would sweep down on the city by way of the river.

But when would this occur? When? She could find no date. She knew she would have to be satisfied with what she had managed to learn. Traggo would be back at any moment, and she could not risk being caught with the scrolls. She rolled up the charts and with trembling hands replaced the ribbons. No one seemed to be paying any attention to her.

It was accomplished just in time. She turned and walked toward the door just as the nobleman returned.

Luti greeted him with a smile as he slipped the cloak over her shoulders.

Then he turned her to face him and peered at her with concern. "Are you all right?" he asked. "You look flushed."

"M-maybe I'm coming down with something," she said. "I was so cold, and then, while you were gone, I felt feverish. But I feel fine now."

He asked her if she wanted to go home, but she said no. They continued the tour only after Luti convinced Traggo that she was perfectly fine, that she just had not eaten yet. But her mind was working furiously. Was there a chance she could get back into that room, alone? Hardly. Did she have enough information to satisfy the priests of Astarte so that they would return Seka to her? Knowing the cruelty of the priests, she knew the answer would be no. She needed the target date of the invasion.

When the tour was finished Traggo escorted Luti back up the stairs. But instead of returning her to her desk, the man brought her into the courtyard, then led her to a divan beside one of the sunken pools. The rain had stopped, but the air was heavy. He asked her to wait there for a few moments and left. When he returned, he was carrying a bowl of sliced fruit over which was sprinkled crushed almonds, then covered with cream. "Here," he said. "This should help you to feel better. You should never go without a morning meal."

Luti smiled wanly, then ate slowly, trying to appear as if she was enjoying the repast. But all she could think about was that fruit and almonds were part of the supplies listed for the Phoenician ships—part of the food that would fuel the Assyrian soldiers who would attack her country.

Then she remembered the third food listed for the Assyrian army: milled grain.

The bowl dropped from her hands and clattered on the courtyard's tiles. Traggo instantly knelt at her side, all concern. "Are you ill, Luti?"

"No! No! I'm fine. It just slipped."

What she could not tell him was that she had solved the puzzle. Today's rain was but an indication of the weather to come. The rainy season was about to start, with downpours every afternoon, without fail. Milled grain could not be shipped during the rainy season because it would mold and rot. That made things clear for Luti: The invasion must be planned for right after the rainy season, in three months' time!

I must tell Drak, she thought, jubilant. *We can return to Ur and claim our child and our fortune.* Her joy was so great that she kissed her friend Traggo soundly on the lips. He lost his balance and fell over the dropped bowl. Luti and he howled with laughter, each for a different and very private reason.

And then her laughter faded as she thought of her husband. Would Micah return to Babylon with her, or would he choose to remain behind, in Tyre, with his new love?

Midnight . . . Micah hesitated before entering the house. He hoped that Luti and Drak were asleep, so he could pick up the rest of his clothes and then leave quickly without any unpleasant confrontation or guilt. Drak would want him to stay. Luti, not even looking at Micah, would try to reason with Drak and protect his feelings. That would make it very difficult for him to leave. It was what always happened; then he would be filled with shame and rage . . . but he would leave anyway. Riza and her world were waiting for him. She had put him back in touch with the beast in him, the wild animal he had been before Luti had put him on a leash and stolen his manhood. It was good to feel the passion! It was exciting to be dangerous and uncaring of those who loved him enough to take his abuse and then wait for more.

He listened by the door. All was quiet. They must be asleep. He slipped inside the house, but immediately a small lamp was lit. Luti. Well, he thought, at least Drak was asleep.

Micah could not look her in the face. He turned away and said, "Sorry. Can't talk now. Can't stay. I have to be someplace soon. We'll talk another time. Tell Drak I miss him."

"Oh, shut up," Luti hissed brutally. "Listen to me. I have found the information! I have learned the date and place of the invasion, everything the priests of Astarte sent us here for! We can go home."

Micah's head whipped around, and he looked at her, dazed. He had forgotten all about Luti's mission. It felt as if she was referring to something that happened years before, to people he did not know and could not care less about.

"Don't you understand, fool?" Luti was at his side in two long strides. She shook him by the shoulder. "We can go home now and get our child back and my houses and all my property."

He could not think. Panic overwhelmed him. All he knew was that he had to get away from her, from this house. "Please! Not now, Luti. I have to meet someone."

He fled the house, but she followed at his heels. "We have to leave tomorrow, Micah. Tomorrow!"

"Tomorrow?" Micah halted and, stifling an urge to laugh, faced the woman who looked like a stranger to him. Had he heard correctly? She wanted him to leave? How could he leave Riza and Tyre? That would be impossible. How could he ever return to a small, dull town like Ur? It did not matter if Luti became the wealthiest woman in the country. Tyre meant freedom, excitement, an opportunity to explore his mind and body. His eyes widened, then hardened as he realized the truth: He had no feelings for this woman.

Suddenly Luti smacked him across the face. He staggered. "Don't you remember our daughter, you bastard? Our lovely Seka? Don't you remember that she was taken from us and is being held hostage? Can't you think any-

more, Micah? Has that whore of yours totally destroyed
your sense? Or have you started thinking with your groin
instead of your head?"

Her words were fully as powerful as her blow. Micah
spun away and started to run. He had to get away from
her. She was confusing him. She was mixing everything up
in his head—Seka and Riza and Drak—everything was all
tumbled up. As he ran, his mind kept racing. How could he
leave Tyre? How could he possibly separate himself from
Riza? Was Luti mad?

The crowd gasped as the two erotic dancers, now totally naked, began to make love on the stage.

"Now watch," Riza said with great amusement to
Micah, who was seated next to her on a divan in the audience. "They will perform a very difficult flip, and the
woman will land on top of the man. Then it'll get wild,
positively wild!"

Micah stared stupidly at his companion. Riza was so
beautiful, he could not believe he was actually in her company. And she was so honest! She was not apologetic that
she lived for pleasure. She made no excuses that she took
life to the limits of passion and sometimes even beyond.
She had brought a wild, indescribable joy to his life that he
had never felt before. Nights became days, and days became nights. Nothing at all mattered except sucking the
most enjoyment from the moment.

He looked away quickly. He could not allow that to be
ended now. He refused to spend his days in Ur with a wife
who felt nothing but contempt for him. Even Drak, at one
time his best pal, had become a disappointment. The boy's
view of him had changed, no doubt of that. Micah reached
for the jug of wine and drank deeply.

"I never saw you drink this much, Micah." Riza giggled as she licked a few errant drops of wine from his chin.

Micah did not answer. He was feeling very calm. As
he watched the sex show on stage, he felt no emotion at all

—as if he were some creature living underwater, in a cold, slow-moving environment.

When the performance was finished, Riza, Micah, and several of her friends went to a tavern. The perception intensified that everything was unreal. Micah's thoughts became fuzzy, and a funny tingling plagued his extremities, but he drank still more. The flute music in the tavern ebbed and flowed, then faded, as if it were coming to him from across the wide, wide sea.

"Where am I?" Micah asked. His cheek was pressed against pebbles and dirt. The first pink rays of dawn were on the horizon. His head ached like thunder.

"You're in front of your house," Riza said. "Inside are your wife and child. Just go now, Micah, and get some sleep. You've been a bad boy. You drank too much wine to make love to me." She nudged him with her sandaled foot. "Shame on you, Micah. I thought you savages from Babylon were insatiable."

Then she left. Micah struggled to his feet, then stumbled toward the door. He was very tired. Sleep . . . he had to sleep. Once inside the house, he felt for the wall, pressed his back to it, and then slid down it.

"Father! Father! Father!"

He did not remember touching the floor. Someone was calling him. Was it a dream? Two desperate hands were clutching at his shoulders. Frightened, Micah fought them, swatting ineffectually with his hands. The sunlight flooded through the window and hurt his eyes. His stomach churned. Too much wine! Too much wine! He opened one eye and found himself staring into the concerned face of his son.

"Why are you pulling at me?" he asked Drak angrily. "Don't you have any respect for your father?"

As Micah sat up, Drak reached out to help him. Again the man slapped his son away. Drak retreated. Micah massaged his temples to clear the fuzziness. "Bring me some water," he ordered.

But Drak just stood there.

"Don't you hear me?" Micah shouted. He was beginning to feel really angry.

Suddenly the boy threw himself on Micah and sobbed wildly.

"Drak! Get hold of yourself." He pushed his son away.

The boy, fighting back the tears, tried to speak. Finally he gasped out, "M-mother was arrested this morning. By the Phoenicians. They've taken her to . . . to that terrible dungeon. I know they're going to hurt her. They said she's a spy!" He stopped for a moment and then screamed out again, "They're going to hurt her!"

Micah scrambled to his feet. "Are you making this up? Did she put you up to this? If she did, I'll—"

But the tear-stained child shook his head vehemently.

Micah closed his eyes. Unable to bear looking at his son's pain, he turned away. His legs felt weak. *Luti . . . Luti . . . Luti . . .* He mouthed her name but couldn't speak it. Bitterness rose to sour his mouth. Finally he turned back to Drak. "Listen to me. What was the name of that man who made friends with your mother?"

"Traggo?"

"Yes, him. Do you know him? Can he be trusted?"

"He is like a father to me," Drak replied coldly.

Micah ignored the criticism in the boy's voice.

"Do you know where to find him?"

"Yes. He works on the ships, in the port. And I know where he lives."

Micah considered going with the boy, but it would be too humiliating. He needed to clean up, to organize himself, in order to present a more respectable, manly image to this Traggo. He had to compose himself, think things out.

"Go on, then, and bring the man here."

Drak ran from the house. Micah stumbled over to the water bucket and submerged his head. When he straightened, tears of shame and rage mixed with the water. It was obvious now what had happened: In his selfish revelry, he had betrayed his marriage and, worse, sentenced his wife to death. During all those hours he was drunk, traveling from tavern to tavern with Riza, he surely revealed the purpose of the family's mission in Tyre. He slowly shook his head, remembering. Maybe Riza was in the pay of Navan. Or maybe she was just a patriotic Phoenician. More likely, the woman had no scruples and had taken advantage of an easy way to get rid of Luti. It did not matter. After he had drunkenly blabbed the secret like the fool he was, Riza would have reported it to Navan.

"No!" The cry of self-loathing tore from his lips as he picked up the water bucket and flung it with all his might against the far wall. A sudden vision of Luti's suffering and terror because of his drunken tongue drove him to his knees. Her imagined screams echoed in his ears more loudly than his own wrenching sobs. "Forgive me, dearest, forgive me," he moaned, banging his head on the hard floor.

Finally, when his tears had been shed and all that was left were dry, heaving sobs, he regained his feet. Weakened, he staggered to the doorway, where a cool breeze moved across his face and eyes.

There, in the morning sunlight, Micah agonized over what to do. He could slink away now and let Traggo take care of Luti now and forever. Or he could stay to save her. He would have to pick up the sword again, to become the swift, deadly killer he once had been. He would need to reassert himself as a great soldier and embrace a new dedication to bloody violence. At one time that core of cold cruelty had enabled him to enter the supposedly impregnable fortress of Eglon of Moab and assassinate the tyrant. If he could kill with dispassion for a political cause, surely he could do it to save his wife's life.

He lifted his head up . . . into the breeze. *So be it!* he thought, throwing back his shoulders and firming his jaw. *There is no other way.*

"I will free you, Luti! I will!" he whispered to the breeze.

"As you can imagine, I was quite interested in meeting you," Traggo said, eyeing Micah coldly. "I am willing to do whatever I can . . . for Luti."

Micah grasped Traggo's hand strongly. "I know that you were my wife's only friend here. And that you've been here for the boy, too, when he, uh, needed someone."

In spite of Micah's earlier resolve, which had not faltered, meeting Traggo was proving to be a damnably uncomfortable experience. The nobleman's dark eyes were nearly impaling him, and the Phoenician's manner with Drak was decidedly protective and proprietary.

Micah, Traggo, and Drak sat on pillows that Micah had arranged on the floor, around a hastily arranged box of sand. The child made a point of settling in closer to Traggo than to his own father.

There was a moment of awkward silence. They cast their eyes downward. Then Micah blew out a breath and drew a rectangle in the center of the smooth sand. "This is the dungeon," he explained. "Tell me everything you can about the approaches and escape routes."

Traggo did not respond immediately, and Micah's mind filled with doubts. Had Traggo and Luti been lovers? Could he trust the nobleman? Traggo would be risking his own life and freedom if anyone were to find out that he had helped Luti. What was the extent of Traggo's commitment?

Suddenly Traggo burst into sobs and embraced Drak. Micah, immediately recognizing the depth and sincerity of the man's love for Luti, turned his face away. Traggo would risk everything to help her.

The Phoenician gently moved the boy away, then pounded his fist into the sand. "Enough tears! Let me tell you what I know, Micah."

Micah leaned forward, his elbows on his knees. He

operated in a terrorist's frame of mind: plan, explore all possibilities, then prepare to act with swift brutality.

"The central dungeon," Traggo began, "is attached to the Palace of Weights and Measures in the port area. It is not heavily fortified, but it is very well guarded by Sea Peoples. There are two soldiers at the entrance to the cell area, three in each passageway, and another five scattered among the three exits, here, here, and here. In addition, ten Sea Peoples guards are always in the weights and measures rooms directly above the cell areas." He paused and glanced at Drak before continuing gravely, "There are three torture cells in the center of the main passageway. If Luti can be rescued from her cell, the two subterranean north exits—here and here—are our best bet. Either way, we'll end up on a broad boulevard that will lead directly out of the city. An overland escape will probably be less risky than one by water; Navan will expect us to have a ship waiting."

Micah had not been sure whether or not Traggo would limit his assistance to the setting of strategy. His words implied that he would be at Micah's side the whole time. He looked Traggo in the eyes. There was no doubt that the Phoenician wanted to participate in the mission, but Micah was not sure he wanted the man's help. As Micah saw it, this was his only chance to redeem himself in his wife's judgment. Otherwise he could risk losing her and the children to this powerful man.

"How about hiding a chariot?" Micah asked.

"Just outside the north exits is a large abandoned inn," Traggo answered. "It has a stable in an alley on the far side. No one will see a chariot there."

"And when is the best time to attack the dungeon?"

"Midnight, after the change in the guards. The upper story of the building will be empty then."

Micah studied the diagrams Traggo had drawn into the sand model. "So I'll be facing two guards at the entrance to the dungeon, three along the passageway, and between two and five between Luti's cell and one of the north exits."

"Why do you say 'I' instead of 'we'?" Traggo asked, angrily.

"I am very appreciative of the information you have given me. But it is not your fight."

Traggo brought his hand down hard in anger on his thigh. "Listen, you idiot: Drak will stay with the chariot and horses. But I am the one who can get you inside the dungeon. And once inside I will fight for you." He paused. "To the death."

"Are you willing to kill your own people?" Micah asked.

"Anyone who would hurt Luti is not my friend." Traggo was silent for a few moments. "On the way over here Drak told me about Luti's purpose in being in Tyre . . . about your daughter and the planned invasion of Ur." He shook his head grimly. "Navan has brought great wealth to the Phoenicians, but the cost in misery for other people is exorbitant. There has to be a moral law in the world—otherwise there will be no future for youngsters like this fine young fellow." He ruffled Drak's hair. "We have to start somewhere."

But Micah was not interested in moral philosophy. "If you help me enter the dungeon and you live, your fate will be sealed. You will lose everything you have here. You will be forced to come with us back to Ur."

"A single chariot cannot hold four people," Traggo replied. "I would be reluctant to try to hide two chariots in the inn's stable."

Micah would accept the Phoenician's help. Traggo was right; going it alone would be nothing more than a suicide. And just as Traggo was willing to risk everything to rescue Luti, so would Micah need to risk losing Luti to Traggo. What would be, would be.

"We'll have to take the chance," Micah replied.

"Then I will be honored to go with you. I will obtain horses and chariots."

Drak pouted. "I will *not* watch the chariots! I will fight for Mother's life."

"Don't be foolish," Micah told him harshly. "You will only hinder us."

"Besides," Traggo said, "we need you to make sure the chariots will be ready."

"Just tether the horses!" Drak insisted. "You said the inn was abandoned."

"No." Micah was firm. "You cannot go with us into the dungeon."

A wave of memories suddenly flooded through him: He remembered Joshua and the powerful force that followed him. He recalled what Joshua's top commanders used to tell the troops: "This is a people's war. You are soldiers in the army of Yahweh. But so are your wives, your sweethearts, your elderly parents, and your young children. We all must fight with whatever strength we have, with whatever weapons we have. The army *is* the people."

The idea of his son dying in a damp, filthy dungeon in a foreign land was horrific. But if a son cannot risk his life for his mother, who can? The steely composure of the bandit blood had taken over. The daring and drive was once again coursing through his body. For that reason he accepted his son's offer. Everyone, he knew, must pick up the sword and be prepared to use it. Everyone must be ready to die. And that included Drak.

"My son will fight alongside us," he said simply.

There was a shocked silence. Drak's bravado faded, as did the color in his face. Then his expression hardened into resolve. Traggo opened his mouth, then shut it again. As the two men and the boy looked at one another, they felt a camaraderie so intense that they could not articulate it.

Finally, Traggo said in a low voice, "Tell me what weapons you want."

"Three double-edged short swords, bronze with iron tips if you can get them. Make sure the hilts are reinforced. Plus at least five throwing daggers and a small ax."

"What about a bow?"

Micah shook his head. "Of no use in such tight surroundings." He narrowed his eyes at the Phoenician. "Traggo, you do know how to use a weapon, don't you? I mean, your education did include—"

"You'll find out soon enough, eh, Micah? I'll get you what you need. Meet me by the abandoned inn about an hour before midnight."

Traggo stood and walked out the door without uttering another word.

Micah slept for two hours. Then he washed, got changed, and found Drak, who was sitting outside by himself, scratching patterns into the dirt with a stick.

"It's time to go," Micah told him.

Drak nodded and stood up.

"You're sure you want to do this?"

The boy nodded. "I'm sure."

"All right, then." He barked out a series of instructions. It was as if he was talking to a soldier, not a twelve-year-old with wide and frightened eyes. "First, wet the bottoms of your sandals so they'll make less noise. Second, make sure the hems of your robes are weighted down. Nothing should be flapping around. Third, smear olive oil over your body, so no one can grab on to you. Oil will also help any wounds to coagulate. Fourth, go pee now. Drink no more water."

Micah accomplished for himself the cautionary steps, so his son could watch him and copy. Drak did everything exactly correct. When their preparations were completed and they were about to leave, Micah took his boy by the shoulders, looked into his young face, and said, "The purpose of our mission is to rescue your mother. If I am lying wounded on the floor of the dungeon, do not go back for me. Get your mother out of there. I promise you, as much as I love you, I will not go back for you. Understand?"

The boy nodded, wide-eyed. His fear was evident.

The moment they left the house Micah broke into a slow trot, the same gait he had used to eat up the desert miles in the Wilderness of Judea between raids. Drak kept pace.

Traggo was waiting for them, as he had promised, in the shadows of the stable by the abandoned inn.

Micah walked around the chariots and horses and carefully studied them for peculiarities, signs of weakness, any defects that could mean the difference between life and death as they attempted their escape. But Traggo, he realized to his satisfaction, had done a very creditable job on such short notice. The chariots were well built, in good condition, and oiled. There were no markings to reflect moonlight, and the sides were a dull gray. As for the horses, they were the very best kind for the purpose— short, powerful northern beasts with massive barrel chests. Their legs were like logs and could take the pounding of hard terrain. Their wide faces were placid and the eyes deep set. Whirling sand would not blind them.

"Well done," Micah approved, nodding.

Traggo, smiling, knelt to unwrap a blanket, which proved to contain the weapons.

Again Micah was pleased. He distributed the short swords. Then he gave Traggo one of the throwing daggers and kept the others for himself, including the powerful short-handled battle-ax, which gleamed in the starlight.

Traggo studied the sky. "Soon . . ." he said. "Very soon."

The three waited. The air was rife with strange sounds. Once, Micah thought he heard screams coming from the direction of the dungeon. Luti? He closed his eyes and forced the vision away. He had to stay calm and totally concentrated on the task at hand.

Finally Traggo looked at Micah and nodded once. Micah said yes quietly, and the three stood up. They moved swiftly to the front entrance of the Palace of Weights and Measures, entered the deserted building, and headed down the hallway toward the steps that led down to the dungeon.

The building was damp, and the walls oozed and sweated. The trio slowly descended in the flickering torchlight. When they reached the subterranean rotunda, Traggo pointed to a thick wooden door that contained a small rectangular opening at eye level.

Micah signaled to Drak to station himself on the right side of the entry and crouch low. Micah did the same on the left side.

Traggo pounded boldly on the door. "Guard! Guard! Come here immediately!"

Eyes showed from the other side. "Who goes?"

"Traggo, aide to Navan. I have been ordered here to continue the interrogation of one Luti of Ur."

"Yes, my lord." The door opened immediately.

Micah felt the hilt of his sword slide on the sweat on his palm. He flexed his fingers nervously. It had been so long since he had held a weapon. It had been almost two years since he had experienced the . . . the total exhilaration that comes only when one drives a blade into another person's body and causes bones to splinter and sinews to be severed.

He hesitated only a moment before he rose up from behind Traggo and struck the guard. As his left hand covered the man's mouth so there would be no screams, the blade of Micah's short sword impaled the soldier deep in the stomach. The dying man bit deep and drew blood from the hand that suffocated him. Then he died convulsively at Micah's feet.

Drak stood shaking at the doorway. His pupils were huge, and his jaw hung slack.

"Get against the wall," Micah whispered urgently. "You'll be all right."

He had to push his son to get him moving. Slowly the three inched their way deeper into the dungeon. When they heard voices, Micah signaled a stop. They waited. From the voices, Micah knew there were two men in the hallway, just around the bend.

"Follow me," Micah said in a low voice. And then

suddenly, unexpectedly, he screamed, *"For Yahweh and His people!"* It was the old war cry of Joshua's great army.

Micah charged, with Traggo and Drak at his heels. The man and boy added their own war cries to Micah's, and the walls of the dungeon seemed to shake from the echoing sounds.

The two soldiers, caught unaware, recovered quickly and fought valiantly. Traggo sliced off the arm of one, but Micah did not fare so well. His opponent's sword grazed Micah's face. As Micah fell back, Drak rushed forward and, in his first thrust, killed his father's attacker. The boy stared, panting, at the man whose throat he had cut. He began to tremble, and his sword hung limply in his hand.

Micah lunged at his bewildered, shocked son and smacked him hard in the face. "Fight! Fight!" he screamed at the boy. As Drak recovered, Micah used his battle-ax to split the skull of the man who had lost his arm to Traggo's thrust.

Encouraged by their success, the three ran toward the cells, but more guards blocked their way. Micah hurled his throwing daggers toward the charging Sea Peoples. Two of the daggers struck home, smashing into throats. The guards pitched forward with gurgling shrieks. Their dying screams alerted reinforcements. Micah and his allies heard the sounds of men running toward them.

"We must get to the cell quick," Traggo shouted.

Micah's sword cut a bloody path toward Luti, clearing the way as they ran forward.

"Over here!" Traggo called out. "It must be one of these!" The Phoenician nobleman slung back the outside latches of the torture cell. He ran inside the first one, while Drak raced inside the second. As Micah entered the third, a dying guard flung himself forward and clung desperately to Micah's ankle. Unstoppable, he swung his battle-ax and split the man's skull with no more thought than swatting an insect. Then Micah looked up. What he saw sent him to his knees. "No," he moaned. "No . . . no."

Luti was unconscious and strapped naked to the wall.

Both eyes were swollen closed from beatings. There were welts from a whip across her thighs.

Micah sank to his knees, then to his belly. He placed his face on the filthy dungeon floor and tried to scrape away the shame from his features.

Then, exerting tremendous willpower, he forced himself to rise, cut Luti down, and lower her gently.

When he walked from the cell, his wife cradled in his embrace, Traggo and Drak were waiting for him and poised to run. A low moan escaped Drak when he saw his mother.

"She's alive, boy," Micah said. "Be grateful."

Traggo's mouth was a thin white line as he took off his robe and covered Luti with it. They fled toward the north exit. But there, facing them, blocking the way, was a squad of Sea Peoples guards, fully armed and in formation.

Micah quickly handed the unconscious Luti to Traggo, and with a terrifying scream, he leaped with ax and sword upon the cohorts.

The five Sea Peoples who bore the brunt of Micah's charge were disciplined, experienced mercenaries. They had faced death many times before. They had fought all kinds of enemies who used a variety of weapons.

But now they found themselves assaulted by a madman. Now they found themselves facing a wild man who was far superior to them in use of weapons, in speed, in boldness of attack—even though he had not raised a weapon in anger for more than a year.

Micah killed the first one with his sword, disemboweling him with a single savage stroke. Then he discarded the blade and wielded only the terrifying short ax. The other soldiers fought their way to him. His face and chest now bloodied by a dozen superficial wounds, Micah swung the weapon in a series of short arcs, pulling back quickly the moment he heard the sickening thud of weapon against flesh.

The old blood lust was upon him. The need for vengeance for his beloved's abused body filled his muscles and bones with enormous strength. Like a scythe moving through wheat, his weapon mowed down the remaining guards. And then he just stood there, staring crazily at the soldiers lying at his feet—the wounded screaming and the dead staring with glazed eyes.

"The exit! Let's go! More are coming!"

Traggo's warning prompted them to run to freedom, pounding out of the dungeon and down the alley to the abandoned inn. The chariots and horses were at the stable, just where they had been left. Micah could hear the clanking of armor as more soldiers ran toward them, only seconds away.

Micah leaped into one chariot and tightly wrapped the reins around one hand. Traggo carefully placed a moaning Luti into the chariot beside her husband. Then the Phoenician lifted Drak and helped the boy into the chariot with his parents.

"Go! Go! Go!" Traggo screamed.

"What about you?" Micah demanded. He turned to look behind him. Soldiers had burst into the courtyard and were heading toward the stable.

"Get in!" Micah urged.

But Traggo whipped the horses' rumps with the flat of his hand, and the beasts lunged forward. Then the Phoenician ran at the approaching soldiers. The nobleman was ready to do battle to the last, to give his companions time to escape.

"Traggo! Please!" Micah shouted. But it was too late. His heart sank. He knew that the man was sacrificing himself to Luti. Micah was left with no choice. He had to move the chariot, or none of them would escape. He whipped the horses. Faster and faster the chariot moved along the open avenue leading to the city gates. Micah wept, tormented by leaving Traggo behind. Tears ran down his bloodied cheeks.

At Micah's side, Drak wept piteously over his mother's inert form. The child grieved for the loss and valor of his friend.

*   *   *

Micah drove the horses for hours, until the chariot was far beyond Tyre. Only when it was obvious to him that the beasts would collapse unless rested did he rein them in at a small olive grove.

Father and son, exhausted by their ordeal, climbed out of the chariot and together carried Luti away and placed her gently on the ground. Micah tried to kiss her, but even the feathery pressure of his lips made her groan with pain. The boy stepped back, his face ashen.

"Will she die?" Drak asked in a whisper.

"No, Son," Micah replied with more confidence than he felt. He did not know how much blood she had lost, whether she had internal injuries, or if the rough escape from Tyre had taken a toll. "But she's been hurt badly. We'll watch her closely."

Micah bent down close to Luti and placed his ear against her heart. The beating was still strong. Suddenly tears filled his eyes. He wanted to apologize to her for his thoughtless cruelty. He wanted to beg again and again for her mercy. He wanted to mutilate himself in penance for what he had done to her and the boy and thank her for her strength in carrying on in spite of him.

"Tell me the truth," Drak demanded. "Will she live?"

Micah stood up and stepped back. If she didn't live, he realized, they would never see Seka again. He assumed that Luti had learned the necessary information for the priests of Astarte—otherwise the accusation would not have outweighed her commendable service to Navan.

Drak was weeping again from exhaustion and terror. Micah, leaving the boy's question unanswered, slung an arm around Drak and held him until he calmed down. Then Micah tried as best he could to evaluate the extent of Luti's injuries. Nothing seemed to be broken, but because she had been flayed, she was bleeding and in great pain. Micah knew, from his many years as a soldier, that her raw flesh would need protection. Otherwise it would become inflamed and she would die.

He stared around. The ground was bare of vegetation. There was nothing with which to treat her wounds or to ease her pain. He did not believe that she would bleed to death; her wounds oozed but did not bubble. His concerns were replenishing her system and protecting it.

The horses caught his eyes. "Come with me," he said to Drak. "Your mother and I need your help."

Drak looked up. His face was swollen from his crying, and as a result he appeared much younger than his twelve years. Micah had not known the boy in his early days, and seeing him now, looking so very, very young, brought a surge of tenderness coursing through the man. Drak stood and meekly followed his father.

Micah unhitched one of the horses from the chariot and led it twenty feet away. "Listen carefully, Son. Hold this beast by the mane. Keep him still. The moment you hear me yell your name, jump away quickly—*very* quickly, as if your life depended upon it."

Drak nodded, then wrapped his fingers in the horse's mane. Micah moved in front of the beast and clucked to it softly. The horse stomped and blew, then calmed down. Micah crouched and slowly, fluidly withdrew a dagger. Then he lunged forward with all his strength behind the thrust, at the same time screaming out Drak's name. His son leaped away. The dagger drove into the heart of the horse, and it sank to its knees, convulsed once, then died. Micah slit the stomach cavity open, threw down the knife, and pulled out the intestines. He ran with the dripping innards to Luti and gently began to cover her with them. The steaming mass penetrated Traggo's robes and allowed Micah to peel them away where they had become stuck to her flesh.

Drak could not watch the nauseating, horrifying spectacle. He turned away, gagging. But Micah called imperatively, "Dig into the corpse. Bring more of the insides here. If we work together, we can help your mother."

Drak regained his composure, and soon both he and Micah were going back and forth, emptying the body cavity of the dead horse and covering Luti with all the removed innards.

Finally the task was accomplished. Father and son, blood dripping from their arms, stood watching Luti. She seemed to have relaxed for the first time and was no longer moaning. Her increased comfort gave Micah and Drak a feeling of camaraderie. Micah felt gratified, realizing that his relationship to his son was being repaired.

Exhausted, all three slept side by side.

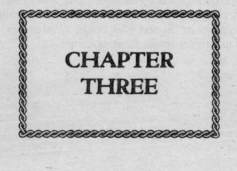

CHAPTER THREE

Canaan

By the time Gaal arrived, the lords of Shechem had already begun their weekly council meeting. He had never been late for such a meeting in all the years of his membership. But it was not Gaal's tardiness that drew uncomprehending stares and stunned silence from his fellow noblemen; it was his mode of dress. Gaal was wearing a long white linen garment that fell in graceful folds to the floor. Gone were his helmet and his body armor. He carried no weapon and wore no shoes.

Zebul broke the silence. "What is this, Gaal? Are you going to a funeral?"

The others laughed appreciatively at Zebul's comment.

Gaal waited until the laughter had subsided. "Yes," he said with grim seriousness. "Your funeral!"

The councilmen recoiled. Something different, weighty and important, gave depth to Gaal's tone. More than one elder shuddered in dread.

"And the funeral of our land," he continued, "for all will be a burning pyre unless Abimelech is destroyed now!"

Zebul looked bored. "Not again," he drawled. "We are tired of your constant complaints."

"Our king has brought law, order, and prosperity to our city," an elder called out.

"He has restored pride to our people!" another council member shouted.

"And promised us that soon the people of Yahweh will become the most powerful nation on the Great Sea!" came another shout.

"Already our borders are expanding!"

"Soon we shall vacation in Egypt and Lebanon and even Damascus!"

As the praises of King Abimelech continued thick and fast, Gaal listened in silence. At last the uproar died down, and he paced in front of the council members. His strides were sure and powerful. An undeniable force emanated from him. So powerful was this quality that many in the chamber cringed.

Gaal raised an arm and proclaimed, "The spirit of Yahweh has come upon me."

The council members looked at one another in astonishment. There were a few nervous chuckles.

Gaal ignored them. "What you will hear from me is the truth of Yahweh, for the Spirit came upon me suddenly. You have allowed a beast to make his lair in our city. That beast is Abimelech. You have enabled him to slaughter the seventy sons of Gideon. You have paid him to bring fire and sword to the countryside. You have given him permission to steal the young men of our land and send them on adventures from which they will never return. Within the past twenty-four hours, two thousand of our youth have been slain on the frontiers—on the north, south, and east, slaughtered by Bedouins and Philistines and Phoenicians. Our young men have been sent without training or weapons into battle. Their only defense was the perverted promises of a madman. Woe unto you, elders of Shechem! You have made a pact with the beast, and the God of Abraham, Isaac, and Jacob will pay you back for your perfidy. Blasphemers! Murderers!"

Gaal's accusations were backed by so powerful a spiritual righteousness that several elders, recognizing the truth when they heard it, simply fell trembling to their knees. They had been growing increasingly aware of the dissatisfaction among the citizenry. For days the families of the young men first impressed into military service, then killed for a cause no one was sure of, had protested loudly. And their faction was gaining strength by the hour.

But up until now no one had had the courage to dispute Abimelech's actions in formal council. The consensus, however, was far from unanimous. A politician who admits a mistake risks losing his power.

Zebul rose and pointed a finger at Gaal. "You have lost your senses. How dare you claim the spirit of Yahweh for your own! King Abimelech embodies the truth of the Lord. He has triumphed over our enemies! What better proof of the Lord's favor can there be?"

"No!" Gaal shouted. "Your gold has triumphed. And to kill the homeless, the unfortunates of our city, along with the thieves and murderers, was inexcusable. Now you must repent! You must pull the mantle of legitimacy from Abimelech. He is out of control. Help me destroy him!"

Zebul started to protest again, but this time he was shouted down by his peers. One after another the nobles rose and asked Gaal, "How can we undo the damage?"

"What do you want of us?"

"Tell us what Yahweh demands!"

When Gaal raised both arms, the voices died down. "First we must pray together, my brothers." He sank to his knees. One by one the others followed—except for Zebul. Glaring, he stood ramrod straight.

"Yahweh," Gaal prayed, "Lord of heaven and earth, forgive us. Deal mercifully with us, for we have sinned. We have been covetous. We have betrayed our people and our families for silver and gold. We have listened to the blandishments of a madman. We have profaned your commandments. Forgive us, have mercy on us, console us. Give us the strength to perform the personal sacrifices necessary to accomplish the greater good."

He stood up. The others did the same. The power of Gaal's presence intensified with each passing moment. These influential, affluent, cynical men knew they were witnessing a most extraordinary transformation when he fastened his eyes upon them. Even the whiteness of his robe was dazzling.

"I leave the city now," he told them. "But I'll return with my own army by nightfall. Tomorrow, we will march out again, but this time Yahweh will be by our side. And we will face the beast who ravages our land, kills our sons, and blasphemes our faith."

Gaal turned and walked out of the chambers, leaving a sobered and frightened audience.

The next night, Zebul, formerly the most high lord of Shechem, watched out a window of his house as hundreds of Gaal's retainers set up camp in the large town square. The blazing torches threw shadows on their faces and along the high stone walls. The eerie, dancing lights merely increased the sense of unreality for Zebul. He was still dazed from the events of the last thirty-six hours. After Gaal had returned with the troops, the young nobleman had usurped Zebul's authority and tossed him out on his ear. The council was now following their new leader unquestioningly. The elders had agreed unanimously to help Gaal destroy Abimelech.

How had this happened so quickly? Zebul wondered. What mysterious power did Gaal wield over his colleagues? How had he gathered such a large force so quickly? Zebul had no idea, especially since Gaal never promised victory. All he promised was personal sacrifice, so that Abimelech would ultimately be destroyed. But Zebul knew all too well that everything he had worked for was threatened—the personal power, his wealth, and the ascendancy of his city. Without Abimelech, everything Zebul had acquired would vanish.

Desperation and anger gave birth to a plan, a foolproof scheme that would protect his interests. Zebul waited until past midnight, when all of Gaal's troops were bedded down within the city.

Then he called for Rafi, his most senior house servant, from the tribe of Dan. The faithful old servant was a war veteran who had lost an arm many years before in some now forgotten battle. He came in and bowed low before Zebul.

"Listen carefully, Rafi. I have a mission of extreme importance for you. Abimelech is camped some eight miles north of the city, planning to assault Thebez in the next few days. Ride to his camp immediately and tell the king that Gaal has raised an army to oppose him. Urge Abimelech to come back here, to gather his forces just before dawn and deploy in the hills east of Shechem. Explain that Gaal's threat to his kingship is very serious."

After Rafi had left, Zebul secreted a small weapon in his clothing, then wrapped a cloak tightly around his shivering frame and left his house, to walk silently among the smoldering campfires of Gaal's troops. What he observed upset him: These were hardened troops, experienced fighters! Again he was amazed that there were many more men than he originally thought Gaal could have gathered on short notice.

His gaze settled on the conical shape of the command tent, erected apart from the others. Even in the near darkness he could make out the form of Gaal, still in his startlingly white robes, sitting within. Why, Zebul wondered angrily, did the fervent followers of Yahweh always cause so much trouble? Why did they always have to force their so-called special relationship with Yahweh on everyone else? Zebul absentmindedly rubbed his stomach. Every time he thought about Gaal in the last day and a half, his stomach burned and ached. He took a deep breath and tried to calm down. Now was not the time, he realized, to fuel his hatred of Gaal. For the plan to work, he would have to fool the usurper, and to fool a man you had to be gentle with him.

Zebul stepped into the shadows, drew out the small, sharp dagger he had brought with him, then shredded his garments. Then Zebul turned the blade on his flesh— scraping the skin until it bled. Now he was ready! He smiled once at the audacity of his plan and then staggered into the command tent.

"What are you doing here?" Gaal demanded, still disgusted with Zebul for having spoken in defense of Abimelech at the council.

"You were right," he said, gasping. He fell at the younger man's feet. "Abimelech is a madman. He had me beaten just for telling him what you said. He had me whipped like a dog."

"When you act the spy, don't expect gratitude." His demeanor softened. "At least you now see the truth, Zebul. Come, rest by my side." Gaal, shaking his head, helped Zebul to sit on a pillow.

"There is no time to rest! While I was in the king's camp, I overheard some important information. Even now Abimelech is marching toward Shechem. He is planning to ambush you outside the west gate of the city."

Gaal accepted the lie without question. It was all Zebul could do not to laugh at the young man's gullibility.

"The west gate, eh?" Excitement shone in Gaal's dark eyes. "Let Abimelech wait! Just past dawn we'll go out the east gate, then circle the walls and attack the king from behind!"

Zebul smiled. This was exactly what he hoped Gaal would say. "A brilliant plan," Zebul remarked.

"Get some rest, Zebul. I'll call someone to treat your wounds. When you wake in the morning, you'll see Abimelech's head on the ground beside you."

After Gaal left to organize his troops, Zebul could not sleep. He slipped from the tent and climbed high onto the east wall. He watched as Gaal's own physician came to the tent and, finding it empty, went back to his own shelter. There was only one final element necessary to Zebul's plan's success: The sun had to rise brilliantly and flood the eastern plain with its light, so that Gaal's horses and men would be blinded when they formed up to face Abimelech. Then the king, hiding in the eastern hills, could swoop down on the blinded army.

The schemer spent restless hours on the wall. By false dawn, he thought the burning sensation in his stomach would force him to go home and get into bed. But he gritted his teeth and endured. Then, at last, dawn came.

The sun did not disappoint him. It rose slowly, peach, pink, and fuchsia. Then its fierce white light flooded the eastern sky.

Zebul grinned nastily as he watched Gaal lead his troops out the east gate. He laughed out loud because Gaal was so totally unaware of what awaited him . . . so sure was he of the rightness of his cause. Gaal rode fifty feet onto the plain. Immediately the horses shied as the sun hurt their eyes. Gaal's troops shouted at their mounts, but the beasts continued to buck and rear. The soldiers tried to locate their leader, but their eyesight was impaired, too.

Zebul, squinting, tenting his hands over his eyes, peered into the eastern distance for the king's men. Suddenly, from across the plain, points of color shone through the sunlight. The dots came closer and closer until at last Zebul could identify them as Abimelech's ferocious troops. Their long clubs and spears swung threateningly over their heads. Within minutes total chaos prevailed. They drove into the confused mass with a brutal thrust, and in seconds

Zebul could see it was a bloodbath. He tried to find Gaal in the midst of the battle. He wanted to watch the nervy upstart get what he deserved. But he could not find the white-robed commander. Zebul shrugged philosophically; Gaal had talked about personal sacrifice, and that was exactly his fate. Abimelech would see to that! The screams of the wounded and dying—both horses and men—could be heard across the land.

Ecstatic that his plan had worked, Zebul scrambled down the walls to await the entrance of Abimelech and to receive the king's gratitude.

He did not have long to wait. Abimelech and his bodyguards galloped triumphantly through the east gate. Zebul waved his arms gleefully and ran—nearly danced—toward him.

The king waited until Zebul was ten feet from his mount, then he flung the throwing dagger. It drove through Zebul's right eye. He fell to the ground and died.

Abimelech kicked his horse forward, then guided the stallion backward, effectively trampling the fallen man under the hooves. Then the king stood up in his stirrups and shouted to his troops, who were entering the city.

"We have only enemies in Shechem! Shechem is our prize. Take no prisoners. Show no mercy."

Abimelech threw his head back and laughed as his troops began their bloody business. He watched as the first Shechemite family—husband, wife, and three small children—was slaughtered on the street. He smiled approvingly as blood flowed into the dirt road and created red furrows. The madness that had always threatened him was now fully upon him. He no longer knew the difference between right or wrong, between God and man, between cause and effect. He had entered another world.

Cotto could not breathe. The burden of his weight was pressing her hard against the earth. She tried to gouge his eyes, but he just laughed.

It seemed to her that the whole world had gone mad.

Outside the king's tent she could hear screams as the victorious troops took vengeance on the city that would have expelled them.

Abimelech's body shuddered in sexual completion, then he rolled off her and lay quietly.

Cotto wished she had a knife. If she could not have killed Abimelech, she would have driven the blade into her own heart, so much did she fear him. She scrambled across the floor to be alone near the wall of the tent. But he crawled on all fours to her, rolled onto his back, and rested his head in her lap.

"I'm going to let you live," he said, grinning up at her. "In a short time, you, a whore, will be the only Israelite left alive. I'm going to wipe my own people off the face of the earth. They have betrayed me and don't deserve to live. After my men are done amusing themselves in Shechem, we'll march out to destroy all the farms, flocks, and workers surrounding the city. Then we'll move north and continue our work. By the time we're done, we'll have circled the entire land of Canaan with flame." He paused, grinning. "By then I will be a worthy foe for Yahweh Himself, wouldn't you agree? Maybe He'll show Himself to me, as He did to Moses. Then I'll slay Yahweh." He laughed. "You see? It is fitting that only a miserable whore like you will survive."

He rolled up lithely to his feet in one surprisingly fluid motion, then stepped around her as if she were a piece of garbage. He snatched up his bow and sword and crumpled robes, and left the tent.

Those who escaped from Shechem and the surrounding villages hurried north, warning the inhabitants as they fled. Soon the entire Jordan valley knew that a madman was coming against them. Most of the refugees headed to the great city of Thebez, for it was rumored that the high priests had escaped from the Temple Mount in Shechem and were seeking sanctuary there. A great tower had been built a generation before in that city. It was thought that the safest place to be in times of great danger was in close proximity to the high priests of Yahweh.

Soon, the narrow streets of Thebez overflowed with refugees. The streets became public bedrooms and bathrooms. The stench was overpowering. Food was in short supply and could be purchased only at great price. As severe as the discomfort was, surprisingly no one really minded. At least they were safe from the certain death that accompanied Abimelech and his legions.

Alas, this safety was soon proved to be an illusion. A tower lookout spotted the columns first. The soldiers were far away but advancing steadily. Abimelech and his men moved with the single-minded intensity of locusts. Every mile they traversed seemed to wither and die. The horses devoured every stalk of grass; the men stole everything worth taking. The soldiers of Abimelech stared straight ahead; their eyes were dull, glazed, lifeless, from having seen too much already; their own sense of humanity had been destroyed by the devastation they themselves had wrought.

As the horde closed in on Thebez, an officer within the city's garrison realized that no one had wetted down the walls or the roofs of the homes near the walls as a precaution against the invaders' inevitable fire arrows.

But the realization had come too late. Within the hour Abimelech's archers sent volley after volley of burning bolts thudding into the thick but dry wood walls. Soon Thebez's fortifications were aflame. Sparks and fiery debris blew onto the miserable refugees and citizens.

Only the massive, sixty-foot-tall cult tower of Yahweh was miraculously protected from the flames. There were five tiers on the tower, the highest being occupied by the priests. Next were the scribes, then the functionaries who conducted the sacrifices. Crowded on the last two tiers were the frantic and the fearful, those who had climbed the rope ladders to safety. Fluttering from the sides of the tower were the gaily colored strips of cloth, which people traditionally hung there as signs of their respect for

Yahweh and as a plea to answer their prayers. The festive look of these bright banners provided a cruel incongruity to the atmosphere that, in truth, prevailed.

Originally each tier had been designed to provide small, self-contained living quarters for about fifty people. Now, of course, each level was bursting with hundreds of desperate men, women, and children. There was no more room for additional people. The high priests on the top tiers had already defied tradition by allowing commoners to seek refuge there. As desperate people climbed the rope ladders to the towers, the lucky ones already there began to push the newcomers off and away, sometimes sending them to their death.

Miriam was one of the lucky ones. She stood on the second tier, holding her child in her arms, and watched in horror and confusion as the burning gates of Thebez weakened, then splintered under the assault of Abimelech's battering rams.

Gaal, she knew, would be dead. But his mission of slowing Abimelech down, forestalling his attack on Thebez until she had arrived to do her job, had been accomplished. But what exactly was her role, she wondered.

With a terrible sound the gates gave way, and the invaders, shouting battle cries, surged into Thebez. Confusion worsened in the narrow streets below the tower. From above, the chants of the priests could be heard as the holy men led their fellow Israelites in the mourner's prayer.

Tears welled in Miriam's eyes, which burned from the thick smoke blowing in from the gates. She hugged her baby to her and agonized, *When will the sufferings of my people end?* She wished that Gideon were alive—he could have stopped this carnage. But Gideon was long dead. There were no heroes anymore. There was no man strong enough to stop Abimelech. Why, she wondered, crying, had Yahweh chosen a woman to gain His revenge?

Suddenly a strong wind gusted, enabling Miriam to see clearly to the ground. Abimelech stood there, gesturing frantically and shouting orders to his men. He wanted them to climb the tower. The people had, of course, pulled up the rope ladders, but the soldiers soon found wooden ladders nearby at a construction site. While a dozen soldiers shot arrows at the people on the lowest tier to prevent them from pushing these replacement ladders away, another dozen climbed up.

The first few soldiers were beaten back by the rain of debris, hot coals, and anything else the defenders could find. But more attackers followed, and soon the bottom tier was overwhelmed. The lucky people scrambled to higher levels. The less fortunate ones were slaughtered and flung over the railings.

"Please, would you help me?" Miriam handed her baby to an elderly woman next to her. She kissed Jeb's face and carefully arranged his blanket. "Be still, darling," she cooed. "Try not to cry."

Then she went to the railing and stared down at the massive figure of Abimelech, exhorting his troops to keep climbing, to take the tower tier by tier until the priests' area had been cleared.

She was weak. She was hungry. The spirit had long since left her. But she knew she had to try. If Gaal had given his life so that she might succeed, then it was up to her to be courageous, for the sake of Gideon's blessed memory and for her child's future—and for all those who had been brutalized. She closed her eyes for a moment, remembering the horror and degradation of the rape. The memory nearly undermined her commitment. So far Abimelech had no idea she was there, within his grasp. If he saw her, recognized her, he would try to hurt her again. But he was doing to Canaan what he had done to her, and it was time to stand up to him. She reminded herself that she and Gideon shared the same blood; perhaps she possessed greater fortitude than she realized or gave herself credit for.

"*Abimelech! Abimelech!*" She leaned out over the railing and, dodging arrows, screamed out his name again and again.

Finally a wondering silence settled as the combatants stared at the strange little woman who, instead of trying to save her skin, was drawing attention to herself.

At last the king heard his name. He peered up at the tower and wiped the blood and sweat from his eyes.

"Miriam? Is that you?"

"Yes! I am here—the woman you always wanted! I am yours! Come to me, Abimelech!"

She opened her garment and extended her arms down to him, as if offering to Abimelech the body he had always yearned for.

A great, deep roar of triumphant laughter burst from Abimelech's throat, and leaving his weapons on the ground and his hands free, he began quickly to climb the ladder to the tower. He pushed aside his own soldiers if they impeded his progress. Screaming, they toppled from the ladder.

Miriam, trembling with fear, turned away. Her eyes cast about, looking for some means of defense. She cursed herself for not thinking of that earlier. Everything that could have been used against the enemies had already been hurled at them or taken along to a higher story for future use. The only thing near her was a massive millstone resting near the edge of the tier. It was about three feet in diameter. It had been left behind because it weighed more than anyone could lift and carry.

She closed her eyes and prayed. "I beseech you, Lord, to grant me the spirit of your power. For the sake of your people, for the sake of children unborn, grant me the power to destroy the blasphemer. O God of Abraham and Isaac and Jacob, Who brought us out of the land of Egypt where we were slaves to the pharaoh, allow me to feel the strength to destroy the beast who would enslave us again."

She opened her eyes and stared upward, at the priests from the top tier. These holy men were leaning out over the ramparts. They were praying or beseeching her to run. Her eyes caught sight of the prayer banners fluttering in the breeze. When she saw these graceful folds of cloth riding the wind, the cries of the people faded from her consciousness. All became blessed silence. Abimelech continued his climb toward her, but for some reason, she knew he posed no threat. His arms and legs moved in slow motion.

She glanced at her baby, resting peacefully in the stranger's arms. Miriam smiled. Total calm enveloped her. It was as if she were far away from Thebez. The peace that pervaded her was one of total and utter trust. It was unlike anything she had experienced since childhood.

She smiled beatifically and walked to the immense millstone. Placing both small hands at its edge, she took a deep breath and raised it effortlessly onto its side. And then, as if the huge stone were a substanceless thing of a dream, she lifted it high over her head.

Abimelech's filthy face appeared just over the rim of the platform. With a heave of his powerful shoulders he started to climb over the railing. His eyes widened in disbelief when he looked at her.

"No!" he cried.

Miriam calmly dropped the stone on his head.

Millstone and man hurtled to the ground together. A scream gurgled in Abimelech's throat until he slammed into the earth, the stone atop him.

Abimelech's soldiers worked furiously to pull the weight off his body. When they finally succeeded, they could see that he would never rise again.

The fallen man reached out, attempting to signal something. Finally one of his bodyguards understood: Abimelech could not bear the ignominy of dying slowly, and by a woman's hand. The bodyguard drew his sword and obligingly slit Abimelech's throat.

His blood flowed onto the same ground where so much other blood had been shed. His men stared down at him. His life force gone, he was utterly transformed—smaller, somehow. One by one the invaders dropped their spears and swords and bows, and abandoned the city. There were no cheers from the populace. All was grimly silent until the last man had left Thebez. Then a great roar of joy erupted from the onlookers. Miriam walked calmly over to the old woman holding Jeb. Tears ran down the crone's furrowed cheeks as she held her charge out to the savior of the city. Miriam, exhausted, unwrapped her little one's blanket. He was sound asleep.

The citizens filed by to kiss Miriam's hand. Above, from the top of the tower, the high priests of Yahweh sang a hymn of thanksgiving. The song brought tears of joy as Miriam felt the power of Yahweh ebb from her body. She had done it!

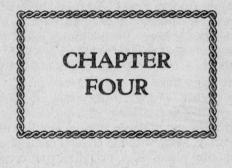

CHAPTER FOUR

Thrace

The chisel slipped from Talus's grasp and clattered onto the hard ground. He stared at the tool and made no move to retrieve it. He spoke quietly to the man next to him. "Theon, I can't do this anymore. I am too weak. My fingers won't bend enough to hold my tools. I can't think straight. I've lost my sense of beauty."

Theon picked up the chisel and handed it to Talus, but the young man refused to take it.

"What's the use, Theon? We'll never get out of this terrible place."

"We're still alive, aren't we, Talus? Your carvings have earned us the food we and our friends needed to stay alive. Our underground organization is growing larger and stronger every day."

"So what?" Talus asked listlessly.

"We have learned to care for one another. Think, my friend! Remember when we first came here? Every day at least one prisoner killed himself. Now none dies by suicide. Your sculptures have brought hope!"

"A plague on your hope!" Talus said bitterly. He sank to his knees and buried his face in his arms.

Theon stared down at the young man. Talus had grown woefully thin in spite of the extra food. His skin had become blotched from the lack of fruit and vegetables. There were open sores on his hands and feet.

Theon sighed, picked up the piece of marble Talus had been carving, and carefully wiped it clean. Sometimes his own strength and patience amazed him. He placed the piece of marble, along with the chisel, beside Talus's knee. "It is a beautiful piece, Talus, like all of your carvings. Not only have you saved many lives by your efforts, you have brought beauty into the world."

"There can be no beauty in a place like this," Talus groaned.

"Oh, no! You are wrong! Only in places like this can men truly appreciate beauty. Please, Talus, do not desert us now."

Talus could not withstand the plea of his mentor. Wearily, he put chisel to marble once again.

It had been an arduous two days' march from the cove where the Cretan ship had deposited Hela and Tuk to the mountain stronghold of the god Dionysus. Now, as the sun rose, its rays bounced blindingly off the beautiful marble columns.

Hela's excitement was intense. Was her mother really there? Would they finally be reunited? Memories walked with her as she and Tuk approached the Temple of Dionysus.

Behind them, the hired laborers grumbled as they drove the donkeys. It was not easy keeping the pace of the fleet-footed golden-haired woman and the little black child.

"Why is it so quiet?" Hela asked Tuk. The woman did not expect an answer. The approach to the temple was as silent as Tuk. There were no voices, no musical instruments —the air was absolutely still.

A shadow suddenly slid across the ground before her. Hela looked up and shuddered. High above were circling vultures. Their presence prompted caution as Hela continued on. She and the others set off up the path that led to the main rotunda. That was when she saw the first corpses. A maenad had fastened her teeth into the throat of a male temple guard, who had driven his short sword into his assailant's stomach.

Hela, cringing and wary, entered the main rotunda. She found it difficult to maintain her balance, for the sight was so overwhelming. It looked to Hela that a war to the death between the sexes had been fought. But why? She turned for illumination to the Thracians who had accompanied her to the temple—after all, this was their land and their people. But the laborers had fled without a word. Well, she could not blame them. She looked down at Tuk, but the child did not seem upset by the sights.

Deeper they moved into the temple proper. Looters had already visited the building—many of the soldiers had been stripped of weapons, breastplates, and helmets.

Then she saw the immense bier, delicately carved, on which lay a decomposing body.

She walked to it slowly. "Grandpa!" she said, gasping, and flung herself on the edge of the bier. Her mind began to race. Something must have happened to her mother! Nuhara would never leave her father's body! She raced willy-nilly through the temple, turning over every corpse in a search for her mother's. Nuhara was not there. Hela did not know whether to feel relieved or saddened.

Exhausted, heartbroken, she sat down on the cool tile floor. A vat of wine was within reach. She rolled onto one hip, grasped the ladle, and dipped it into the wine.

As she brought it to her lips, a sudden blow knocked the ladle from her hands. She looked up, angry. Tuk had struck her.

"What's wrong with you, Tuk?" she screamed, her eyes blazing.

The girl stared at her. Hela shivered because, as always, the child's gaze seemed to bore into her brain. Hela understood in a flash: The wine was poisoned. It would have hurt or killed her.

The clarity of the revelation shook Hela to the core. She had lost her telepathic powers on the day that Gravis fell ill and died. Those special abilities had not returned until this instant, and now she shared them with Tuk!

The child took Hela's hand and pulled. Hela stood and let herself be led out of the temple and to a small ravine where some peasant children were playing. They looked totally unconcerned about the carnage close by.

One of the children was singing a ditty:

> "Nuhara wanted a crown
> on her head
> So she stole the gold and
> left everyone dead."

The lyrics echoed in her ears. Each word felt like a hammer's blow. Slowly the truth sank in. The truth of Nuhara's perfidious life dawned on her. The rumors she had always heard as a child but had discounted suddenly seemed credible. Nuhara *was* cruel. Nuhara *was* unfaithful. Nuhara *was* scheming.

Hela burst into forceful tears. She did not want to think such things about her mother! She loved her mother! She wanted her mother. But under the powerful glare of Tuk's dark eyes, the truth could not be hidden from her.

Hot tears stung her eyes and flowed freely down her cheeks. She staggered away and wandered aimlessly. When she could focus again, she looked around to realize that

Tuk had vanished. Frightened nearly to the point of hysteria, Hela finally spotted the child climbing the far hill.

"Tuk! Don't leave me! Come back!" But the girl kept climbing, oblivious to Hela's pleas. The woman could only follow. "Where are you going?"

Higher and higher they climbed. Hela did not know where strange little Tuk was leading her, but at this point she did not care. Her world had collapsed.

As she followed, Hela slipped deeper and deeper into a depression. Even if her mother was wicked, even if her mother was responsible for the slaughter in the Temple of Dionysus, Hela could not suppress her longing to see Nuhara, to feel her mother's familiar touch, to hear her voice and revel in the security of her presence.

Tuk stopped only to eat fruit she picked along the way and to drink water she obtained from hidden springs. Hela could not imagine what had led the child to water. Tuk would leave the trail and walk with sure steps directly to the springs.

Hela realized with a start that their roles had become totally reversed—Tuk was now in charge. The child was keeping them alive and seemed to know exactly where they were both going.

Having admitted to the repositioning, Hela abandoned herself to the child's authority. They kept climbing; they kept moving. As the air grew colder and thinner, Hela lost track of time. Had it been hours or days since they had left the Temple of the Dead?

Each step caused pain in the lungs and chest. The wind was like a knife along her cheek.

The trees grew sparse, and the shrubbery became small and twisted. It grew flat against the ground, pressed there by the unrelenting wind. Hela no longer saw small mammals or snakes—now all she saw were the soaring mountain birds.

By late in the day the woman and child were in the high rocks. Every step was precarious. Tuk pressed on. Hela's hands bled from grasping the crags by which she pulled herself up and around huge boulders and outcroppings. Her shins were skinned from missteps.

The sun was falling in the afternoon sky. Tuk picked up the speed, and Hela struggled to keep pace. The red sun shone in her eyes.

Finally they reached a hilly expanse. Tuk burst into a run. Hela called out to her. But the child disappeared behind a mound, then, as the rolling terrain dictated, she popped up again and then vanished again. Hela took off after her. When Hela gained the girl's side, Tuk took her hand and led her down the steep path.

Suddenly they saw people—men . . . hundreds of them . . . ragged, disheveled, and painfully thin, with sores and scars on their backs. Each grasped a pick.

Circling these live skeletons were cruel-looking guards wielding whips and spears and prods. The sight was so gruesome and so pathetic that Hela averted her eyes. "Why have you brought us here?" she whispered to Tuk. "What is this place?"

"This is Traxis," Tuk replied quietly.

Flabbergasted, Hela stared at the child. She had finally spoken! Then Hela shook her head, wondering if she had really heard the child speak. Were exhaustion and depression playing tricks on her? No, she knew it had happened.

Even though Tuk had only uttered a single sentence, Hela was struck by the strangeness of her voice. It did not sound like any child's voice she had ever heard. It was deep, gravelly, mature.

"Why have you brought us to this sorry place?" Hela demanded.

Then Tuk smiled at her—emotionless, impassive Tuk. The smile was so deep, so profound, and so beautiful that Hela burst into tears and moved to embrace the child.

But Tuk jumped nimbly away to avoid the hug.

The child smiled radiantly once again, turned toward the prisoners and guards, and began to sing.

Her voice was so pure, so penetrating, so lovely, that

time itself stood still. The lyrics were in a language that
Hela did not know. They did not even sound like a language of this world.

Theon straightened from his labors the moment he
heard the strange melody. All around him the other prisoners did likewise. Whence was it coming? What language
was it? Why did he feel that strange sensation at the base
of his neck? In fact, his whole scalp tingled.

Theon looked up to see that a brutal guard called
One-Eye had unfurled his studded whip. He was about to
bring it down on Theon's back when one of the guard's
legs suddenly gave way. He crashed to the ground.

The threat gone, Theon, amazed at the reprieve, was
free to listen. Beside him, Talus stood with tears in his eyes.
The song continued, sounding for all the world like waves
of love and beauty. They filled Theon with absolute joy.
His weak limbs seemed to be suffused with a sudden energy.

"Look!" Talus whispered and pointed.

Another guard, then another, had fallen to his knees
and convulsed. The overseers' eyes were rolling in their
heads, and they were babbling.

The song was louder now and washed over and
through the emaciated men. It was like a blessed breeze to
the prisoners but, at the same time, like an angel of death
to the guards.

Now! Theon thought. *Now is the time to revolt!*

Gathering his newfound strength and raising his pick
in the air, he called to his fellow sufferers, "Rise up! Kill
them! Kill them!"

Like a legion of spirits who had just emerged from the
netherworld, the prisoners, their limbs resurrected by the
mystic song, attacked the hated guards. The captives' picks
flashed in the sun. The points bit deep into the skulls and
flesh. It was over in moments.

When the last guard was slain, the song stopped. The
prisoners stood and looked at what they had wrought, puz-

zled by their strength, surprised by their daring, befuddled at their freedom. Gaping, their weapons hanging limply from their fingertips, the men watched the golden-haired woman and the black child, who waited quietly.

Talus squinted, then blinked. The woman seemed familiar. . . . Could it be? He took a tentative step, then stopped, then grabbed Theon's arm. "Come with me!" he urged.

The two men walked toward the strangers. Talus increased his pace. Yes! He remembered her clearly. She was one of Nuhara's twins, one of the pair on Home who used to bring him food. "Theon!" he cried out joyously. "Your daughter is alive!"

The two men broke into a run. At first Hela could not recognize the bleeding, emaciated young man. But then he called out, "It's me, Hela! Talus!"

She cried out his name and, so happy was she at last to have found someone she knew, embraced him.

Then Talus stepped aside and pointed to the older man. "This is Theon, Hela. Your father."

Eyes narrowed, Theon edged close. He had not seen his daughter in more than ten years. She had been a little girl. "Do you remember me?" he asked.

She wrung her hands, confused, distressed. "You were a wonderful father. But Mother said you had died in a shipwreck. Just a few weeks ago I heard rumors of your survival, but I didn't believe them."

"Your brother?" he asked gently.

"Dead," she whispered, a catch in her throat.

"And your mother?"

"I came to Thrace to find her, but she's gone. Grandfather's dead. There was no sign of Mother."

"She's done terrible things, Hela," Theon told her sadly.

"I know." There was an awkward silence. So many years separated them.

"I am sorry about Nuhara," Theon said. "She is evil. She's murdered and betrayed those who trusted and loved her. She sentenced Talus and me here to die, and she plotted to steal the birthright of all Children of the Lion."

Theon lowered his eyes. He had to tell her the truth. Maybe, he thought, he should not have blurted it out like that, but it was necessary for him, if not better for her. Would he ever be able to resurrect the love between Hela and himself? he wondered.

He felt someone tugging at his arm. He looked down. "Daddy! Daddy!" The little black child reached up with her delicate hands. She seemed to weigh nothing as he scooped her up into an embrace. He looked at Hela. Questions were in his eyes. The woman pushed aside Tuk's little garment and bared the child's flesh. Theon stared down at the lion's paw-print birthmark of the Children of the Lion. The girl's mark was yellowish.

Long-repressed memories suddenly flooded Theon's vision. He knew that he had been an amnesiac for ten years, but now, for the first time, he remembered clearly the woman he had married when he lived his interim existence as Zeno, a ship's captain. The sweat broke out on his body. He held the child away from him.

"Where is your mother? Where is Dulana?" He remembered her name. He remembered her breathtaking dark-skinned beauty. "And where are your sisters?"

Tuk wiped her eyes with the heels of her tiny hands. She sniffed.

"Dead. Nuhara sent killers. They murdered my sisters and my mama. I escaped with our neighbor."

"What happened then?"

All the tears Tuk had not cried suddenly burst forth in a deluge of grief. Theon held the small, quivering frame tightly against his chest, and Hela came to wrap her arms around both of them.

Talus stroked the child's head. It was a new family formed out of horror of the past.

"It must have been her neighbor who died of the plague in the Egyptian desert," Hela explained quietly. "As did Gravis, shortly afterward."

Theon's eyes closed in sad remembrance, and he laid his cheek against the top of Tuk's head.

"What do you want to do now?" Talus asked.

"Find Nuhara," Theon answered resolutely.

"Oh, no!" Talus said. "Count me out. She is too strong for me. And you should forget about her, too."

Theon smiled grimly, secretively, and did not reply. He knew what Talus did not know—that the child, his little daughter Tuk, was not merely a waif with a beautiful voice. She was something special—her mark showed that. She was a throwback to the old ways—Theon's father, the great Seth. Tuk harkened back to the time when the Children of the Lion possessed the secrets of the mystics—magical powers that could neutralize and triumph over all the gold and ships and armies that Nuhara could muster.

"The game is not yet lost, Son," Theon finally replied. He smiled as he saw Hela reach out a hand to Talus, to bring him into their family embrace.

For a moment he hesitated, and then he took a bold step forward, his eyes glittering with unshed tears.

CHAPTER FIVE

Syrian Wilderness

When Micah woke, the sun was already up. He looked at Luti, just as he had for the last several mornings. She was smiling wanly at him.

"Is the pain gone, beloved?" he asked.

"Yes, it's gone. I am just very weak. And I smell terrible." She pointed at the crusted entrails that covered her body.

He shrugged.

"We should go soon. I have to deliver the information and get Seka back."

"We can't risk your health, Luti. Rest! I will get you home. I promise you."

"We must go now, Micah. There is little time," she pleaded with him.

He did not reply. He knew she was right.

Micah saw Drak tending to the remaining horse. He was glad the boy had taken on this responsibility without having been asked. Micah left Luti's side and walked over to the dead horse. He began to skin the beast, and when the entire hide was off he scraped it clean with the edge of his blade. Then he set the hide as a blanket on the chariot floor. He picked up Luti and carried her to the vehicle and placed her gently inside it.

He bundled up the horsemeat, their provisions, around her. Then he motioned to Drak to bring the horse over and hitch it to the chariot. At last they headed deeper into the brutal Syrian desert.

They kept moving, hour after hour, stopping only to eat. The desert floor was like stone, and the sun was like a knife. The horse stumbled often and appeared to be blinded.

Near dusk Micah called a halt. Luti seemed to have fared well. She smiled at him encouragingly. Micah and Drak carried her to an area where large boulders would provide some protection from the night wind. The family sat together, huddled over a small fire, as the temperature plummeted and the chill swirled around them.

Micah stared broodingly in the fire. His fatigue was understandable but not welcome. The last few weeks had been filled with enormous bouts of violence, both physical and emotional. He needed peace and quiet. So did Luti and the boy. The few days they had spent in the wilderness after their escape did not even begin to scratch the surface of the rest they needed. But all that would have to wait. Now that Luti could travel, their only goal must be the ransom of little Seka. They had to reach Ur quickly.

He looked over at his wife. She had already fallen asleep. That was good. She was healing; there was no doubt about that. Pink new skin was beginning to form. Micah smiled as he noted Drak, lying next to his mother, also fast asleep. The boy had turned out to be a tiger in battle and a dependable companion. He was growing up.

Micah's thoughts went to poor, brave Traggo, who had sacrificed himself so they might escape. If the soldiers caught him alive he would be subjected to horrible torture. Micah's eyes misted with tears at the thought.

Total darkness enveloped them. The moon and the stars were obscured by thick clouds. The cold wind gusted with a vengeance. Micah folded his arms and slept a fitful, anxious sleep.

Suddenly a nearby sound woke him. He peered with concern at Luti, worried that she was in pain. But she seemed to be sleeping. He turned his head away.

The blade of a spear greeted his eyes. It moved to aim at his throat. Every muscle in Micah's body stiffened as he looked up. The man who held the spear was dressed in the flowing robes of a Bedouin. Slowly, slowly, Micah sat up. The small camp was completely surrounded. He counted nine men with spears, standing quietly but threateningly.

Then he heard Luti's quavering voice. "Who are you? What do you want? We have no money. We are poor travelers going home to Ur."

None of the men spoke or moved. Micah realized with a start that their Bedouin dress was a disguise. Bedouins do not wear shoes, and these men all had sturdy sandals, exactly alike. No, they were professional soldiers, not tribesmen.

Minutes passed. Not one of the soldiers spoke, but every time Micah, Luti, or Drak moved or tried to say something, the spears were pressed brutally against them.

The night slipped away in terror. Luti began to weep. Drak shivered. Micah kept watching . . . waiting . . . hoping, but for what?

The sun rose and burned away the chill. Now the captors' grim faces became visible.

Dry sounds came from Luti's throat.

"Water," Micah cried out. "Will you give the woman water?"

But before an answer could be obtained, he heard chariots approaching. The spearmen tensed.

Micah saw them—five chariots. They halted about fifty yards away. A figure climbed down and strode toward them. Because the sun was in his eyes, Micah couldn't see clearly. All he could see was the color yellow.

"It's Akkad!" Luti exclaimed. "The priest of Astarte!"

Yes. It was Akkad, wearing the long yellow robe. He strode into the small camp and stared around fiercely. He walked to Luti and said, "A stroke of good fortune. My spies told me that you had been captured but managed to escape. Is the invasion about to begin? I sent out patrols into the desert hoping that you would have the information we need."

"My child!" she rasped. "Where is Seka! Where is my child?"

Akkad gestured to one of his men to give Luti a bladder of water. She drank greedily. Other bladders were given to Micah and Drak. "She is well. I promise you," the priest said impatiently. "Now tell me what you have learned, woman. Time is short!"

"I have learned that a large ship convoy will be sent to Antioch. From there, the food and weapons will be carried overland to Ashur to meet the Assyrian army. They will attack by the river."

"You lie!" Akkad shouted and his troops brandished their spears.

"No! I tell you what I have learned," Luti replied in a fury, raising herself up.

"The Assyrians have no riverboats."

"The Phoenicians are supplying the vessels. They will be carried with the convoy."

Akkad's face lit up at this information. He slapped his side with joy.

"That makes sense. Ah ha! We can send the chariot units of the Babylonian army to the ravines west of Ashur and intercept the convoy. We can destroy the boats before they reach the Assyrians. We will abort the invasion before it even begins."

Akkad turned and signaled to his charioteer. A figure ran toward them, holding something in his arms.

Drak leaped up and began to dance and shout. "It's Seka! It's Seka!"

Seconds later, the brawny trooper carefully placed the young child in her father's arms. Micah brought the child to her mother. Luti burst into tears.

Akkad bowed low. "My chariots will take you all to Ur. Your lands, your houses, and your wealth will be restored. All I have promised will be yours. And you will have once again the love and honor of your grateful nation."

Luti turned her smile upon Micah. The family was whole at last. They must never be separated again.

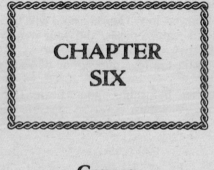

CHAPTER SIX

Canaan

Hand in hand, the couple slowly explored the dreadful streets of the once-thriving city of Shechem. Fires still burned everywhere, unchecked, and the loud *crack* of splitting wood rent the air.

"I have to rest," Cotto said. The smoke made breathing difficult.

Purah helped her to sit down on the rubble of a destroyed building. They stared around at the destruction, their faces pale beneath the sooty smudges.

Cotto tiredly leaned against the man, who stood beside her. He gently stroked her head and said, "There, there, I know. . . ."

The beauty asked with despair, "Do you? Can you possibly know how I feel?" Then she sighed as she felt him stiffen. "I'm sorry, Purah. You probably *do* know. Well, I'm done with it! Never again will I sell myself to Yahweh's enemies. Never!"

"Dearest," Purah replied, sinking down and bringing her hand to his lips, "marry me! Together we can forge a new life."

Cotto started. "How could a good man like you ever want me?" She pulled her hand back roughly.

"I've been Navan's pawn, too, remember. But it's not that we're both so terrible that we deserve each other; it's just that we're weak and fell under the influence of a terrible man. We can make a new start together. Please, Cotto!"

She knew she would never be able to love Purah with the passion a young woman can feel for a man her own age. And he would never have the wealth and power that excited her. But he had been kind and caring. She owed him her affection. Without his support and empathy, she would never have endured her degradation at Abimelech's hands. She probably would have killed herself. Sadly, she knew she would have to perform one last deed of betrayal before their new life could begin.

"I will marry you, Purah. I will be a faithful and loving wife. I will bear your children." She spoke the words softly, and Purah buried his face in her lap.

Her fingers combed through his graying hair. "But first we must settle accounts."

He looked up anxiously. "What do you mean?"

"We pay Navan back in full, blood for blood. We'll kill that Phoenician bastard."

"Yes! Yes!" Purah agreed.

Cotto stood up and kissed Purah slowly, lingeringly, deeply. Then, hand in hand, they left the ruined city of Shechem and headed north toward Tyre.

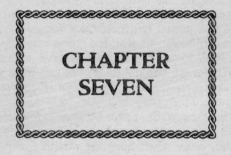

CHAPTER
SEVEN

Thrace

"The mountain path has lost its terror," Talus remarked to Theon. The younger man was holding Hela's hand.

Theon laughed. "That's because we are going downhill rather than uphill, and we're walking as free men. The last time we were on this path we were being driven to our enslavement." Then he called out to Tuk, who was leading the march, "Slow down, little one. Your father is not a young man anymore."

They had left the liberated prison camp only hours before, after two days of revelry. Their good-byes to their fellow inmates had been heartfelt, but now they had a task to perform: They had to retrieve the treasure of the Children of the Lion.

284

Theon wiped his brow. "Let's rest for a while," he said, and they all sat down together right on the rough trail and ate the cheese and olives and drank the goat's milk that had been liberated from the guards' stores.

Talus kept staring in wonderment at his new companion. Hela was the most beautiful woman he had ever seen. She was so different now from when he knew her on the island Home. She was so assured and kindly. He wondered how awful he looked. All that time in the penal colony had probably turned him into a bearded filthy madman. But she seemed to want to know him better . . . to stay with him . . . to walk with him.

"Are you hungry, Tuk?" Theon asked.

His mysterious daughter shook her head. She had lapsed into silence. Theon watched her as he ate. How much occult power did this child possess? Could she be trusted at her young age to use it wisely? Could he control her? Did her love for him supersede all her other loyalties?

After a time, the four of them started up again, headed south, always south, toward the plateau that fronted the shoreline. There they could obtain a boat to a busier port and begin their search for Nuhara in earnest.

They walked for several hours, then stopped for the night. Talus built a rough lean-to for them, and Theon regaled them with wondrous stories of how it had been when the Children of the Lion were a powerful political and economic force in the world.

They slept the sleep of the just, woke refreshed, and started off again in high spirits. The trail was becoming easier and the weather milder.

"We are close to water now," Talus remarked. "Can you smell it? And look there, by those large trees."

There were several birds circling low. Their harsh calls carried on the wind. "Yes. You're right," Theon said. "Gulls. We must be close."

Heartened, Theon increased his pace, and the others did likewise. Little Tuk grasped his hand tightly.

The trail began to curve and move at a steeper slope.

"Aaiiiiiieeee!" Theon's scream of pain was so sudden and so horrible that it froze his companions.

He fell to the ground, and his fingers clutched at the arrow shaft that had penetrated his thigh.

Out of the shrubbery and vines that lined the path came five bowmen—ugly, powerful, small men carrying the stout Thracian bows and arrows with the jagged points. Each one had an arrow nocked and ready.

Seconds later Nuhara appeared and walked swiftly to the wounded Theon. She kicked him savagely in the side and laughed as he rolled over.

"Stupid fool," she said. "Did you think I would leave Thrace without making sure that you were dead?" She turned to signal to her bowmen to loose the rest of their murderous shafts.

"Mother! No!"

Nuhara turned and when her eyes rested on the young blond woman, Nuhara's face drained of color.

"Is that you, Hela? I don't believe it! Is that you, my darling?"

Hela, mute, shrank back, holding on to Talus.

"Where is your brother? Where is Gravis?"

Hela found her voice. "Dead, Mother. He died of the plague."

"Not the plague!" Nuhara screamed. "*You* murdered him, didn't you? That is why you have thrown your lot with your father!" She kicked Theon again, this time in the shoulder.

Talus made a move toward Nuhara, but the bowmen made a convincing case for staying where he was.

Nuhara turned back to her daughter. "I will kill you all," she vowed.

Suddenly she noticed Tuk standing on the far side of the writhing Theon. "Who is she? What is she doing here?"

No one replied. Instead, Tuk kicked her father in the ribs with all her might. Theon screamed. His legs were now drenched with blood from the deeply penetrating arrow.

"Tuk!" Hela shouted. "Get over here!"

But Nuhara applauded the child's action and laughed. "No, child, you belong here with *me*. Anyone who kicks a fool is a friend of mine. Come over and stand by me. Tuk, is it? I think you'll like what will happen next."

Tuk crossed over her father, brutally stepping on him. Nuhara laughed again. She reached out with a hand to welcome the child. Tuk skipped the last few feet and took the proffered hand. The girl's lips moved, but no sound came out.

"What, dear?" Nuhara asked.

Again Tuk's lips moved without sound. Nuhara bent to put her ear by the girl's mouth.

Suddenly Tuk's free hand whipped around. Something gleamed in her palm. There was a gasp of fear from Nuhara. But her experience, her cruelty, and her skill at deception could not help her now. Tuk drove a thin blade into the side of Nuhara's skull. She crumbled, blood and froth coming from the corners of her mouth. Hela screamed and hid her face in Talus's chest.

The bowmen, seeing their leader on the ground, vanished quickly off the path. The sound of their crashing through the foliage soon faded.

Tuk returned to her father and with miraculously gentle yet powerful hands twisted the arrow from his thigh, then cleansed and healed it.

Hela could not move. Her wide, dilated eyes sought the face of her dead mother. Why had all this happened? Why had she become an evil murderess? Why had she caused all this misery?

Talus thought of the port ahead. "No doubt Nuhara has loaded the ships and hidden them along the coastline. They'll be easy to find, and on them will be the family's treasure."

As Theon climbed to his feet, he felt an immense surge of victorious pride. He knew that Talus was right.

The Children of the Lion were about to rise again . . . to play their rightful role on the world scene. The race, he realized, is not always won by the swiftest. He patted Talus on the shoulder as the young man held Hela tightly while she wept.

CHAPTER EIGHT

Tyre

"You did not seem to enjoy yourself as much as you used to," Riza said quietly to the naked man in the large bed with her.

"You are a very beautiful woman, Riza," Navan soothed. "It is just that I have many things on my mind."

"Did Traggo talk?" she asked.

"No. He died under torture without saying a word. He was a brave fool. Almost twelve days he survived."

Riza turned away. She was glad Micah had escaped. She was sorry she had had to betray him. But she was a Phoenician, and she would not protect spies against her people, no matter what.

"My lord Navan!"

Both occupants of the bed sat up, startled. Navan glared at the small figure of his ancient adviser, Sutt.

"How dare you enter my chambers, Sutt!"

"Forgive me, Lord Navan," the old man apologized. "But I have two important messages from the council."

"The council? *I* am the head of the Phoenicians' council! How could it meet without my consent or presence?"

Sutt moved deeper into the chambers. "It was an emergency session, my lord. There was no time."

Navan was clearly furious. "What are the messages?"

"Two Babylonian chariot brigades attacked our convoy five miles west of Ashur. They destroyed the longboats and all the provisions. The Assyrians will be unable to launch their river attack. The entire invasion must be canceled. Our losses in money and goods are enormous."

Navan stood up slowly. The sheet that fell away from his body was as white as his face. His eyes reflected horrible disbelief. "How could this happen? What went wrong?"

"The spies must have gotten access to the chart room," Sutt said.

Navan began to pace furiously. The Phoenicians had floated huge loans to pay for this expedition and the coming invasion. To remain solvent they were depending upon the enormous booty they would receive after emptying the Babylonian coffers. If the invasion had failed, Navan was ruined.

"And the second message, Sutt? Spit it out."

Sutt smiled enigmatically and did not reply.

"Speak up, man! Speak up!" Navan demanded.

Sutt motioned, and a Sea Peoples spearman moved from the shadows into the chambers. He hesitated for just a moment, then without warning he charged Navan, driving the short spear through the Phoenician's breast.

Navan died instantly.

Sutt slowly walked to the fallen body and tested it with his sandaled toe. He was satisfied. "That was the council's second message, Navan. You have made your last mistake."

Riza cringed among the blood-splattered pillows. But Sutt was not interested in her. He spoke to the assassin. "Good job. Remove the body. If you want the woman, she's yours."

The moment they entered Tyre, Purah and Cotto went immediately to Navan's estate. Something was going on. Soldiers were everywhere, and the windows were shuttered.

The gates opened, and house servants filed out, all carrying piles of clothes that the master had worn when he was alive.

Flabbergasted, Cotto and Purah backed away into an inn. After setting their traveling packs on the ground, they ordered some new wine in shallow bowls.

"Something must have happened to Navan," Cotto said.

Purah nodded. "Actually, it's no wonder. Considering our enmity for him—and we were so insignificant in his organization—it's surprising he lasted this long."

"I wonder if he was murdered or died of natural causes."

"Oh, please, Cotto." Purah snorted.

"I'm sure you're right. Men like Navan don't die of old age in their sleep."

Suddenly the unmistakable sound of deep bass drums reverberated in the distance.

"It's a funeral!" Purah exclaimed.

From where they sat they could see the procession wind around the inner walls of Tyre. Six white horses led the procession, followed by the Phoenician elite in their long robes and conical hats, and then armed contingents of soldiers who were allied with the Phoenicians. Finally came the magnificent coffin, borne on a wagon pulled by enormous oxen with garlands of flowers about their necks.

Purah squeezed Cotto's arm. "We are watching the funeral of the man we had sworn to kill."

"Praise to Yahweh. He has done our work for us."

Purah stood and gathered the bundles with furious speed. "Let's get out of here, beloved. The child growing in your womb will be poisoned by this city of intrigue and death and betrayal. We can go home now. All is well."

Like children, laughing and singing, they left the city of Tyre forever.

Epilogue

~~~~~~

The Teller of Tales stared out at the ring of rapt faces.
The gathering had hung on his every word. He was tired and
thirsty; the cold night dew made his ancient bones ache.

"And so it happened," he said, "that the beast of Canaan, the self-crowned king Abimelech, was destroyed by a
gentle woman. And noble Theon was reunited with his own
true daughters. Young Talus found purpose, love, and happiness at long last. The Israelite whore Cotto sought redemp-
tion, both in the loving arms of an older man and in an
ambitious desire for vengeance. The evil Nuhara was proved
not to be shrewd enough for her enemies."

He stopped, took a deep breath, and stared into the
glowing embers at the heart of the dying campfire. From the
darkness the hunting wolves of the desert called one another.
These were terrible sounds, deep and riveting, and his listeners
drew closer together.

"Do you hear those howls of death?" the Teller of Tales
called out. "They are nothing compared to the wolves who
were gathering around the Great Sea to confront the Children
of the Lion and the people of Yahweh. To the south rose the
Philistines. To the north, the Assyrians. They brought fire and
chariots and machines of destruction the likes of which the
world had never seen."

The Teller of Tales smiled in the darkness at his audience. "And their adversary was a tall and handsome young

293

man, propelled by a national emergency into a kingly office he resisted. His name was Saul."

A murmuring of recognition could be heard. They knew that name.

"Think of him," the Teller advised, "when you rise up and when you lie down. Contemplate his great deeds, which will free you from self-loathing and impotence. But remember, too, his folly."

He bowed his head. "I speak no more. All these wondrous tales we shall save until the morrow, after I have rested and tasted the first milk of the morning."

Upon his final word, the last of the embers flickered and died, leaving the travelers in silence and darkness and to sleep.

DEPARTED GLORY
VOLUME XVI
of the breathtaking Biblical saga
THE CHILDREN OF THE LION
by Peter Danielson

It is 1050 BC. The tribes of Israel dwell in hillside settlements in the Promised Land of Canaan, but Philistine armies are laying waste to their towns and slaughtering their armies. At a bloody battle near Eben-Ezer, the Philistines seize the precious Ark of the Covenant and turn it over to their pagan priests. The young Israelite Saul, obedient to God's instructions, sets out to recover the Ark for his people.

Two Children of the Lion, a father and a son, are also victims of the Philistines. Urnan, the father, is condemned to crushing labor in the copper mines of Cyprus. His son, Eri, is taken to the Philistine city of Ashdod, where he is enslaved in the house of a man of great wealth but corrupt morals. After escaping his bondage, Eri meets Saul in the streets of the city. The youths join forces to outwit the Philistines and recover the Ark.

As adults, years later, Saul and Eri wage war against the Philistines, driving them from the land and thus launching the era of Israel's great Age of Kings.

Read this exciting book, available summer 1993 wherever Bantam Books are sold.